CONTINUING

BOOK FIVE of *THE STARLIGHT CHRONICLES*

C. S. Johnson

Ebook ISBN: 978-1-948464-05-5
Paperback ISBN: 978-1-948464-06-2

THE STARLIGHT CHRONICLES

The story continues on, for Sam.

It continues on, too, with the help of a new friend and fellow writer, Krissy, who has helped encourage me much in the short time we have been friends.

THE STARLIGHT CHRONICLES

To Get *Awakening* (A Special Christmas Episode of The *Starlight Chronicles*) as a bonus for picking up this book,

Download It At:
https://www.csjohnson.me/awakening

Don't forget to check out *Belonging* (A Date Night Episode of The *Starlight Chronicles*), a short story that takes place before Book 5!

5

THE STARLIGHT CHRONICLES

☼<u>1</u>☼
New Year

I was standing before the entrance to my high school, staring into space and sloshing my feet further into the cold wetness of the surrounding slush, when a foreboding premonition settled on me like softly falling snowflakes.

I'm alone.

Even as a chorus of my cohorts joined me, pushing past me in the crowded halls, surrounding me in a sea of familiar faces, I felt alone—utterly alone. It was hard to say whether or not their presence compounded the empty feeling inside of me.

If nothing else, I thought as I made my way through the familiar halls, *they aren't doing anything to make me feel better.*

Those self-absorbed jerks.

I supposed I couldn't blame them entirely. It wasn't my personal choice to be back at school, any more than it was anyone else's. It was the end of winter break. That probably made things harder than they had to be, even though they were already hard enough.

"It's time to just suck it up and deal with it, Hamilton," I muttered to myself as I pulled some books out of my locker. "Doesn't matter if you're unhappy right now."

"Hey, Dinger!" Drew McGill nodded toward me as I stepped inside the school. "You got Elm's AP Chem assignment done? I'm going to need your help."

"Well, hello to you, too," I replied with a half-instinctive, half-hearted, half-smirk. "Can't even get to first period before you need help, Drew? Pathetic."

He laughed. "At least it's predictable."

If Drew expected a grin, he was sorely gratified, even if it was a hollow one.

Everything that was wrong about this day was predictable.

I received an email regarding the swim meets for the next month, I desperately needed coffee, and Cheryl, always the lawyer-more-than-mother, insisted that I somehow convince the immutable laws of space and time to bend to her will and add three hours onto the day, just so I could put in more work at City Hall.

All of this was completely predictable, right down to the hapless friend asking for basic homework answers standing before me, only three months before our SATs were scheduled to take place.

How is it only seven-thirty in the morning?

"Got it when you need it," I assured Drew, before heading toward my first class.

"Hey."

"What?" I turned to Drew and he shrugged.

"I'm glad you're doing okay, man."

"What are you talking about?" I asked, suddenly alarmed. *There's no way he would know about ...*

"I mean, I'm glad to see you're doing okay. With Mikey in the hospital still, and Gwen, you know, with the illness and all, I thought, you know, maybe the holidays would be … "

His voice trailed off, and I suddenly understood. *He* didn't, and none of my other friends did either, but *I* did, and that was enough to prompt me to respond accordingly.

"I'm fine," I lied. "People depend on me, Drew. Where would Central be without me on the swim team this year?"

"Yeah, true. I guess especially so, since Mike's not on it."

I nodded, as if to make my point clear on the matter.

"Well, see you later, then." He waved, and I felt a tug in the back of my conscience.

I reached out, my hand slapping down on his shoulder in a brotherly way. "Thanks, Drew."

"No problem."

"I got to go," I muttered. "Martha's class and all that, you know. AP Gov's not going to wait, even if it is me. That's saying something, too, because I'm Martha's favorite."

Drew laughed. "Sure. See you later, man."

"Bye." I turned and headed off quickly. *Well, that wasn't awkward at all.*

"Hey, Poncey's on the lookout for you, too," Drew called back.

THE STARLIGHT CHRONICLES

"He'll get his homework help, same as you." As Drew turned the corner, my grin turned into a grimace.

Routine was unsettling, and not just because it was the official deathblow to the holidays. Everything was the same as before the break.

January in northern Ohio, even with the lake effect currently in effect, was no warmer than usual. Nothing out of the ordinary happened to me as I walked to school; my steps had been the same as the previous year's, as carefully measured out as the sugar and creamer in my coffee.

On some level, it was a good thing that my best friend, Mikey, and my ex-girlfriend, Gwen, were still hospitalized from the demon monster attack last semester. It would give me room to mope, and everyone would still think of me as this great, tragic, wonderful guy.

Last year, I would have lapped that up like cream. But I knew it was no longer the truth. I was no longer that guy.

Walking into Mrs. Smithe's room for AP Gov, I knew immediately there was no longer any use for pretending everything wasn't somehow worse.

Everything was the same—except for one major thing: Raiya's seat was empty. I sat down in my seat, the one in front of hers, and tried not to dwell on my dismay.

I could agree that lady troubles were the source of my sadness, but it had nothing to do with Gwen or any guilt over her fate.

THE STARLIGHT CHRONICLES

Love has a strange way of changing people, and I was no exception.

It was amusing to me on some level that even this time last year, I would have welcomed Raiya's absence. Falling in love with her—accidentally and intentionally all at once—changed me, changed my life.

Thank goodness I had my Game Pac. I pulled out my gaming device and sinking my mind into a routine game of Tetris.

This year, I thought as I skillfully maneuvered the colored blocks around on my screen, *I know I'm not as great as I thought, but it doesn't matter quite so much*. Part of it came with the territory of growing up, some of it came from falling in love, and the rest of it probably came from other things—with "other things" the most understated way of saying my supernatural powers. Life was not easy when it was your duty to fight evil and seal away demons as the city's resident superhero.

I smirked to myself. Of all things, finding out about my supernatural powers and my life as a fallen Star on Earth—not to mention running around town in a super-cool, super-goofy costume topped off with a feather-crown—would have been the *last* possible thing on my list of what would change me.

Right up there with true love, I thought, recalling the cynical ramblings of my past.

Bearing the superhero calling of Wingdinger, and carrying out its duties, had pushed me to be a better person, ironically showing me how not so great I'd been before.

Thinking over it, it was good that I knew I wasn't a good person. What kind of person would actually be happy at the thought of his best friend suffering from a mental breakdown and PTSD, and his ex-girlfriend getting her soul sucked out?

Even if it would add a nice subplot to my legend.

"Hamilton Dinger, are you paying attention?"

"Huh?" I jerked my eyes off the screen (just as I managed to make it to the next level) and looked up to see Martha Smithe giving me one of her famous glares over the top of her thick glasses.

"I asked if you were paying attention," Mrs. Smithe repeated. "I'm on a coffee-fueled lecture here; you'd better be paying attention."

"Oh. Yeah, I am," I remarked, giving her a teasing smirk. "You can count on me."

She pursed her lips. "Why don't we have a chat after class, anyway?"

"There's no need," I assured her. "I'm listening."

This seemed to placate her, as predictable as it was.

I stole a glance at the empty seat behind me, as though I could wish Raiya into reality.

THE STARLIGHT CHRONICLES

No such luck, even for a fallen Star, I thought to myself. Of course, every Star is only allowed one wish, and I'd already used mine.

That was part of the reason Raiya had to go. She had to go and see Alora, the Star of Time, to see about getting another wish. She told me she needed it to earn her place back in the Celestial Kingdom.

I glumly turned around, pretending to take notes in my notebook.

But it wasn't long before my mind wandered off to better times and stranger places, and settled on a memory less than a month before …

THE STARLIGHT CHRONICLES

Farewell

"Are you sure about this?"

Raiya arched her brow at me as she stood in the moonlight of the winter solstice, just beneath the trees near the Apollo City marina. It was the same place, months prior, I'd fallen back to Earth after visiting with Aleia's sister, only to find Raiya—then in her Starlight Warrior form, Starry Knight—waiting for me in the rain.

"I told you before, I'm not exactly sure of this, but it's the best shot we have." Her violet eyes darkened against the night sky as the fog began pouring in.

"What am I going to do without you?" I asked, shoving my hands in my pockets.

"Watch over the city," she told me simply. "We both know it's a full-time job, even with only Asteropy and Elektra left to stop."

"They haven't made a lot of commotion lately."

"But there are other demons making trouble, and there is that possibility that they've found a new leader," Raiya reminded me. She leaned against the trunk of a tree. "And there is always Elysian to look after, right?"

I snorted. "That's another full-time job in itself, or even two if you count feeding him. There's no denying he's got a sweet tooth. I'll need backup when I go to Rachel's."

"You just might get some," Raiya said with a small smile, making me wonder what she meant. "I have to admit, after this past month, I'm surprised you're not tired of me."

I came over and leaned beside her, taking her hand in mine. "It still wasn't enough time." After all the time we'd been apart, both on this side of Time and the other, I was more than adamant about making up for lost moments.

"We've seen each other nearly every day for the last six weeks," she reminded me. "Sometimes more than once. I'll be back soon enough."

"That's not soon enough."

Raiya laughed. "I'll miss you," she admitted. "More than you know. But this is the only way I can see about getting a new wish, so I can be restored to the Celestial Kingdom, same as you are."

I shifted against the hard bark of the tree behind us. "Being forgiven by Adonaias doesn't seem like it would be something that would need a Star's wish."

A scowl crossed her face. "I used to judge people, and a price always had to be given. There's no way to survive and still get everything you want. But if I can get a new wish, I'll be able to get there."

"I'm not so sure about that."

"That's because you've seen him, talked with him. Adonaias," she clarified. "What do you need to fear, having been remade and recreated already? Your Starsoul—all of it,

THE STARLIGHT CHRONICLES

including your Starfire, soul, and spirit—is alive; mine is not. My spirit has been dead since I was born into this world."

"This is confusing, all this Star stuff," I said with small sigh. I didn't see why she thought I was in any better of a position, since she seemed to know more about the Prince of Stars than I did.

"I was going to recapture the Sinisters and seal them away. Presenting them might have helped me earn back my life on the other side of Time, in the Immortal Realm."

"We're not that far from getting the last two," I pointed out.

"Thank goodness for that," Raiya said, her voice bitter. "If it wasn't for Aleia's desperation, I wouldn't have agreed to this until they were all captured."

"But you did," I said, realizing it was indeed out of character for her. "Why does Aleia have the power to change your mind so easily?"

"Because I love her, of course. She is among my best friends. I have damned myself, but if she has a chance at happiness with Orpheus, who was to be her match on the other side, then I have nothing to lose."

"Nothing but your pride," I teased.

Raiya glared at me, but I knew it was more because she knew I was right.

"You did end up falling in the first place," I reminded her.

"Be careful, or I'll have to beat you up when I get back."

15

"Something to look forward to," I remarked, trying to be cheerful.

A Star's wish had great power, I knew, and the misuse of that power had brought us here. But I was sure Adonaias, the Prince of Stars, and our master, would understand Raiya's actions. She'd used her power to stop the Seven Deadly Sinisters from escaping her power.

I shifted closer to her and leaned against her. In the cool night air, this close to Christmas, the extra warmth was inviting. "You know, there are a lot of things I never realized I didn't know about you."

"That's because you like to talk about yourself," Raiya bantered back. "You have a hard time talking with me, instead of at me."

"I do not. We've talked about you plenty of times."

"It's still more of a 70-30 split."

"You don't always like to tell me things."

"That doesn't mean you shouldn't ask."

"Is that supposed to be a trick of some kind?" I asked.

"Well, it was the same with Gwen for that matter," Raiya mused, and I shook my head.

"I'd rather not recall my past mistakes," I contended, "but since you brought it up, I'll keep it in mind."

She sneered at me. "I'd appreciate it."

"It would be my pleasure," I promised, sealing it with a quick, pressing kiss—which quickly turned into several, each one longer and sweeter than the last.

We were quite breathless by the time the Apollo City Time Tower chimed, and we knew we only had fifteen minutes before eleven o'clock.

"You never did tell me why you had to supernova before," I said, awkwardly backing away from her.

She went quiet for a moment, a contemplative expression on her pretty face. "My sisters had been held prisoner with me for a long time," Raiya said. "They managed to find a weakness."

"What was it?"

"You."

"Huh?" I reeled back, turning to face her. "What happened?"

"Orpheus tricked me." She twirled her fingers around a loosely bound lock of hair. "He gave me one of your feathers and said it was all that was left of you after he attacked. I knew by then Orpheus was a traitor, but … "

She shrugged as her voice trailed off.

I thought about the first time I'd seen Starry Knight, when she came barreling into my life. She had a long, red feather in her hair. I took it back some time ago, seeing it as part of my own fire-feather wings. She'd kept it, I realized, even as she

THE STARLIGHT CHRONICLES

ripped through Space-time, getting reborn into a human existence.

I squeezed her hand. "You really didn't expect to ever see me again."

"No."

"That monster." I shook my head. "I can't believe Orpheus and I were ever friends."

"He was different before. You know as well as I do that our decisions have strange ways of marking us and changing us."

I nodded. "That I do."

Raiya glanced around the tree, gazing over at the marina. "Speaking of Orpheus, he should be coming with Aleia soon."

"Elysian, too," I added. "He said he'd bring the rest of the sealed Sinisters with him so you can have them."

"We'd better transform."

A flash of light and blast of power later, we both stood together, face-to-face with our fallen Star forms. Her bow was out, and my sword was ready. Before she could step out of the shadows of the trees, I took hold of her arm.

"You know," I said, "I really like being with you, like this."

"You always did," she said with a smirk, "until we met last year."

"I would've liked you better before if you hadn't insisted on calling me a child," I told her.

"I would've liked you better before if you hadn't insisted on acting like one," she easily countered.

"Ha! You were worse." But I couldn't hold back a smile, because she just made arguing more fun than it already was.

"I have been who I am for all my life," Raiya replied. "Though, of course, down here on Earth, my purpose has changed."

"My purpose has changed, too," I remarked, "and it guides the rest of me as I go along, I suppose. But I still think there is enough wiggle room for fun and happiness. And hope," I added, recalling how many of our trials had become victories.

"People who think they are not beyond mercy or grace often think that way."

"Well, I am the Star of Mercy, technically. So I know you are not beyond me."

She giggled, surprising me. "I see why you still want to work in law."

"Well, it is hard to break the habit, after thinking it for so long," I conceded. "And it is not like we will be superheroes forever, right?"

"And what if we are?" Raiya asked. "Are you prepared to do it until your body submits to death and your spirit is taken back to the other side of Time's power? Would hope be enough to carry you through, despite pain?"

My real answer, I decided, was not one what I wanted to know. Or maybe it wasn't what she wanted to hear.

I figured charm was the best way to respond to that. After pulling her close, I gently kissed her cheek. "I'd do it forever, so long as you're with me."

When she only looked at me somberly, I sighed and looked skyward. "That's why these next few days are going to be hard."

"It'll be alright, in the end," Raiya said, her voice quiet as her eyes held mine. "You'll see."

"I'll be waiting for you," I told her, gripping my arms more tightly around her.

Before we could say anything else, Aleia came up beside us. Her blonde hair was bound back with her small crown of starlight, and her eyes were wide and awake. She was bursting with energy, and some part of me envied her anticipation.

Behind her, I could see the outline of the *Meallán*, St. Brendan the Navigator's ship, as it finished casting its grand anchor into Lake Erie.

She waved excitedly. "Are you coming?" she asked.

☼<u>3</u>☼
Mary

"Are you coming?" Mrs. Smithe's voice cut through my subconscious viciously in its professionalism, like a doctor handing out a sad diagnosis. "Hello, Dinger, are you there?"

"Huh?" I blinked, and suddenly I was back in my world, days and weeks apart from Raiya's departure, alone in my class, with my Game Pac beeping and flashing the "Game Over" signal over the screen.

Martha was waving her hand in front of my face. "I asked you to come and see me once class was over, remember?"

"Oh. Yeah." I stood up, vaguely realizing class was over, and I was the only one left. "Sorry."

I wanted to see Raiya again. It had been a couple weeks, moving closer to a month. There's something about seeing others—hearing their voice, feeling the warmth of their being, seeing their smiles—something you can only get when they are with you in real life.

I wanted to see her again, but I couldn't. I had to continue on, working to keep the city safe, my schoolwork finished, and my career focus sharp. While I didn't often have time to mope at missing her, it still didn't seem fair. Not in the least, if you can imagine it.

The only good part about getting through this, I thought forlornly, is that she should be back soon.

My feet shuffled, appropriately, I thought, as I sauntered up to Martha's desk.

21

"I would ask you if you were amused by the section on bureaucracy and media in the lecture," Mrs. Smithe began, "but I have a feeling you're not even thinking about that, are you?"

"If you're worried about my performance because of Gwen—"

"I've known for some time now, Dinger, that you've got a new girlfriend, despite what you want your friends, and Gwen's friends, to think."

Shocked at hearing her say it, I nearly hissed at her. I'd forgotten that I'd taken Raiya out on a date to a football game, shortly after finding out she was Starry Knight (it was not her first choice of date nights, but I'd convinced her to go for my sake.) We'd had a really lovely time together, but we'd been more than surprised to find Martha sitting in the visitor section behind us. "I would appreciate your silence on the matter."

"There's no need to worry," she snapped. "I know that it's better to avoid trouble. There's no use in making your life more difficult than it has to be." For a brief moment, her eyes glazed over, before she wrinkled her nose. "I know that better than most, too."

I wondered if she was thinking about her time in the hospital last year. "I guess I should have known that," I muttered, somewhat apologetic.

Her eyes narrowed as they gazed at me over thick, black frames. "A teacher knows these things," she murmured, "and other things as well, Hamilton. There comes a point when the

THE STARLIGHT CHRONICLES

price is too high, and it's better to figure it out before it's paid."

Martha always made me nervous when she said my first name. Recalling how she helped Raiya and me sneak away to attend to some Starlight Warrior business last semester, I frowned. *Is she trying to tell me something?*

"Mikey might know something of that too, considering how often he has been in detention," Mrs. Smithe added, breaking me from my thoughts.

When I remembered what Raiya had said before about payment and punishment, I almost flinched.

"I asked you up here because of Mikey," she continued. "I know he's your best friend, and he's been in the hospital for more than two months now. Given the circumstances," she said, nodding in the direction of my seat, "especially after your lack of performance today, I thought I'd check in."

I looked at her for a long moment before dropping my eyes to the ground. "He's not well."

"I'll bet he could use a visit from you, and Raiya, too. Just like how you came to see me when I was in the hospital before. Have you visited him lately?"

"I was thinking of going again soon," I promised, trying to avoid answering that directly. The truth was, he wasn't keen on seeing me, and Raiya, despite everything her healing powers were capable of doing, wasn't able to heal him.

"And Raiya? Will she be back in school tomorrow?" Mrs. Smithe asked as she started stacking up several papers and evening them out into a neat pile.

"I don't know."

"Do you know where she is?" Mrs. Smithe asked. "The principal told me she has used up all the days she's allowed, before they drop her from school."

"What?" I asked. "They can't do that."

"That's the attendance policy of the school," she asserted, tweaking her glasses. "I thought I'd let you know, so you might be able to let her know."

"She has medical reasons."

"True, but she also has responsibilities here at school." Martha's eyes, dark but soft, flickered to mine. "I think it would help," she said through pursed lips, "if you let her know."

Panic hit me harder than I would've liked. *I can't do anything about that! She's not even in this dimension!*

Before I could form a logical, non-stammering reaction to Martha's information, the door burst open.

And Raiya—or rather, a girl who *looked* like Raiya—walked in.

"Hi, Mrs. Smithe," she said. "I was hoping to catch you. I'm sorry I missed class today."

My head nearly exploded. *This is not Raiya. What's going on!?*

The girl had the same long, golden brown hair as Raiya—right down to the dark, copper undertones and the loosely bound bun; she was of similar, if not exact, height, and her face even seemed relatively similar. Or at least, it would have been, if I didn't know every sparkle and slant of Raiya's eyes, the slope of all her different smiles.

The girl standing before me was even wearing a Rosemont uniform!

If this is a joke, Raiya has outdone herself.

My fists clenched. *If this is a demon*, I thought angrily, *I'm going to make her suffer so much she'll willingly succumb to a fate of nothingness.*

I looked back and forth between Mrs. Smithe and the would-be Raiya, and I didn't know what to do.

Martha, ever the voice of reason, spoke up. "*Ferme ta bouche*, Dinger. It's hardly an attractive look."

I clasped my mouth shut as Mrs. Smithe began going over what "Raiya" had missed in class.

"Thanks for all the help, Mrs. Smithe," the girl replied, more chipper than Raiya would have been. "I'll get the work back to you as soon as I can."

"I'm sure Dinger here will be more than happy to help you out," Mrs. Smithe replied, making me nearly gape at her again.

Am I the only one who sees that this is not *Raiya?*

"In fact," Mrs. Smithe continued, "I'll write passes for you both, so he can catch you up with the notes he took today."

"Humdinger here actually took notes?"

Hearing Raiya's evil twin use the real Raiya's endearment for me made my fists flex involuntarily.

"Sure," I agreed through gritted teeth. "Let's talk for a few moments."

"Don't forget to hurry," Mrs. Smithe reminded us as she grabbed her presumably empty coffee mug and her papers. "You need to skedaddle to your next class."

"Right," I agreed.

"Thanks, Mrs. Smithe!"

My eyes, narrowed and angry, fixated on her the moment the door shut behind Martha. "Alright, what's your deal?"

Her eyes, so similar to springtime violets, glittered with amusement. "I'm glad to see that there's no fooling you," she said slowly. "You must really, truly be in love. Aren't you, Almeisan?"

I was nearly knocked down by the use of my Star name. "How—?" I stammered. "How do you know who I am? Who are you?"

She giggled. "I mean you no harm," she replied. "My name is Mary."

"Mary?" I repeated the sound of her name, as if it was completely alien. "Mary who?"

"I actually have quite a following," she murmured, her eyes brimming with humility, "but I can understand your situation. I know you have not remembered your time in the Immortal Realm. This world's pull is quite influential."

"That doesn't answer my question."

"It's hard to explain," she said, "but I have been sent here. Your Raiya needs more time with Alora. I have come to take her place until she returns."

"You'll never take her place," I asserted, my tone full of vitriol.

"There's no need to think that," she said gently, making my anger flame into shame and sadness. "I'm here to make it easier on her, as much as you."

"This seems to make it harder for me."

"Raiya won't have to worry about re-enrolling in school if I'm here for the next few weeks," Mary pointed out.

"A few weeks?" I repeated. "What's going on up there, at Time's Star? What could be taking her so long?"

"Choice, for one," Mary surmised.

Unexpectedly, I faltered. Aleia had once told me how Raiya longed to return to the Immortal Realm, where the Celestial Kingdom was located. This was her chance to go home—or at least, it was the closest she was able to get for now. I shouldn't hold it against her if she wanted to stay for a bit longer.

THE STARLIGHT CHRONICLES

"I guess," I grumbled. "If you're here until she comes back, that at least tells me she will be coming back."

"Of course." Mary nodded. "I wouldn't have come if she wasn't coming back. I've been substituting for people for years, some of them while they have wandered from their paths or went on great journeys into other realms."

I just stared at her, no doubt an odd look on my face.

"It might be helpful to have me around," Mary continued, "in a practical sense. I can help watch your brother, for example, while you work on fighting off the Sinisters. I might even be able to help Rachel in her café. I think Raiya would like that, don't you? Her cousin is one of her favorite people."

Practicality was a necessity in the superhero business. And there was no denying that I was tired of watching Adam and seeing if Letty, Raiya's aunt, and Rachel's mother could take care of him for a few hours while we fought off demons (while she thought we at the movies or doing homework, of course.)

"You're sure you're not a demon?" I asked slowly.

Her smile was immediate; something she would have to work on if she was going to imitate Raiya for the next couple of weeks. "Of course. You know that. Your mark hasn't signaled to you that I'm a threat."

I glanced down at the Emblem of the Prince, blood-red mark, the four-point star on the underside of my wrist. "I suppose," I replied, still frowning. It seemed she knew about me, and about my supernatural abilities. "Still, I'm going to see Aleia about this."

Mary nodded. "I understand. You can check with Elysian, too. He might even remember me."

"Oh, I will," I assured her. I glanced at the clock, somewhat desperate to get away. "I gotta go. I'll see you later."

"At Rachel's, I'm sure."

I hated that she seemed to know me so well. I also hated that I had a feeling she was telling the truth, and while I had every reason in the world to hope and eagerly look for Raiya's return, I was more than upset at hearing she would not be back as soon as I thought.

There are other things I need to think about right now, I reminded myself as I headed off to my next class. *I'll get more answers when I talk to Aleia.*

THE STARLIGHT CHRONICLES

Investigation

All throughout the day, as I ran into Mary, I went through the different steps of excitement, as I mistook her for Raiya, and then disappointment, as I realized she wasn't; this was followed by suspicion and unease, as I wondered again what was happening that required Raiya's absence for so long, or if she was in trouble.

Mary made it worse when she would talk to me. I think she took the hint around eighth period because she stopped.

I almost wished that Elysian would come and try to coerce me into skipping class.

It was, I argued with myself, still possible Mary was an imposter. Part of me half-hoped she was, just so I could get rid of her, along with the resulting ache in my chest.

When the last bell of the day rang, I hurried out of the school. Not even Jason and Poncey were able to catch up with me. I could hear them calling—and my ego loved them for it—but my feet were determined to take me to the answers pulsating through my mind.

Ironic, I'm headed for a church. I almost felt like it was something like going to confession.

"Kid." I jumped as Elysian came along side me out of the darkness.

"Elysian." I slowed down some. "What are you doing here?"

"Aleia sent me to get you once school was out."

"I'm headed her way now."

"I noticed. I almost missed you as you left. You're in hurry today." He looked over at me, his dragon teeth exposed in a teasing grin. "Bad day?"

"I didn't miss you, if that's what you're worried about," I said. "But yes, I did have a bad day."

"Any demons?" He frowned. "I didn't sense anything wrong while I was waiting for you."

"I wish," I scoffed. "It's worse."

"I know it's your first day back," Elysian grumbled, "but surely even those college prep tests you complain about——"

"I met Starry Knight's replacement," I interrupted. "She looks like her, but it's not her. And other people think it is her."

"What are you talking about?" Elysian asked, stopping short as we headed through the shadowed gate, the one I knew from past meetings led through the cathedral's gardens in the back. "Starry Knight has a replacement?"

"I see you've met Mary, then," Aleia spoke up from behind us.

Elysian and I turned simultaneously to see Aleia, in her nun's habit, working with a basket of flowers and herbs by her side.

THE STARLIGHT CHRONICLES

"Yes," I grumbled, deciding to forgo any greetings, especially as her remark managed to further send my mood plummeting.

Aleia sighed. "I warned her that you would be difficult."

"She's real then? She's not a demon monster attempting to fool us?"

"I'm sorry, Hamilton, but no. She's come to help us out. We need to be grateful."

"I'm grateful that she'll be helping us out," I corrected her, "but this means something is keeping Raiya, and Orpheus, too, from returning."

"So that's why you're being a bitter-butt about the whole thing," Elysian said.

"Excuse me?" I turned to him. "You're not worried that something is wrong?"

"There's very little we can do if there is something wrong," Aleia said ruefully. "And just because they have been delayed longer, there's no need to assume that something has gone wrong." She looked pointedly at me. "Even in Eternity, things have their appointed time."

"There's still no reason to think something *hasn't* gone wrong. How do we fix it?" I asked.

Elysian stuck his tongue out at me before making kissing noises. I glared at him, but he only attempted to keep his giggles inside of his fat mouth.

I (eventually) ignored him. As much as I missed Raiya, I was sure Aleia wanted to see Orpheus again, too. After all, he had been her intended, her match on the other side of Time.

"I am not sure," Aleia said quietly. "And again, I'm not sure something *has* gone wrong."

"I don't think you should waste the time worrying about it." Elysian sneered. "After all, Starry Knight did say she has to earn a new wish. That could be something that would delay her."

"What? She said that?" Aleia blinked. "I know she wanted to see about returning to the Celestial Kingdom, but earning a new wish isn't possible."

"What do you mean?" I asked. "Aren't a lot of things that are supposed to be impossible just actually highly improbable?"

"Some things," Aleia admitted tersely, her lips pursed in irritation. "But that would be a call of the Prince, or even his father."

"There's a king?" I asked, surprised I hadn't thought of that earlier.

"Yes, there is."

"What's he like?" I asked. *Maybe we can appeal to him if the Prince of Stars doesn't feel like catering to us.*

"If you have met the Prince, you know what the father is like."

"What kind of ruler sends his son to oversee his fallen Stars?" That was something I wouldn't know. I wanted to run for president one day, not king or emperor ... although it could be a nice fantasy.

"You know the answer to that," Aleia assured me as she turned back to her gardening.

I hated it when she used that tone with me. *What if I don't actually know what you're talking about? Or what if I don't want to waste the time trying to figure out the answer when you could just tell me?*

I sighed. "It's still hard to think of that kind of stuff," I finally said.

Elysian rolled his eyes. "It must be hard for you to come out into the real world, where you can't be as selfish and self-absorbed as usual."

"Hey! I've gotten better," I objected.

"Yes, I've noticed. You haven't planned any social coups or popular party politics of late."

"The first step to getting better is to stop doing the bad things," I countered. "Something you still need to learn, apparently."

"Me? I have stopped letting my brother betray me," Elysian snorted. "*And* I've started the second part of being better—the part where you actually start doing good things."

"Like what?"

"Like babysitting you!"

THE STARLIGHT CHRONICLES

"Like judging me, you mean!" I shot back.

"Children, children. Come on," Aleia interrupted. "Can't we agree we all have been less than good at times?"

"Yes, but he's worse," Elysian asserted, flicking his tail at me.

"Just stop, both of you. Hamilton, why don't you leave this to me? I know it's hard on you, being without Raiya," Aleia suggested. "Let me talk with Mary again and check in with Alora, and I'll get back to you in a few days."

"Seriously? You need a few days to find out what's going on?"

She shrugged. "It might be sooner. But Elysian's right in this case. There's no need to worry. Just yet, anyway. That's why I need the time to investigate."

I took it as a cue to leave. If Aleia wanted to spend the next hour or so on some kind of interdimensional phone call with her sister, I'd let her.

"Don't forget," I added, "you promised me that you'd watch my brother while I have work this week."

Aleia gave me a smile. "I'll be at Rachel's when you come by to get your brother. Maybe Mary can help you out with caring for him, too, while she's here."

I wisely decided not to comment on that. I knew Aleia was trying to make things more easy for me, and I hated to be placated when all I wanted to do was complain until I got my way.

Glancing at the clock, I saw that it was almost time for me to be at work. *I'd better get going. Don't want to keep the paperwork waiting.*

☼<u>5</u>☼
Visiting Hours

The onward march of time was relentless as the next days passed without much (more) pain or interruption. Eventually, between my work at the mayor's office with my paid internship/job, school, and supernatural duties, I was able to forget that Raiya was supposed to be back, and Mary, in her own way, was almost tolerable.

I think I would've liked her better if she didn't manage to fool so many people into thinking she *was* Raiya. Everyone we passed in school had no inkling of the truth—our teachers, our peers, and even Rachel and her family didn't seem to notice at all.

"That's annoying," I muttered under my breath as Mary finished pouring me my afternoon coffee.

"What is?" she asked.

"You're fitting in so well here," I told her begrudgingly. "Even Rachel doesn't bat an eye at you."

"Sometimes people don't always let you know they've been fooled," Mary said gently. "If it makes you feel better, I don't think everyone has been completely won over."

I looked closer to see Rachel glancing in our direction, looking at us out of the corner of her eye. She flinched as she saw me looking, and then hurried away.

"I guess you're right," I admitted. "Rachel does seem confused."

"Of course," Mary speculated, "it could be because you've been in here for about an hour, just glaring at me."

"That's how I normally treated Raiya," I said.

"Not recently."

I narrowed my gaze at her as she poured herself a cup of mocha and sat down across the booth from me. "Just how much do you know about me? About me and Raiya?"

Mary's eyes twinkled. "Everything, of course. You know I've already proved it to you."

"I need more than proof."

She shrugged. "I can't offer anything else to you, Hamilton. It's better that you just accept it for now."

"I should," I acquiesced. "But I was wondering if you could give me more information. If you do know her thoughts on such things—"

"I don't have specific thoughts," she said. "Just feelings and experiences."

"Oh. Bummer."

"It's best if you don't get that information from me, anyway," she said gently. "You might wish you could, but things don't always happen the way we wish. And that can be a *good* thing."

I didn't know if she said it that way intentionally, bringing up the reminder of wishes to a fallen Star; it didn't make me feel good, that's for sure.

THE STARLIGHT CHRONICLES

I finally shrugged and chugged down a large gulp of coffee.

"Maybe we should go and do something together," Mary suggested. "It might help Rachel believe that I'm really Raiya."

"I don't get it," I said. "If the Prince did allow you to come, doesn't it bother you that you're lying to people about who you are?"

"Things are never as simple as they seem," Mary told me. She flicked her hair out of her face. "This is part of my mission. I take care of people, helping them where I can, while they've been taken away from their destinies." She took another sip. "You know what complicated lives that you and Raiya have lived so far."

"I'm not deriding you," I insisted. "I'm just surprised."

"The truth is that Raiya and you both have destinies that are split between the realms. Stepping in for her here will help bring about resolution for her fate."

The way she said it made me wince. Like it was a death sentence or something.

I frowned at that thought. Raiya had told me before that she was prepared to sacrifice her life, her mortal life, in order to get back to the Celestial Kingdom where the other Stars resided. Was it possible … ?

I shook my head. "I need a distraction," I declared.

Mary smiled. "How can I help?"

"Let's go and visit Mikey in the hospital." As I said the words, my own sense of resolve overtook me. After all, I promised Martha I'd go see him.

Why not now?

It wasn't like I had to work that night, and Aleia was still able to take care of Adam.

"That's a good idea," Mary agreed. "He's probably bored."

"Not if there are any hot nurses around," I mused aloud, managing to smile despite my mood. "Of course, he's probably gotten better about hitting on them since I went to see him last."

I'd seen him plenty of times, but it had been some time since I went to see him with the real Raiya, I recalled. I figured it had been about six weeks since then. I tried to recall the visit as I watched Mary scoop up her bag and head out the door with me.

Hopefully, he'll be in better shape this time.

"I'm sure he'll get better," Raiya told me, as she reached over and took my arm in comfort.

I latched onto her, uncomfortable to see my best friend in such rough shape. But I tried not to let it show. "I'm sure you're right," I said, "considering how well the other

THE STARLIGHT CHRONICLES

'sickness' victims are randomly waking up from time to time, as we defeat the demons who are using their Soulfire."

"There's more to it than that, in Mikey's case."

"Dinger?" Mikey mumbled. "S'at you?"

"Hey, Mikey," I said, trying not to let my voice crack. "Yeah, it's me."

"Shut up," he muttered, as he rolled over and gazed up at me. "Go home."

Raiya stepped forward before I could answer (good thing, too, because I wasn't in the best of moods after that greeting.)

She touched his forehead. "How are you feeling today?"

He shifted away from her. "If you're not going to heal me," he muttered darkly, "you can leave, too."

Raiya stepped back and sighed.

"Come on, Mikey," I argued. "Don't get mad at her."

When Gwen's Soulfire was taken, Mikey completely lost it. I couldn't blame him; he likely thought he could have prevented it, and he probably felt a lot of it was his fault in the first place. Either that, or it was my fault.

Mikey probably thought it was my fault.

When he had gone into the hospital for traumatic shock, I'd never expected he would collapse into a full-blown mental breakdown. A few days after he'd been admitted, I found out they were keeping him longer.

I watched as he peeked back at me, before sticking his tongue out and then huddling even more deeply into his blankets.

"It just seems weird to me," I whispered to Raiya. "I mean, he didn't have his soul ripped or anything."

"He did watch as the one he loved had hers ripped out though. You might have some sympathy for him in that regard."

"You mean because I saw you blow up your star?" I asked, reaching out and shifting her wayward bangs out of her eyes.

"And then tried to follow me."

"Well, when you put it like that," I murmured, "yes, you would think I would have more sympathy for him. And I would, if it was anyone other than Gwen."

Gwen had been my girlfriend for several months when she'd apparently found out I was Wingdinger. As she realized I was no longer interested in dating her—which she honestly must have realized before I did—she'd tried to blackmail me into doing her bidding, more or less.

Why she thought that was a good idea, I'll likely never know. But anger teased at the forefront of my mind again, when I remembered how insistent she was about me staying away from Raiya.

Not too many people had even realized we had broken up before Taygetay, the Sinister of Rage, had taken Gwen's Soulfire from her in an attack at the Apollo City Time Tower.

"Even if it was Via Dolorosa?" Raiya asked me with a skeptical look on her face, as her question drew me out of my own murky thoughts.

I smothered a chuckle. "You know me so well."

"Yes, I know," she agreed cheerfully. "But I love you anyway."

People can tell you all sorts of things about being in love that sound terrible and mushy-gushy and disgusting. I'd spent a good portion of my teen years arguing against them. Most of my opponents, the ones who didn't change their minds after I presented my arguments, just smiled a smile of smug superiority at, and told me I would feel differently when I was in love for real.

I hated them, completely disagreed with them, and thought they were stupid and were just being mean.

Turns out, they were right. I still hated them for it, but it was true. I could understand and even agree (tacitly) with Rachel, the most ardent and hopeless of all the romantics I'd ever known, and all her "true love" spiel.

It wasn't easy to admit they were right, but it was better than saying I had been wrong. I considered it a mark of maturity that I was able to admit that.

THE STARLIGHT CHRONICLES

"Do you have an appointment today?" I asked, tapping the smooth skin just above Raiya's heart. I'd learned that she often went to the hospital for appointments.

She knocked away my hand. "Not today."

"Tell me again; what is wrong with you?"

"Besides the fact I can deal with you?" Raiya smirked. "I told you before; the only pain I can't heal a broken heart. Something is just broken about mine, so the doctors monitor it and take my blood and blood pressure once in a while to make sure it's okay."

"Is that is what Mikey is suffering from? And why you can't heal him?"

"Possibly." She seemed a bit miffed at the suggestion, but conceded to my point. Eventually. "They keep tabs on my physical condition here, but it's brokenness will only get worse. Unless a miracle happens."

"Why not ask the Prince? He seems pretty capable of miracles."

"I like you better now that you've fallen in love," Raiya whispered softly, leaning her head against my shoulder, letting me wrap my arm around her and hold her close. "But you still need to recognize there are certain truths and realities that can't be changed without sacrifice, assuming they can change at all. Submission is another part of our calling."

"I know that." I rolled my eyes, remembering some of that quite clearly.

She gave me her best skeptical look. "Sure sounds like it."

"Can you guys just go?" Mikey snapped from his pile of blankets. "You're making me feel worse."

"You should be glad we're here," I retorted. "If this is how you're going to act, I can't imagine you've had a lot of visitors. Besides your mother."

"I've had plenty of visitors!" Mikey snapped. "Everyone from Grandpa Odd to Patricia Rookwood and even *my father* has come by."

"Grandpa?" Raiya raised her brows in surprise.

"Patricia Rookwood came to see you?" I asked. "You mean the anchorwoman from the city news station? The one who supposedly offered you a book deal? What does she want?"

"What else? The same thing *my father* apparently wants." Mikey spat. "The identity of Wingdinger and Starry Knight."

Raiya and I exchanged worried glances. "You haven't said anything, have you?" I finally asked.

"No." Mikey snorted. "But you shouldn't tempt me. Go away."

Raiya didn't budge. "What happened with Patricia Rookwood?"

"She came in, disguised as a nurse, if you can believe it," Mikey muttered. "She was hounding me for questions, until they came in and gave me my medicine."

THE STARLIGHT CHRONICLES

"How did she know about you?" I asked. "I thought you published stuff anonymously on your blog."

If that stupid blog of his was how she found him, I thought, I'm going to hit him as soon as he gets out of the hospital.

"I don't know. Someone gave her a hot tip, I guess," Mikey replied. "I sure didn't. I don't know about the blog. Apparently, she's been following the story since the beginning."

"Who was it that told her about you?" Raiya asked. "Was it your dad?"

"Why would Dante send in a journalist?" I asked. "And one who's a hack, at that?"

Raiya shrugged. "Journalists are good at getting tough answers out of people. Maybe he thought she would be successful. She does have a good record behind her."

"You mean like the mafia?"

"I don't know who told her," Mikey snapped. "You guys should go. It's almost time for them to give me my medicine again."

"What did Dante do while he was here?" I asked. "I don't think there's much Patricia Rookwood can do; I'd be more concerned about SWORD at this point."

Mikey frowned. "I don't want to talk about this with you anymore," he insisted. "You've already done enough damage."

"It's not me," I fought back. "It's the Sinisters, and all their minions, and their leader—"

"Seems like a good person to blame," Mikey argued.

"Hamilton is telling the truth," Raiya said. "The Sinisters need to steal the souls of people in order to remain alive here. Without the power Soulfire can provide, they will wither away. It's instinctive for them to steal in order to live, even if they have to leech onto someone in the meantime."

"Ew," I muttered.

"You've known about that for over a year now," Raiya reminded me.

"I know, and it's still gross."

She just stared at me for a long moment, before turning back to Mikey. "You're lucky they haven't come to attack you," she said. "They will recognize you from the attack at the Time Tower."

"Is that your way of warning me?" Mikey asked. "Just like you did with Gwen?"

"For all the fat load of good it did her," I grumbled.

Raiya frowned at me. "Come on, Humdinger. Behave. Compassion, please."

"Fine."

She turned back to Mikey. "We can still help Gwen," she said. "We just need to capture Asteropy and Elektra, and then all of the Soulfire will be released back to their owners. Tell us what you know. It might help point us in the right direction."

Mikey turned away and bundled himself in a cocoon of covers. A moment of silence passed as he seemed to weigh out his options. "I didn't say anything. The TV lady left after the real nurses came in, and Dante even left after I made it clear I didn't know anything—anything I was going to tell him, at least—he just left. Didn't even really say goodbye. He just slammed my file down on the table and left."

I frowned, moving closer. "Do you think he was acting on orders or working against SWORD?"

"*I* wouldn't know that," Mikey sputtered. "Remember? *You're* the one who he talks to."

"Because SWORD is trying to protect me, for some reason," I said. "They're on my side."

"No, they're not," Raiya muttered as she leaned against the night table. She stumbled for a moment as her hand slipped.

"Those are my records," Mikey told her. "Watch what you're doing."

"Sorry," she said. "Anyway, SWORD is a touchy subject. It has its own agenda. Which involves Wingdinger, apparently."

"Can we assume they are after you, too?" I asked her.

She folded her arms across her chest. "I don't know. It's not a large leap to make, but it's not something you want to assume, either."

The door opened, making all of us jump.

THE STARLIGHT CHRONICLES

I blinked in surprised. "Dad."

Mark waltzed through the door. "Hamilton," he said. "What are you doing here?"

"Mikey's my friend."

Mikey snorted behind me, the sound muffled by his covers.

"I see." Mark glanced over at Raiya, who quickly looked away. "I suppose this is not the best time to remind you of your mother's rules about dating?"

"Please." I rolled my eyes. "Don't bother."

For some reason, my mother disapproved of Raiya. Cheryl refused to tell me why, but I had a feeling it had to do with my brother. Way back at the beginning, Adam had recognized Raiya before I did. And of course, since it was Adam, who was only four years old now, I didn't take him seriously.

I wouldn't actually take him seriously for years, actually, which was unfortunate.

"Well then," Mark said, "why don't you go downstairs, in the cantina area, while I run checks on your friend here?"

I glanced at Raiya; she gave me the slightest nod of approval. "Alright," I agreed. I never needed much incentive to leave my parents. I headed out the door and waited, while Raiya conveyed our good-byes to Mikey and skirted around my dad.

I saw her downcast expression as we left. "Sorry about that. You don't need to worry about my parents," I told her. "Cheryl's never been one to let me be happy."

49

"I don't like getting you in trouble," Raiya said.

"Like I said, don't worry about them." I took her hand as we walked down the hall. "If time and space can't seem to separate us, I'm not about to let Mark and Cheryl."

She still seemed troubled, but her eyes lit up with a quiet joy. "Maybe they'll come around, one day."

I smirked. "Yeah, maybe after we've been married for ten years and have kids. But until then, you'll have to deal with their disapproval."

"More like you will," she corrected.

"I can handle it. I've dealt with it for years." I shrugged. "Besides, I fight demons and monsters from other realms, and I've taken Martha's tests. This is a walk in the park by comparison."

Raiya laughed before she dropped my hand. "I have to go and check on something," she said. "Can I call you later?"

"Sure." I glanced at her for a long moment, until I could see the emotions flickering off her face. *One of the cooler things about being Wingdinger*, I thought to myself.

I was surprised to see confusion, despair, and suspicion leap off from her expression. *What? What did I say?*

I reached for her hand again. "What do you need? Maybe I can help."

"No, it's just medical stuff here," she promised, backing away from me. "I'll see you soon, okay?"

THE STARLIGHT CHRONICLES

"Okay." I watched as she hurried away to the elevator and took off.

Was it something I said? I wondered. *Did she think I was serious about wanting to marry her?*

Replaying our conversation over in my head, I decided it sounded weird. Not because I didn't want to, but ... just because of everything.

I mean, come on. I was seventeen years old. I grew up in a home where family was placed behind work and school and accomplishment, and in a culture where we had forever to worry about the future, so there was little need to consider marriage.

But that didn't mean I wouldn't want it eventually, right? Someone to build a future and a family with. Someone to laugh with, cry with, fight with, stand with ... someone I could look at and know she would take me as close to forever as this body would let me go.

I stopped short in my tracks as I stepped outside the hospital.

This has never happened before, I realized. I've never wanted a family of my own. I've never wanted someone to share in my future.

Until now.

I felt sheer terror hit me the same moment soothing joy embraced me.

The concept which had once terrified me suddenly didn't seem so unusual or scary or even silly. I'd grown up thinking it was not natural—but then, at that moment, I realized I'd had enough experience with the supernatural that I should have been able to recognize it when I stumbled upon it.

☼<u>6</u>☼
Broken

I didn't mention the topic of marriage to Raiya again, even in jest. It wasn't that hard; in the days and weeks that followed our visit to Mikey, it got easier to ignore the idea all over again.

As Mary and I entered the hospital and headed up to see Mikey this time, I thought about that. *Maybe I should ... I don't know, ask Raiya what she thinks about it when she gets back?*

I knew she was risking a lot to live for me already. But I also knew she loved me, and I was more than able to feel her joy when we were together.

Would it really be too much to ask her to marry me? Or if she'd like to, maybe, one day? One day in the far-off future? After we'd graduated? From college? Grad school?

I sighed. I didn't know much about asking people to marry you, but I definitely didn't think I'd need to worry about it for several more years. Decades, even.

This is going to require some time.

"It seems unusual that they've kept him here for so long," Mary said as we arrived at his room.

"Huh?" I jerked my attention back to her.

"Mikey," she explained. "Why has he been held here for so long? Don't you think nearly three months is a long time?"

"I don't know," I admitted. "PTSD and trauma has some counseling involved."

53

"How often has he been to see one while he's here?"

"I don't know." I shrugged. "I don't come to see him a lot. He's been upset with me, mostly about Gwen. And some other stuff. To be honest, I can't say he'd want to talk about that, even with a counselor."

"We should try to find out."

I only nodded. *It is kinda weird that he's been in here for so long. I guess.*

We walked into the room, and there he was. Mikey was sitting up in his bed, reading through a magazine. He *looked* normal.

"Hey, Mike." I greeted him with a forced grin.

"Ugh," he groaned as he glanced over and saw us. "Can't you guys just leave me alone? I would've thought after the last visit you would have let me be."

"Your mom invited me for Christmas," I reminded him. "And this time, I brought, uh, Raiya, to see how you were doing."

"I don't know why you bothered. She can't heal me anyway," he muttered back. He nodded toward Mary. "She told me that several times."

I guess Mikey doesn't realize that Mary isn't actually Raiya, either. Huh. I looked over at Mary as she stepped forward to fluff his pillows.

I wasn't that surprised at it, after seeing so many of our other friends fail to see anything amiss. But Mikey, true to himself, had developed quite a crush on Starry Knight before he realized she was in love with me. I'd been expecting a little more from him than others.

"Stop," he said, waving her away. "I'm fine."

"Why are they keeping you here, then?" I asked. "I mean, why bother if you're doing fine? You even look like you're normal."

"They keep talking about discharging me," Mikey admitted, "but they won't. Something to do with the medicine I'm taking. It has to be given under a doctor's guidance. Specifically, your dad's."

"Really?" I asked. "Wonder why." Mark was a cardiologist. Why was he supervising Mikey's treatment? Didn't Mikey have a counselor or mental health nurse who could do that?

"Medicine is a big deal." Mikey shrugged. "It doesn't help that they lost my written records a few weeks ago. They were scrambling around trying to find them. They keep looking around, too, when they come and give me my daily dosage."

"What happens if you go off of it?" I asked.

"I don't know." He pointed to the computer open on the counter by his bed. "It's all in there, if you're really that curious."

"I can check it? Cool." I reached for the keyboard. "Looks like your nurse is still logged in. Isn't that dangerous?"

"Come on, are you actually going to look? I was just kidding."

"I'm curious," I replied. "And your nurse conveniently left it open for me to look. If nothing else, this is an invitation to read through everything."

"Even if they forgot to log out, it's still against the law for you to read it," Mikey reminded me. "Those HIPPA laws."

"Please. I work for the government," I said, opening the files. "It's practically a given that I'm going to break the law. Actually, I probably already have."

I thought about all the time I'd spent looking up Apollo City's budget and expense reports, looking for some evidence of the front company Dante worked for while he was a part of SWORD. He told me once, when I was on duty at City Hall, that he did some "security consulting" for the city, under a company called Otherworld, Inc. I'd spent weeks searching for some sign of payment to them, only to come up with nothing.

Even the Internet wasn't helpful. I Googled and Binged and Yahooed and Safaried a bunch of times, only to come up with nothing. Nothing coherent, I mentally corrected myself, thinking of the Norse/Latin/Finnish webpages that didn't make sense, even when they *were* translated.

That wasn't the worst of it, either; when I Firefoxed I did find some conspiracy theory webpages. Always fun to see those.

I scrolled down through the medical records, while Mary asked Mikey about his schoolwork and the selection of food the hospital offered. He wasn't happy, clearly, but he was polite enough to answer her questions as I read through his last several check-ups.

Mary is clever, I thought appreciatively. *Smart, to get Mikey's attention off me.*

I skimmed the electronic paperwork, looking for Mark's signature. If he was in charge of the medicine, seeing his familiar scrawl would likely help me find the information I needed.

My eyes stopped moving when they caught sight of a familiar logo.

The medicine Mikey was prescribed came from the Skarmastad Foundation.

What are they doing in medicine? I silently wondered.

Decades ago—or possibly centuries, I didn't really remember—an old Norwegian man named Ogden Skarmastad came to America and founded a lot of research about astronomy. That was the reason that the Lakeview Observatory was built, the Time Tower was kept up and running, and a lot of the northern part of the city was reserved for research and other related causes. It was also part of the reason that that area of the city was sort of slummy now.

Although, my mind reminded me, Logan did say that the area around the observatory was getting more and more gentrified since the Skarmastad Foundation was providing more astronomy scholarships to the city college.

But why was the foundation making medicine?

I guess it's more profitable. If it wasn't for the meteorite, they wouldn't likely have any interest at all in keeping their astronomy division open.

I took note of the address and decided to check it out later. (Thank goodness for my mad study skills.) I glanced further down the sheet, only to see red as I saw the name at the bottom of the report.

"Dante's the one who's approving you for this treatment, not your mom," I exclaimed, glancing up at Mikey. "Did you know that?"

"My mom comes in all the time to visit and to talk to the doctors," Mikey murmured. "I don't know what she knows."

"Did you know it?" Mary asked. "That your father was the one who approved the form?"

He bolted upright in his bed. "I don't care," he snapped. "Don't you get it? *I don't care.*"

"This is bad, Mikey," I told him. "Your dad doesn't have custody. This is illegal. Especially if your mom doesn't know. She's your legal guardian, even if Dante's your dad."

He crossed his arms over his chest. "I don't care. It makes the pain go away."

"What pain?" I asked. "You've got PTSD!"

"Exactly," Mikey yelled back. "I saw someone I really care about get her soul sucked out. It hurts. It *really* hurts, Dinger. Get your face out of your butt and see that I'm *hurting.* I'm not stuck in the hospital because I want to be here!"

THE STARLIGHT CHRONICLES

"The medicine isn't helping the root cause of your pain," Mary informed him quietly. "Doesn't that bother you?"

"No." He huffed. "No, so long as I don't have to think or feel it." He glared at me. "Something bad happened to me, and I can't help it. I can't change it. I might as well suffer for it."

"That kind of attitude will keep you in here for years," I argued. I wondered at that for a moment; maybe that was what he wanted. He was technically closer to Gwen while he was here. She had been placed in the hospice wing of the hospital, with all the other victims of the so-called sleeping sickness. Mikey might have even been able to go see her from time to time. I doubted he would confess to that, let alone to me.

"It doesn't matter," Mikey insisted, turning away from me again.

"Well," I said slowly, "then I guess it's no wonder why you don't like it when I visit."

There was a muffled snort from under his blanket. "No kidding."

"I do find it hard to believe I'm the worst guest you have," I mumbled. "Considering how much you hate your dad."

"He left me and my family; I expect him to be horrible." Mikey narrowed his eyes at me. "I don't think I ever expected you to betray me."

I said nothing. All the arguing in the world wouldn't have made him believe otherwise—and I might not have believed it myself. I knew I'd disappointed him.

But, on the other hand, it wasn't like I was feeding him to the wolves.

The more I thought about it, the more it seemed that Mikey was at the mercy of his dad and whatever scheme SWORD had ready for him.

"Well, I'm sorry," I finally spoke up, turning off the computer, before moving toward the door. "I didn't mean for you to get dragged into all this, you know. Gwen, either."

He said nothing, but I thought I spied a softening within his gaze. Maybe it was just wishful thinking.

Mary patted his hand. "I'll try to come and see you again soon. If for no other reason than to help you with your math homework."

Mikey frowned. "Yeah, fine," he muttered. "That stupid teacher they're sending to tutor me is annoying. She isn't even hot like Ms. Darlington."

"Careful," I told him. "Simon's living proof ugly teachers might be better for you if you're thinking along those lines."

"He seems pretty happy, even though he wasn't accepted into college. I heard he's working at his dad's office now."

"Being a CNA seems to fit him," I agreed. It had been interesting to see the mix of pride and uncertainty on Simon's dad's face when Simon told Poncey, Jason, and me about his big news when we visited him during winter break. "Though I knew his family was hoping he'd go into family practice, so he could take over their business."

"Well, I'll never have to worry about that."

I smiled. "I'd hope so."

As we were walking out the door, Mikey spoke up again. "For what it's worth," he said, "Patricia Rookwood was the worst visitor I've had, not you. She was practically throttling me, trying to get me to confess what I knew." He turned toward the window. "I'm glad she hasn't come back. If Grandpa Odd hadn't been here when the doctors came in to give me a transfusion, I'm not sure she would have left."

I paused at the door, but moved out as he turned on his stomach, facing away from me again.

"He's hurting still," Mary whispered beside me.

"Raiya thinks he has a broken heart, and that's why she couldn't heal him."

"That makes sense," Mary agreed.

"We can't do much, other than capture the other Sinisters, I guess," I said. "And we can't do that while they're not really active. Aleia told me she couldn't detect anything from either Elektra or Asteropy."

"They'll come out when they need power again," Mary assured me. "It shouldn't be too much longer."

THE STARLIGHT CHRONICLES

"In the meantime," I said, "I'm going to check into a few things. There are some loose ends with SWORD I'd like to solve."

"Anything I can do to help?" Mary asked.

A rush of longing ran through me. *She's starting to sound a lot more like Raiya.* I shook my head. "Just keep up what you're doing. I'll handle the rest."

"Hamilton."

I whirled around to see Mark standing behind me. "Dad."

"Back visiting your friend?" Mark asked. His gaze stayed focused on me; I took it as a sign he was desperately trying to ignore the fact I was still breaking Cheryl's stupid rules.

"Oh, um, yeah. We were—I was just leaving."

Mark smiled. "You have good timing. I was just about to give him another round of his medicine."

I glanced at the IV therapy bag Mark had in his hand. The clear liquid would have seemed harmless enough—if I didn't see the faint glow around it.

My breath caught in my throat as the pieces fell into place.

I hurriedly nodded. "Well, that's good then," I muttered. "I'll see you later." I tugged at Mary's arm, and as naturally as I could, I sped away.

"What's wrong?" Mary asked.

"The bag, with Mikey's stuff in it. It was *glowing.*"

THE STARLIGHT CHRONICLES

"It was approved by Dante," Mary said. "Do you think it is a special kind of medicine?"

I shook my head. "That's not medicine. Or at least, it's not *just* medicine. That's Star blood. And not just any Star's blood. That was Raiya's blood. Or it had some of her blood plasma in it, at least."

"What?" Mary's eyes widened. "How do you know?"

"It was glowing, Mary," I said. "I could see it. That's how I've always seen Raiya's power." I thought about the glow I once saw around Gwen's hand all over Mrs. Smithe when she came back out of the hospital, and even Adam. "That's got to be her blood."

"I know she comes in here regularly," Mary admitted softly. "And she's been doing it for years. Do you think they've been experimenting with her blood?"

"Maybe." I thought about Raiya's healing powers, how she was connected to my family, and her regular appointments at the hospital.

Then I thought about Taygetay, about how SWORD had managed to capture her for a time using Star blood, about how Elysian had found a bill from the hospital.

I frowned. The blood keeping Taygetay locked down before wasn't glowing like the medicine. Aleia had said that it was possible there were other fallen Stars that were giving blood. But just how many were there?

I put my head in my hands. *This just got a lot more complicated.*

"Everything will be alright," Mary said softly. I peeked up at her through my fingers and frowned. I remembered before what Raiya had said, about how I might get help when it came to handling Rachel and Elysian. Had she known Mary might come and take her place even before she left?

I *knew* Raiya had her secrets. She wasn't always comfortable telling them to me, and I wasn't always comfortable hearing them.

But was it possible Raiya was *aware* of what they were doing with her blood?

Anger hit me, hard and fast. "Just how much," I muttered, "will she insist on keeping from me?"

If we're going to continue to be together, we're going to have to be more open with each other.

My hands curled into fists as I turned to Mary again. She was right about before—I didn't want to hear that Raiya had betrayed me again from anyone else but her. "Is there any way we can talk to Raiya?"

"Alora and Aleia would be the best people to consult on that matter. While I am here, I am bound by the same laws of time and space that affect humans, same as you," Mary told me.

"I'll have to do that, then. We need some answers."

Before Mary could respond, something unusual happened.

A whisper of a *boom* echoed through me, as there was a large shift in the ground beneath my feet, and I felt my consciousness ripple awkwardly through my skin.

Mary gripped onto my arm. "Are you okay?" she asked.

I glanced around and wondered if a small earthquake had bustled through the building. That was when I noticed.

Nothing was moving. *Nothing.*

There was no sound, there was no movement; there was only a silent stillness that seemed to stall all of humanity in between the seconds of time.

I saw shadows of light and shifting winds of different emotions, spirits, and demonic auras as they stayed hovered around other people.

"What happened?" I asked. "Is it a demon?" I glanced at Mary again, and then down at myself. There was no burning from the mark on my wrist.

Mary hurried toward a window. "No," she whispered. "Look at the Time Tower."

I glanced up at the tower's famous sparkling white face. The second hand, always winding its way around in perpetual circles, had stopped. "It stopped."

"It appears time has stopped," Mary clarified.

"Why are we still able to move?"

"We are not bound by temporal means." Mary gestured to my mark. "We are both servants of the Prince of Stars. As his

THE STARLIGHT CHRONICLES

ward, I do not live in the human realm in the same way as a human would. As a fallen Star, you face the same circumstances.”

“What happened? I mean, I know *what* happened. But why?” I glanced back up at the sky, looking for Alora’s star. In the winter evening, I could see it, shimmering out in flickering light. I turned back to Mary. “Something’s wrong, isn’t it?”

“I don’t know,” she admitted. “This doesn’t happen very often.”

“It’s happened before?!”

“Sure it has.” Mary gave me a quick smile. “There are some days which are battles, and some battles require longer moments of sunshine to resolve themselves.”

I said nothing about that; obviously, it was some kind of secret joke between her and the rest of the universe.

“We should go find Aleia,” I said. “If it is a battle, then I want to go and fight.”

Time Stops

As much as I began to worry, I couldn't help but admire the beauty in the stillness of the cityscape as I flew over it. With the time stop, rainbows of auras painted over the mundane, gathering in different clouds and curls of color, adding a layer of otherworldliness to my view.

"Awesome," I muttered, looking down at the skyline underneath me. The feathers of my wings, once black and stubby, were now long, blood-colored flames. I imagined I looked like a true falling star as I sped through the time-frozen clouds of Apollo City.

Or maybe closer to a meteorite, I thought, just a bit deviously.

"You okay?" I called back to Mary, whose arms were tightly wound around my back, as we flew through the air.

"I'm fine," Mary assured me, spitting some of her hair out of her mouth as the wind whipped through its wayward strands. "I could use a hair wrap about now, though."

"I don't think it's Raiya's style," I said with a laugh. "But don't worry, we're almost back at Rachel's."

As I said it, the familiar sight of my favorite home away from home came into view. At first glance, the cozy brick, the ancient shutters, and the darkened window at the top didn't seem like much. It seemed like an old building in an old district.

I half-expected Raiya's light to flicker on as she stuck her head out the window in greeting.

What is going on with you, Raiya? Is this part of your doing? Or has something else going terribly, terribly wrong?

I didn't believe in gambling; it seemed too much of a scam and too easy of a way to lose your money. But I would have bet millions something was wrong.

And I would have won.

Mary slid off my back just as Aleia came rushing out of the building. "Oh, good," she exclaimed. "You're here. Something's wrong; something's terribly, terribly wrong."

Uncanny.

I felt shock push through me, launching out anger.

"What do you know?" Mary asked, before I could issue any angry demands.

"Take a look for yourself." She pulled out her memory bubble, the small crystal ball I'd seen her take out hundreds of times as we fought battles and looked for Sinisters. Instantly, I knew she had a right to be concerned.

The small bubble had blackened on the inside, as if it had been punctured by darkness. The oozing shadow seemed to be consuming it …

As we watched, the dark matter inside reached the outside. Aleia shrieked and dropped it, then she grabbed her hands.

"It burns," she moaned, and looked to see her hands, half-gloved like my own, were burnt with searing scars.

THE STARLIGHT CHRONICLES

"Ouch." I shuttered, before looking at the ball. It rolled away, leaving scorching marks along the road.

"Are you okay?" Mary asked, hurrying over.

"Can you heal her?" I asked Mary.

"No." Mary shook her head sympathetically. "I came here to help Raiya, not Starry Knight. I am unable to transform into her other self."

"It's fine," Aleia said, even if her voice caught in her throat some. "But I can't touch it without getting burned."

"I'll seal it away!" I volunteered, whipping out my sword. "Surely that'll be able to contain it."

Before I was able to move, a new voice snapped out. "Stop it, boy, if you know what's good for you."

All of us turned to see Grandpa Odd, lurking in the doorway to Rachel's Café.

It took a long moment for me to process his appearance, and even more so his words. My mouth dropped open and slammed shut several times before I managed to speak again. "You!"

The old man grinned at me as he gave me a mocking bow. "At your service, young Hamilton." He arched a wrinkled brow at me. "Or should I say Almeisan, the Phoenix Star, who died of Fire and was reborn into Mercy?"

"You knew it was me?" I really, really hoped my voice didn't squeak in shock.

THE STARLIGHT CHRONICLES

"Of course." A look of smugness passed onto his features. "I have to confess, I was worried that my beloved granddaughter might have revealed me even though I asked her not to. But I can see I was right to trust her to keep her word."

Raiya.

"She knew?" I blustered. "She knew about you?"

"Naturally," he assured me. "Who do you think it was that taught her how to fight?"

"So you're one of us?" Aleia asked, speaking up, reminding me that other people were with us. "You're a—"

"I know of the Celestial Kingdom," Grandpa Odd said. "And I am here as an ambassador of sorts. I cannot reveal much more at this time."

"If you're from there, then why did Raiya have to go and see Alora?" I yelled, suddenly bitter and frustrated and angry.

"Who do you think it was that convinced her to go?" Grandpa Odd retorted. "She was very adamant that there was no mercy left for her there, until she could earn it."

"Mercy earned is not mercy," I argued.

"I know that as well as you do," he countered. "But you know Raiya. She is very stubborn. It's no wonder to me why you like her; she is as legalistic as you, with all your lawyerspeak."

For no clear reason, the old man's comments sounded more like taunting than anything. (Maybe that was because

70

he'd done little but make silly comments to me since I'd met
him.)

I sputtered at his gall. "That's—Raiya wouldn't—she—"

"Hamilton!" Aleia, thankfully, interrupted me and my
sputtering madness. "This is no time to worry about this. We
need to take care—"

A small *boom!* lashed out from where Aleia's memory
bubble had rolled. Immediately, we all ducked, as a gray cloud
swallowed up the area.

Ash choked me and burned my eyes; my wings wrapped
around my face and arms as the wind of the explosion sent
me staggering.

Fire spurted up from where the small orb had been.
Squinting behind my hands, I looked over.

It was gone, with only malicious clouds wafting up from a
pile of ashes. I shivered at the sight and turned away.

Later on, I would think about how many people in the
world look for signs—signs of providence, signs of favor,
signs of love. Very rarely do people ask for signs signaling evil
is out there, and it is waiting; we don't want to be reminded it
is a force to be reckoned with in this life.

"What happened?" I asked, my ears ringing at the sound of
my own voice.

"It exploded," Grandpa Odd said from behind me. "It was
poisoned."

"Poisoned?" I glanced over at Aleia, who nodded.

"Yes," Grandpa Odd answered. "It's a good thing you didn't use your sword on it, or you might have been poisoned, too." He nodded toward the remnants of the crystal. "That's a dangerous substance; it acts as a vacuum."

"Huh?"

"The Master of the Void cannot 'unmake' creation," Grandpa Odd said. "It's a matter of physics and nature: Matter cannot be destroyed."

"I remember thermodynamics," I assured him. "What's that got to do with this?"

"If you want to go against someone who made everything, and you cannot 'unmake' his creation, how do you win?" Grandpa Odd asked.

I frowned. "I don't know."

"You hide it. You crush it, you disfigure it, you crucify it. You smoosh it into a point of singularity, and use it as a point of victory, before cutting it off from the rest of creation." Grandpa Odd pointed to where the orb had been. "That's what the darkness does; it's not darkness itself, but what it is used for."

"That's true," Aleia said quietly.

We turned to look over at her. Aleia's disposition was daunting, her normal cheeriness displaced by damaged sorrow.

"Are you okay?" I asked.

"Something must have happened to Alora," Aleia said. "I can't communicate with her anymore."

"We need to get up there," I declared. I shook my head, looking down at the ground, helpless. "I shouldn't have let Raiya go. It was stupid. We could've just waited for Elektra and Asteropy to be captured, and then all of us could have gone."

"There's no need to despair," Mary said. "Raiya will come back."

"That's not enough for me anymore. She could be in danger, too," I said, terrified by the thought of living through that possibility.

Aleia pursed her lips together. "I agree with Hamilton," she said. "With the memory bubble's destruction, there's no telling how much trouble Elektra and Asteropy will give us. When they came to this Realm, there was a restraint we pressed into them. They would have seen it as a curse," she explained.

"I remember. Orpheus mentioned it before. He thought it was Starry Knight's power," I said, recalling the battle after Starry Knight and I had been captured by SWORD.

"It was my power, and Alora's," Aleia said. "If they manage to break both my power and hers, there's no telling what kind of trouble we'll be faced with."

"What will happen?" I asked.

"Their full power will return. They'll likely destroy Orpheus, too, if they get the chance."

"Why?"

"He acts as a vessel—or he did, anyway—for their power," Aleia said. "Much as they act as a power source for other demon monsters."

"I see," I said. "So they wouldn't need him."

"And they would get rid of him to gain his power. And then they could take souls from people, and be able to keep them."

"What do you mean, keep them?"

"A human soul's final fate is decided during the course of this life here on Earth." Aleia frowned. "If the body dies, the soul goes to its resting place. With my power broken, Elektra and Asteropy would be able to take the Soulfire from humans and kill them, but still keep the Soulfire from leaving."

"That's not good," Mary said.

"No, it's not." Aleia shook her head. "And I have no control over the passage of time without my orb."

"The passage of Time is an enduring power," Grandpa Odd said softly. He reached out and put a comforting hand on her shoulder. "Alora's power should resume shortly."

"That's good to know," I said.

"She might still run into trouble," Aleia said. "We'll need to go and help her."

"Call St. Brendan," Grandpa Odd said. "If Alora is in trouble and needs help, I'm sure he'll be glad to lend his hand."

"The *Meallán* doesn't just come for no reason," I recalled. "He has to pass by this way, doesn't he?"

"That is the rule, yes," Grandpa Odd said. "But with Time's power unstable, chances are he'll be able to get here sooner than usual."

Aleia nodded. "I'll go and summon him," she said. "I might not have my orb, but I should still be able to contact him." She turned and hurried off before I could say anything else.

I thought I saw a shiny sheen of tears in her eyes as she left, and I wondered if she was thinking of Orpheus or Alora, or both.

"We should check around the city, Hamilton," Mary reminded me before I could call after Aleia.

"Yeah, I guess so. It wouldn't be good to stay here when we could be looking for Asteropy or Elektra," I agreed. I glanced over at Grandpa Odd. "So, how long have you known about me?"

"I've been waiting for you, actually," he said with a smirk. "Just as I'd been waiting for Raiya."

An odd feeling washed over me; I felt irritation surge inside of me, but I didn't say anything. Raiya told me how Grandpa Odd had been the one to pick her up after her parents died, and how he had been the one who raised her before Rachel

THE STARLIGHT CHRONICLES

and Letty welcomed them into their home more than ten years before.

As much as I thought he was a grotesque, irritating old man, he was the one who had protected Raiya—and advised her—for her entire life on Earth. I owed him something for that. I supposed. Right?

"I must say, I didn't expect your little dragon friend to be here, too. He was the surprise between the three of you."

"Elysian?" I frowned. "That's right. Where is he?"

As if to answer that question, my mark burned in pain.

"Never mind," I said. "I'll go and get him."

"Just so you know, I wouldn't worry about me if I were you, Hamilton," Grandpa Odd assured me. "I'm just a silly old man, after all. There's no need to think anyone would concern me about your identity."

I snorted as my mark burned again, this time hotter and harder. "I'll keep that in mind," I told him. "But right now, I get to go see if either of the Sinisters just got a power boost."

I grabbed Mary and carefully perched her on my back. "Come with me and help me look," I said. "I know Raiya would appreciate your help. We'll see if we can find a Sinister before Alora's power starts up again."

"Alora is a fighter," Mary said. "I'm sure she will be able to fight off what has come against her."

"I agree," I said. "I just hope it's not Orpheus. Raiya will feel terrible if she caused Alora anymore pain, especially since she managed to rip through her power before."

Mary tucked her head against my back. "We all make choices, Hamilton."

"I know," I said with a grimace, "but you just can't live with some decisions."

☼8☼
Asteropy

It didn't take me long to drop Mary off. I put her down at Lakeview Observatory, in hopes that she would be able to check in on Logan. Time remained stopped between the seconds of my world as I headed off to find any sign of an active enemy.

They've been getting worse with each attack, but they have been good about waiting.

If there's a downside to being good, I thought bitterly, *it's that you don't need to change.* If you don't need to change once you reach perfection, you don't have to wait, either.

Evil seemed to be really good at waiting to pick its battles.

As I passed through midtown, following the pulsating pain of the mark under my wrist, I finally saw Elysian.

"Elysian!" I called out.

He was transformed, the same as I was, but he was rolling on the ground and shaking.

Fear momentarily bit at me. Demons had managed to hurt both of us, significantly, before, and there was no Starry Knight to help us out this time.

I dropped to the ground beside his head and hurried over.

His head lolled back and forth, and I finally caught him between the nostrils. "Are you okay?!" I shouted down at him.

He puffed out a stream of mucus in reply.

"Ugh! Gross!" I lashed out. "Come on, Ely, don't do that."

"What else do you expect me to do when you're grabbing at my face?" Elysian's voice, deeper and gruffer than usual, was underscored with irritation.

"I suppose you're fine then," I muttered.

"Better than fine," Elysian barked. "I was laughing."

"Why?" I asked. "There's a demon nearby. And it's a big one, from what my mark seems to think."

Elysian snickered. "I know. She's right there." He flicked his tail to the woman in front of me.

It took me a moment, but I saw why Elysian was laughing. Asteropy was half-trapped in a woman's body. She looked much like a ghost would, her aura hanging out of the body of a woman.

A woman who looked a bit familiar to me, actually.

"You!" Asteropy's yellow-toned skin was gray with rage as she tried to get the human stuck in time to move.

"Asteropy," I greeted, stepping forth with my sword. "Stuck, are you?"

"This is just great," she muttered, trying to pull herself free from the woman. "First the dragon, and now you. I don't need this."

"I'm as surprised as you are," I admitted. "I thought you would have been more clever with your disguise. Hiding in a regular human doesn't seem like you at all."

"I'll agree she is a really unspectacular, regular human," Asteropy said with a smirk. "But this one has a pretty sweet arrangement."

I frowned at the woman's face again. And then it clicked.

"That's Patricia Rookwood," I yelled. "You tried to use her to attack my friend in the hospital, didn't you?!"

I nearly lashed out and hit her, but Elysian's tail swept me off my feet before I could get close enough.

"Come on," Elysian murmured to me. "Just because the woman in question is a bad person, doesn't mean you should attack her, too."

"I'm perfectly okay with it," I grumbled back.

"Well, I don't think you should be. We'll have to wait for time to resume."

"Ugh … you're no fun, Elysian," I growled.

"I haven't attacked anyone, unless you count this lady," Asteropy said, drawing my attention back to her. "I've been using her ego to feed. That largely means that people bring her stuff to say in front of a camera and she says it. There's nothing like the rush of small fame and the constant desire for more to replenish my supply."

THE STARLIGHT CHRONICLES

"How long have you been using her?" I asked, suddenly cringing. *It must feel terrible*, I thought, *for someone to use you as a puppet through your soul.*

Although I had to wonder if Patricia even realized it. Surely some people could shrink their souls small enough that if it got infected by a powerful presence of evil, they wouldn't feel it. Or notice it.

"Long enough," Asteropy assured me. "I'd break out of her completely, right now, if I could."

"I'll stick around to watch," I promised, waving my sword at her face. "Believe me, this is worth waiting for."

She narrowed her eyes at me, but I only smirked. I knew that if I could catch her, Gwen would be able to wake up once more.

"It is strange," I said to Elysian, "that even with the curse over them broken, Asteropy can't break free from Patricia."

"I told you once," Elysian reminded me, "that humans have the greater power between us, and it is largely because of how Time affects this world."

"So when Time stops, the Sinisters are at a loss?" I chuckled. "That's perfect."

"We're not helpless," Asteropy shouted bitterly. "*I* am, at the moment, because I decided to hide inside this infernal mortal! I never should have listened to that repulsive man about hiding from—"

THE STARLIGHT CHRONICLES

"What?" My attention snapped back to her face. "What man?"

"There was a man," Asteropy said, "who told me that I could operate under your radar, so to speak, but hiding inside a human, not merely overshadowing them with a minion."

Elysian and I exchanged glances.

"What did he look like?" I asked.

"He wore a dark cloak," Asteropy said, "and he hid his face from me. But he said he knew of the fallen Stars, and he knew I needed a new master since Orpheus was 'unavailable' at the time."

"Where did you see him?" I asked.

"I don't know," Asteropy muttered. "Just around here."

"Near the hospital?" I asked. "The building, with all the sick people in it?"

"I know what a hospital is," Asteropy asserted. "I've sent plenty of people there."

I looked at Elysian. "What are your thoughts on coincidences?" I asked. "I was just visiting Mikey and he said that his dad had come to see him."

"Dante?" Elysian's pointy dragon nose shifted thoughtfully. "He would fit the profile."

"I know he knows about fallen Stars," I agreed. "He told me so."

"And he does tend to favor darker colors."

"Hmm." *He* did *wear a black suit,* I thought. Maybe that was what someone like Asteropy would call a "cloak."

"I say it's worth checking out," Elysian said. "You know, if you're up for ambushing him at his house."

A bright light suddenly dashed across the sky, sending vibrations and ripples of light through Apollo City.

"What was that?!" Elysian screeched.

"Aleia is calling St. Brendan," I told him. "I was just talking with her. Her memory bubble is broken."

"That explains why she can't jumpstart time," Elysian muttered.

"She said it was poisoned."

"Alküzor's forces."

Elysian's dark whisper sent chills down my spine. "You think so?" I asked. "That's more or less what we thought, I guess."

"He wants to be free of his prison," Elysian agreed. "There's no telling how many he has in working toward that goal."

"I know we have to stop him."

"Alküzor won't be stopped, even if you manage to derail his plans this time," Asteropy said.

"I guess you would know," I said.

"I do," she agreed. "But that doesn't mean I want him to escape, either."

"What do you mean?"

"All I want is to be free of him," Asteropy admitted.

I considered that for a long moment. "But you can't be?" I asked.

"No, and if you weren't forgiven, you would know what that feels like," Asteropy said. "The Prince has accepted you back into his fold. You work for him."

"Yes, but you could, too, if you wanted," I insisted. "After all, I purified Orpheus, didn't I? I made him useless to you."

"As a vessel, sure," Asteropy agreed. "But he still didn't accept the Prince as his master, did he?"

No. He didn't.

"I don't know about that," I admitted.

"He still serves Alküzor, then," Asteropy said. "I wouldn't be surprised if he betrayed you. Once I learned how to hide from Time's scrutiny, I knew he'd likely known how to do that, too. Especially with Memory acting as his cheerleader."

Before I could retaliate against her for her derision toward Aleia, I felt Elysian go completely still beside me.

"What's wrong?" I asked.

His dragon eyes narrowed into dangerous slits. "There's only a couple of beings who know how to hide from Time's power," he said. "And only a couple that are connected to us."

"What is it?" I asked. "We know that already. That's why it's got to be Dante who told her."

"It could be someone else," Elysian said.

I didn't think so. "What are you talking about? It's got to be Dante. Who else would have the audacity to cozy on up to power, no matter who it was?"

His voice, deep and gruff, whittled down to the barest of sound. "Draco."

"Draco?" I repeated. "Draco who?"

"My brother, idiot," Elysian snarled. "He's been dodging Time for years. I never even thought about him. But he works for Alküzor, too, even as he might wish, as Asteropy does, to be his own master."

I thought about what Elysian told me before. His brother, consumed by Alküzor's promise for power, had driven Elysian to steal sacred water from Aleia's home star, damning both of them at the same time. When he drank it, he became immortal and powerful, and he slipped down to Earth, shedding his dragon skin and leaving it around Alora, protecting her and warning others at the same time.

"You're the only changeling dragon I've seen," I assured him. "I doubt it's him."

Elysian growled. "Draco was much more powerful than me," he admitted. "He might have found a way to live here."

THE STARLIGHT CHRONICLES

"Come on," I argued. "Asteropy said that a man told her how to avoid our detection. Besides, why would your brother come crawling out of nowhere now? He seems to have had plenty of time to hide away—"

"I don't know—"

"And Dante's doing something with Raiya's blood. I just know it. He's signed off for Mikey to have 'special medicine,' and it's made of Star blood—"

"What? What are you talking—"

"He's got Mikey in the hospital!" I shouted over Elysian's questions. "I saw his name on the records. Mikey's getting treated with—"

The world shook, and the streets rumbled; I felt the spirit of the world groan angrily as it was shaken from its still and silent slumber.

"Look out!" I cried, nearly falling over as the ground wobbled and Time resumed her power over the earth.

"Ouch," Elysian muttered, his long body flipping over itself as he was flung forward.

Asteropy's laugh echoed ominously as she collapsed back into Patricia's body and then took off.

"Get her!" Elysian roared.

We took off after her, and others began to move as though nothing had happened. I glanced around briefly to see no one was curious why their legs were stiff or their heads seemed to ache from Time's power. Several close by swiveled at the

THE STARLIGHT CHRONICLES

sight of Elysian and me, having seemingly appeared out of nowhere, halfway through battle.

"She ducked over there!" I called, pointing toward a corner.

Elysian snorted in reply, and sped past me. I followed his lead and jumped, taking flight.

But it was too late.

As we swung around the corner, we only came face-to-face with Patricia Rookwood's body, once more stiff and unmoving; this time, rather than having her body trapped by time, Asteropy had stolen her Soulfire away.

Odd Stories

My sigh was loud against the empty air as I walked out of school the next day, holding the dreaded piece of pink paper in my fist. I nearly hung my head in shame, but I was still close enough to the school some of my friends might've seen me.

"Detention?" I wailed to myself. "Again?"

This is the thanks I get for saving the world.

It was so unfair!

"Maybe you can protest it," Mary said, as she came up from behind me.

"It's fine," I said. "I'll just take it. Maybe that will help me feel better about missing so much class. I'm still acing them all, so that doesn't seem to be enough to make me feel like I'm making 'bad choices.' I told them I'd schedule it later this week."

"I'm still sure you can think of a good excuse for getting out of class this morning, if you change your mind."

"It's unlikely," I admitted. "I've used a *lot* of excuses already this year, thanks to Orpheus and his stupid charges."

"You still suspect him?" Mary asked.

"I told you what Asteropy said," I reminded her. "She said he was still able to betray the Prince, even though his power had been purified."

When Mary said nothing, I added, "And I don't think it's likely that Raiya would be the one to harm Lady Time. She was the one who wanted a new wish from Alora."

"What did Orpheus want?"

I frowned. "I guess he wanted the same thing," I said slowly. "He wanted to be given another chance, according to what Aleia said."

"And she wanted that for him?"

"Yeah, so she could marry him or be with him or whatever," I mumbled, not wanting to think about that. I was still mad at myself for making Raiya uneasy about that particular topic.

I glanced up. "Here's what I think. I think he lied to her, to get the Sinister crystals," I said. "Elysian brought them to the marina when St. Brendan came. He gave them to Starry Knight. He could've stolen them and then used his power to release them on Alora. She's powerful, but the Sinisters we captured could collectively have done something to damage her, possibly."

"Cutting Aleia off from communication does seem intentional," Mary agreed. "And with the power it used, it especially seems unprecedented and malevolent."

I thought about the darkened ooze and the shattered crystal, and the clouds that had formed from its expelled power. "I'll agree with that."

I saw similar clouds when the meteorite hit the town, I remembered, and I'd seen them again, when I was submerged in Alora's time pool. Was it possible Alküzor was responsible?

Something inside of me broke. *I have to stop asking questions that I know the answers to.*

"I'm off to help Rachel," Mary said, diverting my attention from my own tangled thoughts.

"Okay," I said. "I've got work tonight; Aleia's getting Adam tonight. You might see her at Rachel's."

"Will you come, too?"

"I don't know. I don't really want to hang around Grandpa Odd for a while."

"For what it's worth, he was very good to Raiya," Mary said. "He was always protective of her, like a father. While I'm sure he's happy that you make her happy, I can't imagine he looks forward to the day when she will no longer be content with just his love."

"I can forgive her for keeping his secret," I told her. "But I want to talk to her about so much."

"I know you miss her," Mary said. "But she's in your heart."

Yeah, in my heart, not actually *here.*

"I've got to go. I'll see you later." She smiled and waved, and then headed off and left me all alone.

I nearly picked up my phone, tempted to listen to music or to text or call someone. Bravely, I dismissed the urge.

I always hated being alone before this whole superhero thing started. I wanted the constant assurance of other people's care and concern and admiration, so I couldn't hear just how lonely my own self actually was, inside of me.

Now I knew what it was to be truly alone. And I was okay. I was not afraid. I had a whole universe of people around me, and tethered to me, so deeply and intimately I was okay with moments like these.

Besides, Raiya wasn't going to answer her phone; Mary would.

I glanced up at the sky. "So, how long will it be, Adonaias?" I asked. "How long will it be until Raiya comes back?"

I didn't really get much of an answer from him, either.

I dismissed it a moment later, but as I gazed out, I saw a glinting light out on the horizon.

Squinting, I saw the light was flickering off the rounded top of Lakeview Observatory.

I hadn't been there since Raiya left, I realized. *I wonder if Logan misses us.*

She'd charged me to keep watch over the city, and that included Rachel's brother-in-law and the meteorite he kept in the observatory's lab.

I glanced at the time. "I can head over and check in after work," I said. It wasn't like I had a plan for the rest of the day anyway, after my obligatory four hours of shuffling papers around at City Hall. Aleia was getting Adam, Elysian was off "investigating" or something (probably just at my house watching TV), and Mary was helping out at Rachel's. I had to work, and then I thought about going home and studying for my upcoming SATs.

Glancing back at the observatory, I reasoned that I'd get to studying eventually.

I'll wait for Raiya to get back, I thought with an idiotic grin, *so we can spend the time studying together.*

I would have to work it so Grandpa Odd doesn't decide to "help" us, too, I added silently to myself, recalling the last time he interrupted us.

"Come on, Humdinger," Raiya hissed at me some weeks before as she pushed a mug of fresh coffee into my hands. "Grandpa Odd means well, in his own way."

"He didn't have to start quoting *Romeo and Juliet* right as we entered," I said through gritted teeth.

Her eyes shined with devious laughter. "That wasn't *Romeo and Juliet*. It was *The Tempest*."

"All of Shakespeare's work sounds like *Romeo and Juliet*," I argued.

"He was quoting the scene of *The Tempest* when Ferdinand, having seen and fallen in love with Miranda, tells her he

92

THE STARLIGHT CHRONICLES

doesn't mind her deceitful father's insistence that he work to prove himself worthy of her."

"I still don't see why he did it in front of everyone here."

"*The Tempest* is partially about suffering temporarily in order to gain a reward that lasts." Raiya smiled. "I would think, likely, he thought it was an ironic way of teasing you."

"In a way that would please you, no doubt," I accused.

"Probably," Raiya admitted with a small laugh. "We have a lot of running jokes between us. He's the one who came and brought me here, you know."

"Brought you here? From where?" I asked.

"I told you before, my parents died in a car crash when I was seven," she reminded me. "They were on a trip to Norway when it happened."

I didn't say anything at first; I didn't remember that part. "I'm sorry," I finally said.

"It's okay." She patted my hand. "It's an old pain."

Despite her insistence, I had a feeling it stayed with her more than she would admit to. "Why were your parents in Norway?" I asked.

"Grandpa said it was for a second honeymoon," she said. "I thought that was incredibly romantic."

"Seems a bit odd."

"Not really. The country is beautiful, from what I remember of it."

I shifted in my seat, uncomfortable with the topic of death. "I'll take your word for it."

"Their car tumbled into one of the bay areas on a moonlit night. I was the only one who survived. I had no siblings, and no parents, and no identification, since it likely went down with my parents."

I didn't think I could say anything to that. Most of my near-brushes with tragedy couldn't compare to Raiya's. So I just leaned forward and listened intently, squeezing her hand as she continued.

"They kept me at the American embassy, since I spoke English. And then, a week later, Grandpa Odd showed up. He had married an American long ago, and had been living in the States as an English teacher. He grew concerned when he couldn't get a hold of his son, who was my father. So they discharged me to him, and I've been with him ever since."

"What happened then?" I asked.

"We moved in with Rachel and Aunt Letty soon after we got back to America. A social worker saw me arrive with him at school. Grandpa grumbled but accepted that he is terribly old," Raiya said with a small laugh. "Letty tried to get him to go to a retirement home a couple of times, but he never stayed. I'm not even sure how old he is some days, even if he is still pretty lucid."

I snorted.

Raiya gave me a proud look. "He's the reason I did so well in Mrs. Night's class last year."

"I can well believe that," I said. "It certainly wasn't because of Mrs. Night."

"Come on, she's a nice lady."

"Doesn't make her a good teacher."

"Good students make good teachers," she argued.

"Well, it's still English. Even a good teacher probably isn't able to make me like it. Even if Grandpa Odd was teaching," I insisted.

Raiya took the smart road on that argument and changed topics. She smiled into her coffee mug. "He's part of the reason I have an interest in the arts, too."

I thought of her moniker, Starry Knight, and recalled meeting her by a mural of Vincent van Gogh's *Starry Night* before one of our battles with the Sinisters. "I should've guessed," I murmured. "So he introduced you to painting?"

"Technically, Rachel was the one who suggested painting for me once I came here."

Reaching out, she showed me her wrist, the one which was marked nearly the same as mine; the Emblem of the Prince glittered, a silver shadow on her skin. Hiding the mark was a bracelet, the one I first saw when she showed up at Central for the first time.

She pointed toward the bracelet. "Rachel gave this to me when I came here. She made me feel not quite so alone."

THE STARLIGHT CHRONICLES

"But you still keep secrets from her," I pointed out. "Doesn't that make you feel more alone?"

"Sometimes," Raiya admitted, ruefully and reluctantly. "But we all have secrets." She glanced over at Grandpa Odd as he sat down on his stool by the coffee bar, obviously deep in thought. Or maybe asleep.

I could forgive Raiya—again, it seemed—for keeping Grandpa Odd's real identity from me. She obviously loved the man who had comforted her and took her in when she had no one else; it wasn't a huge leap for me to see she wanted to honor his request, even if it did mean plaguing me with esoteric taunts and overly-blown literary devices.

Besides, I had secrets from her, too. At least, I was pretty sure I did.

"Yes," I muttered to myself as I keyed in the code to my mother's work computer, "we all have secrets."

Fortunately for me, my mother's master password was not one of them. I'd known it for years, and that knowledge had come in handy years before I thought dementia would set in.

I scrolled through Cheryl's files. If someone had told me earlier that I would be ruffling through my mother's massive collection of paperwork and documents on my way out from

THE STARLIGHT CHRONICLES

work, I would've been less surprised by the impulse to do just that.

It made sense, I decided. "After all, if I am going to fight demons and seal away Sinisters," I grumbled to myself, "I might as well live dangerously."

Months earlier, when I set out to find the connection between Dante and the Apollo City government, I wasn't sure what I would discover. But I was pretty sure I would find *something*, and in all the weeks and days and shifts I'd been looking, in all the piles of files and rackets of reports, I hadn't found anything.

Dante had told me before, in a rare situation where he assumed I was under Cheryl's tutelage, that he worked for a security consulting company called "Otherworld." Ever since then, I'd been dying to find it.

Of course, Dante had told me, as a prisoner in one of SWORD's no doubt various black sites, that SWORD was an international company with no one clear affiliation, but they were supported by others around the world as they worked with the supernatural, the paranormal, etc.

I took that to mean they were paid a lot of money.

"And that means," I muttered, "there has to be a paper trail here somewhere."

There was a shuffling sound outside of my mother's office. I froze and stopped breathing.

Silence has an eerie way of being suffocating. During the next few moments, I felt my heart rate rapidly rise.

Thank goodness I left the lights off.

After several more frightening moments, I gradually resumed my search. To be on the safe side, I went through a memorized script of what to say if I was caught.

My treachery against my mother was instantly rewarded when I saw the records from City Hall's last fiscal year. *Just around the time Dante had shown up*, I thought with a grin.

My grin collapsed into a frown as I read through the statements. There was a huge payment *from* the Skarmastad Foundation to City Hall listed under "security consultation."

As confused as I was, I nearly shouted in triumph. After months of searching, there was no evidence that suggested that Dante and his semi-imaginary company had been hired by the City.

Because they weren't, I now realized. The Skarmastad Foundation had been sending money to City Hall for security consultations. That meant that the Skarmastad Foundation was the one who had technically hired Otherworld, or more likely SWORD.

The Skarmastad Foundation was already working with both SWORD and City Hall, I recalled. They were the ones who were keeping the meteorite and tracking all the outer-dimensional radiation flowing around the town.

That has to be it, I thought as the pieces began to fall together.

Immediately, a sociopathic sense of appreciation settled on me. The government had been paid off by a private company to hire a loose-cannon operation to take care of the company's interests, an operation that would then in turn use the private company's resources, giving them a financial kickback.

City Hall would get money in, they could look good while still denying all charges if there was any trouble, and they reaped the benefit of working with the Skarmastad Foundation's resources and SWORD/Otherworld's manpower. Obviously, Otherworld would get hired to investigate, and it seemed to be right up their ally, with the special concerns of the supernatural and the power that came with it.

It was similar to a building company funding terrorists to blow things up and then having the terrorists pay for the lobbying fees it took for the government to hire the building company to rebuild the city.

But what was in it for the Skarmastad Foundation? That was the only piece I wasn't entirely sure of. I knew enough from TV and movies to know that they likely just wanted the political maneuverability.

"Still, that is *genius*," I muttered, quickly making a copy and sending it to Mikey's email. I figured that if anyone would be protected from SWORD's wrath, it would be him. "That is one huge story. Too bad Patricia Rookwood's out of commission for a while; I could've used her prestige as a member of the local press."

Recalling how the Skarmastad Foundation was also responsible for Mikey's "special medicine," I decided it was

THE STARLIGHT CHRONICLES

best, as a safety, and to show Aleia, Mary, and Elysian, to take a picture of the screen with my phone.

Of course, I would need more proof. So far, all my evidence was based on my own experiences and only a few concrete connections. Most of which only *I* seemed to know about, so it would do me no favor to call attention to myself.

I'll need to get copies of the Skarmastad Foundation's files.

I recalled their address from the label on Mikey's medicine. I wasn't exactly sure where it was, but I knew it was in the downtown area, not too far down from the hospital.

Another sound hummed from outside the office. I quickly closed the files and ducked under the desk as footsteps sauntered down the hall.

☼<u>10</u>☼

Connections

The growing lump in my throat matched the bubble of fear in my chest. My stress shot up again as another pair of footsteps turned the far corner and joined in with them.

"Dante," a voice called out. "I've been looking for you."

"Stefano," Dante answered.

I'd recognize his voice anywhere, after dealing with it enough in the past months. I swiveled around in Cheryl's chair and tucked my legs up, so I was unable to be seen dancing in the mix of shadows and light in her office.

"I heard about Patricia," Dante continued.

"Yes," Stefano confirmed. "I was hoping she would have gotten us that information before she had her soul sucked out." He laughed, forcibly, as he added, "I guess it was a shame, but only to be expected that her soul would get taken up by demons, especially after reading some of her past editorials."

What's Stefano talking about?

Mayor Mills hadn't struck me as the superstitious type when I first met him months ago. How would he know about Patricia's "real" fate, anyway? Wouldn't he have seen her as another victim of the sleeping sickness?

He'd certainly given me *that* impression before.

"I know her skill was why you wanted her on the case," Dante said, "despite my recommendation not to include her."

101

"She was blackmailing me," Stefano admitted. "Had some stuff on me from twenty years back, believe it or not."

"Oh, I believe it," Dante assured him, probably too easily, because I heard Stefano choke on a response. "But we can't move further on the Flying Angels' case until we know for sure who they are," Dante was saying, interrupting my suspicious thoughts.

Covered in darkness, I rolled my eyes. Why was Stefano actually worried about the case Apollo City was pursuing against Starry Knight and Wingdinger?

"With this, and the other setback at Lakeview, we can't sustain these losses, Dante."

"What do you want of me?" Dante asked. "That kid with the blog is stuck in the hospital for severe trauma. There's nothing we can do while he's there, and he's the only lead we have left."

"Mikey," I half-whispered to myself. A shiver went down my spine.

A new, terrifying thought hit me. What if Dante, in prescribing him them medication, was actually *protecting* Mikey? It wasn't like Dante would know that Raiya's power couldn't heal him. I slipped down onto the floor and crawled closer to the door so I could hear their conversation better.

"Well, I wouldn't say that we can't do *nothing*, Dante—"

"Patricia Rookwood was the best investigative reporter in town," Dante interjected. "And she wasn't able to get it out

THE STARLIGHT CHRONICLES

of him. That should be proof enough that we're just going to
have to wait this one out for a bit."

Stefano grumbled, surprising me. When I first met him,
he'd been such a jolly character.

Was he always this bad?

"I'm surprised Cheryl's not beating it out of him," Stefano
admitted a moment later.

"She's married to his doctor," Dante gruffly replied. "I
don't think that's a good idea. The defense will bring up a
conflict of interest."

"Why?" Stefano demanded. "Someone's marital bliss
shouldn't stand in the way of our cause. Can't we get her off
the case?"

I nearly laughed. Cheryl would've likely sued *him* if he tried
that.

"You can suggest it to her," Dante said with a sigh. "After
all, she's on your payroll."

Dante had been friends with my parents, I remembered,
recalling how he'd mentioned my dad once. There was also
the matter of that one dinner at my house, where Dante had
come. I hadn't been there; I'd invited Gwen, and both my
parents were there, but I had been out with Starry Knight.

Correction, I guess he is *friends with Mark and Cheryl.*

"I thought this case wasn't such a big deal to you before,"
Dante added, after a long moment of silence. "Why the

THE STARLIGHT CHRONICLES

sudden change of heart? The polls haven't changed that much in recent weeks."

"That's *my* business," Stefano snapped, "and you'll do well to remember that."

"Certainly, sir," Dante agreed readily, but I knew him well enough (to my disgust) to recognize his placating tone, even while I was smooshed against the floor on my stomach, trying to hear through the crack at the bottom of a door.

"Find the superheroes," Stefano ordered. "I don't care about the demons anymore. Find the superheroes, and then we'll take care of them."

"In court," Dante clarified.

"Yes, yes, of course, in court," Stefano huffed. I heard him turn on his heel and head down the hall once more. "Tell Cheryl to come and see me next time you see her. I want an update on the Flying Angels case by Monday."

"Yes, sir," Dante repeated.

There was silence for a long moment. I thought I was once again alone when I heard Dante mutter, "You pompous little puppet."

And then he walked out, slamming the door behind him.

My breath slowly left me.

Dante's not as chummy with Stefano as I thought.

"Well," I said, speaking into the open air, "neither am I."

And then it was my turn. I hit the print button, stood up, and headed for the window. Once the printer was finished pushing out its publication, I was ready to go.

Pressing my mark, my fire-sheathed wings sprouted with determination.

I was going to ask Dante some questions of my own. It was time to find out more specifics to this quest of mine. If I was going to keep Apollo City safe—whether from supernatural beings of inconceivable horror or a power-hungry suit—I had to be thorough.

I carefully slipped out of the building and took off, heading for the side entrance to City Hall.

I heard his shoes on the pavement outside shortly after siding up to the building.

This was my chance to get to Dante.

Hiding in the shadows, I waited until the exit door shut before stepping forward.

Only to nearly trip and fall as another voice called out to him.

"Dante Salyards," the voice called. "You and I have some things to discuss."

I jerked to the side to see Elysian falling out of the night sky off to the side, swiping up Dante as he went down.

What's Elysian doing here?!

"What are you doing here?" Dante asked, irritating me as he echoed my thoughts.

I said nothing, just slipping deeper into the shadows for the moment.

"It's time that we had a talk," Elysian said. "After all, you only seem to show up when it's useful to you, and I've decided to change that."

"I'm quite satisfied by our current level of communication," Dante said with a grunt as he struggled to unwrap himself from Elysian's tail.

"That's because you've been calling the shots."

"I'm well connected to the other agents," Dante assured him. "They'll be here soon to back me up if I need it."

"Then I'll work quickly." Elysian's sharp-toothed grin would have made a lesser man weep. "I want to know if you've been in contact with my brother."

"I didn't know there were other changeling dragons down here," Dante replied, still trying to struggle free.

"The kid's told me that you've mentioned you know a lot about the fallen Stars," Elysian continued. "I want to know how."

"Years of observation and extensive training," Dante answered, easily enough. "SWORD has been around for a long time."

"Too long, by the sound of it." Elysian bore down on him. "Who is your leader?"

THE STARLIGHT CHRONICLES

"The Director is a highly accomplished leader," Dante said. "And she has been, for the last twenty years or so. But I hardly see what this has to do with you or your brother."

"My brother was a changeling dragon with more power than me," Elysian explained. "I was wondering if he managed to find a human owner of his own to manipulate and control. SWORD seems like a good fit, especially if they have been around for as long as you're insinuating."

I felt my brow furrow over in anger. *A human owner? To manipulate and control?! He better not try that funny stuff with me.*

Dante shook his head. "I don't have direct contact with the Director. SWORD was started as an international business group, to detect and control the supernatural."

"As a way of eliminating the competition, perhaps?" Elysian asked. "You believe in power. Why would it be so hard to see it be used for evil, all without your knowledge, especially with one as clever as my brother at the helm?"

Dante shook his head. "I've never seen him. I know a lot about the Stars and the Celestial Kingdom. I've never met a Draco, or another changeling dragon."

"Starry Knight told me the same thing," Elysian said, further making me blister over in frustration. "With the demons hiding from us and our capabilities to detect them diminished, it is imperative we find out who is behind them. Draco is one of the only ones who would know how to hide from us, and he is in a position to teach them."

"You're making assumptions. Maybe he just ran away," Dante suggested. "Or maybe—"

THE STARLIGHT CHRONICLES

"Maybe what?" Elysian snorted.

"You're a dragon," Dante scoffed. "You could have been teaching the demons how to avoid you if you really wanted."

I remembered before that Alora warned me Elysian might be a suspect.

"It was *not* me," Elysian spat.

Recalling Elysian's weakness for sweets and his temper, I was inclined to agree with him. Elysian did not have the self-discipline to be a double agent.

"But you know as I do that changeling dragons are rare, even in the Celestial Kingdom," Dante remarked. "There are not many other immortals that would have the power to hide from other Stars."

I shuddered. Dante and I were thinking too much along the same lines tonight; it wasn't comforting.

"Why do you think I suspect Draco?" Elysian shot back. "He was more powerful than me, even before we were cast away."

I decided it was time to join the conversation as an active voice rather than an active eavesdropper.

"Elysian has a point," I said, stepping out from behind.

"Kid," Elysian greeted. He lost his grin, and the sudden surprise was clearly written on his scaly face.

After giving him a glowering look, I turned my attention to Dante. "Asteropy told me that she was taught how to conceal

THE STARLIGHT CHRONICLES

herself from us, and she said Orpheus had learned too. They have a new master here. We're looking for him. That is," I said pointedly, "if we're not looking *at* him."

"I've been looking for the Sinisters, too," Dante insisted, "while protecting you and controlling their influence over the city."

"Then it's in your best interest to tell us what you know and what you're really doing," I said. I held up the paper I'd printed from Cheryl's computer. "Tell me why your company, *Otherworld*, is getting its payday from the Skarmastad Foundation."

If looks could kill, I would have been dead at that moment; Dante looked flustered and angry. "How did you get that? Who told you?"

"I have my sources," I said. "Namely, your son, whose getting treated with some strange medicine at the hospital, also from the Skarmastad Foundation. He has a copy of this in his email."

"I told you to leave him out of this!" Dante roared.

"Leave him out of this so you can keep poisoning him with Star blood?" I asked. "After you forced a Sinister to take the soul of one of his best friends?"

I was really enjoying making Dante angry. After being his captive, it felt nice to have the roles switched. The fact that he'd run out on Mikey and his mom when Mikey was younger just made it sweeter.

I'll have to tell him about this later.

THE STARLIGHT CHRONICLES

Dante struggled against Elysian's hold again, this time violently.

"Give up," Elysian muttered. "I'd hate to crush you now that the kid's ready to get some answers." I met his yellow-green gaze, and I knew what he was thinking of—the one time he captured Starry Knight, I demanded she go free in an effort to win her trust.

I don't need Dante's trust.

Considering he'd run out on his marriage vows and his family, I didn't think he had much credibility to begin with.

"Fine," Dante muttered. "Fine. The Skarmastad Foundation is paying SWORD's bills. They've been around since the city was founded, so they worked out a deal with the city to give funds for different projects, so long as they were approved and available for their organization. One of the deals was for SWORD to come in and keep tabs on the demon monsters after the meteorite smashed into the city."

"So it's like a pay-to-play scheme?" I asked. "Only the Foundation is calling the shots instead of the politicians?"

"They're a real thing," Dante assured me, his tone disgusted. "Why do you think there are so many conspiracies about it?"

"I thought they were a science-based organization."

"To find the answers to the secrets of the universe," Dante reminded me. "They didn't believe science gave a complete picture to the world. It helps with the physical, but there is plenty that's real that you can't see."

"Like love," I muttered, thinking briefly of Raiya.

Dante huffed. "Sure, kid, whatever."

"Why is SWORD giving Mikey Star blood medicine?" I asked. "It's not working to heal his broken heart at all."

"SWORD is not giving him anything," Dante hissed. "*I* am."

"Why?"

"Because, as long as he's in the hospital, Stefano, the media, the Sinisters, and even SWORD can't get to him," he explained. "At least, not easily. He's safe there."

"So you *do* care about him?"

Dante glared at me. "Next question."

I frowned, but let it slide. Some things were hard to admit, even to yourself. "Why are you protecting me? And why are you doing this as you work with Sinisters like Taygetay?"

"I told you before. If something happens to you, we're all done for." Dante struggled again. "That's the only reason I'm answering your questions right now, by the way."

"What about Taygetay? Why did you set up Mikey?"

"I didn't set him up. I took an opportunity," Dante told me through gritted teeth. "I still have a job to do here, and if I don't, things will get worse. For you and Mikey, both. So despite what you think, you should be grateful for my interference."

I didn't know what to think about that.

For the moment, I decided not to tell him about the time stop. I glanced at Elysian, before asking, "Do you know about Elysian's brother?"

"No," he answered, simply and surely. "I don't. I didn't, before he brought it up."

"Do you have any more questions, Ely?" I asked.

"No." He sighed. "I guess not."

"Then let's go. We don't need his help anymore."

Dante snorted as Elysian dropped him. He straightened out his coat and stuck his hands defiantly in his pockets. "We'll see about that, Wingdinger. We'll see about that."

Elysian and I watched as he got into his car and left.

"You'd think he'd be worried that we would follow him in the car, especially after we found their black site before," Elysian muttered.

"Yeah," I agreed. Then I turned on him. "Why are you so worried about Draco now? I don't think it's something you should let SWORD know about."

Elysian shrank down to a smaller size as we stood there. "Ever since we've been back from Alora's Star," he said, "I've been wondering about him."

"Do you miss him?"

"We all miss people we love, and the people we used to love are hardly the exceptions," Elysian said bitterly.

I thought about what Raiya told me about Orpheus—how he'd been my friend, and how he was different before Alküzor enticed him into falling.

"I guess that's true," I murmured. "Why did you talk to Starry Knight about it?"

"She knows more than we do," Elysian replied. "She was able to hang onto to a lot of her memory when she fell. She told me that she didn't know of it, but she'd look into it and let me know if she heard anything."

I frowned. "When did you ask her?"

"I asked her weeks ago," Elysian said. "Not too long after Thanksgiving. She wasn't able to give me any new information."

"Huh." I sighed. "Why didn't you tell me?"

Elysian shrugged. "It wasn't completely relevant," he admitted. "And I'm still not sure it is. But Orpheus, if he did indeed hide his intentions from Aleia, and if the remaining Sinisters are hiding from Time and our detection, it is highly unlikely that they learned about that ability from just anybody."

"I'll agree with you there," I said.

"Thanks for backing me up," he grumbled.

"No problem." I smiled at him. "Come on. We learned some good things from Dante."

Elysian snorted. "Assuming he was telling the truth."

"I guess." I frowned. "I wouldn't mind if he was," I admitted. "It would be nice to see he still cares for Mikey."

"Enough to sneak Star blood medicine into him?" Elysian sighed. "I swear, humans are so funny. They'll destroy justice to carry out justice, they'll redefine truth until it's nothing but lies, and they'll love people in the most hateful ways."

"Life is full of weird stuff," I said. "But the Star blood shouldn't hurt him, right?"

"It likely won't have any effect on him," Elysian said. "Especially if Starry Knight said she couldn't heal him to begin with."

"Good to hear."

"Still, I'd keep an eye on him. Just to make sure."

I nodded. "I'll go visit him more often," I said.

"You might want to make sure your friends are with you. I'd hate to think Dante would figure out who you are."

"I'd hate to think that too," I agreed. "Especially since that's the assignment the mayor gave him earlier tonight."

"The mayor?"

"Yeah, I overheard Stefano talking to him earlier. He's going just a bit crazy. He's desperate, after all these months, to move the Flying Angels case along. He went so far as to threaten to remove Cheryl from the case."

THE STARLIGHT CHRONICLES

Elysian snickered into his claws. "I'd almost pay to see that."

"That's part of the reason I'm hoping Dante wasn't lying," I admitted. "He said to Stefano earlier it was likely Cheryl could get the truth out of him."

"Hopefully he was right, and the hospital will be able to keep Mikey out of more harm."

"I can only hope," I said. "There's little that can stop my mother if she wants something badly enough."

"She is a determined woman," Elysian agreed. "Which I'm sure you'll remember if we don't get back to your house for curfew soon."

"Good point," I said with a laugh.

Stolen

It was only later in the week that I realized I'd forgotten to check in on Logan at the observatory.

To be fair, I had a lot on my mind. As the week crept to a close, I began to fear that Mary would be here forever; while she was certainly nice enough, and certainly helpful, my SATs were coming up, and I was supposed to study for them ("supposed to" being the operative phrase there). And for some reason, I wanted to study with Raiya for them. I didn't know why, exactly, that it appealed to me.

In addition, I had regular schoolwork (which, okay, was honestly a joke for me), a detention, swim meets, and regular social niceties, even if I did them with a surprising amount of disdain. (Who would have thought that girls trying to flirtatiously banter with me would feel so terrible?)

"Hey, Dinger," Jason called after me as I headed out of the school. "Hold up a sec."

"What's up?" I asked as he finally caught up. "You want to study for the SATs with me, too?"

Jason grinned. "I wouldn't say no, especially if it's true that Laura's is going to be joining you."

"Laura?" I raised a skeptical brow. "Gwen's best friend, Laura Nelson?"

"Sure," Jason said. "She's hot."

"I guess beauty is in the eye of the beholder," I muttered, realizing for the first time how stupid that sounded. "But I'm going to disappoint you on that matter. She's not in any study group with me, despite what the rumors say."

"Too bad." He laughed. "I should have guessed when Via was the one who said it. Anyway, I was wondering if you were doing okay."

"Drew ask you to check up on me?" I waved him off. "I'm okay. Gwen and I weren't going anywhere. I'm sorry she got sick, but I'm not devastated."

"Oh, I know about that," he said. "But I was actually wondering if it was the mayor who was giving you a hard time. I know that he's been pretty hard on my dad."

"He has been acting weird," I admitted, more to myself than Jason. "Why? What happened?"

"Right before Christmas, someone stole the meteorite," Jason said. He looked at me quizzically. "You didn't hear?"

"No." *That was probably one of the "losses" he was talking about with Dante the other night.*

"Oh, well, supposedly some teenagers stole the meteorite a couple days before Christmas," Jason explained. "The police thought it was just one of those senior pranks. I mean, who would steal a meteorite, right?"

"Yeah." I laughed, but I felt hollow inside.

"Dad said Mayor Mills was having a fit over it."

THE STARLIGHT CHRONICLES

I nodded. "I hadn't noticed," I lied easily enough. "But then, I've been studying."

"Even at work?" Jason asked.

I grinned, my first genuine one in some time. "You know it," I said. "Come on, it's not like it's hard work. It's just busy work."

"With your brain, I don't even know why you study at all," Jason admitted.

"Same reason I practice football and swimming," I said. "So I'm the best."

Jason laughed. "I did miss you some on the football team this year," he admitted. "But not much."

"I figured."

"Are you going to play next year?" Jason asked.

"I don't know," I said honestly, surprising him as much as myself. "I'll have to see about it when the time comes."

"As much as I'd love to win a Heisman," Jason said, "we need a new quarterback."

"I liked being the wide receiver," I said.

"Oh, totally. I meant me." Jason grinned. "I think I'd make a great quarterback."

"I'll campaign for you if it comes to a vote," I said. "I got to head out and get some work done."

THE STARLIGHT CHRONICLES

"Cool. See you, man," Jason said, waving as he began to wander away.

So the meteorite has been stolen.

Why?

I mean really, why would someone steal a hunk of space rock? And right before Christmas? It'd been in Apollo City since the beginning of my sophomore year.

Sure, Stefano was upset. He was the one who had been using Otherworld to track the town's radiation patterns or whatever that were syncing up with the meteorite. I could understand the loss of revenue … assuming he'd been making any money off of it. *Well, he was certainly sinking enough money into it*, I thought.

Or the Skarmastad Foundation was, anyway. They might've picked up that bill, too, especially since the meteorite was being held in the Lakeview Observatory, and they owned that.

A thought struck me as I glanced up toward Rachel's.

Could Raiya or Orpheus have taken the meteorite?

I dismissed the idea almost immediately. Raiya had been with me at the marina when St. Brendan arrived, and she didn't have the meteorite at that point. It would have been too large for her to hide.

The same thing was true of Orpheus.

Although, he could have taken it and given it off to one of his wards. Asteropy or Elektra might have it. Or even one of

THE STARLIGHT CHRONICLES

their seemingly endless minions. Hadn't the team and I stopped a demon or two from stealing it before?

Aleia had mentioned once, I recalled, that some demons might want the meteorite for its potential power.

Turning away from Rachel's, I made my way toward the observatory. I decided to go and investigate for myself. It was the only prudent thing to do; when you are hiding information from the rest of the world, it isn't hard to have high standards for who to trust.

I also had a new appreciation for who I was, and what that meant for the people in my circles of association. So I pressed the mark under my wrist and transformed, knowing Logan was more likely to open up to Wingdinger than he was to Hamilton.

The observatory was still open to the public, but, surprisingly, I managed to slip in unnoticed; that's hard to do when you've got a pair of fire-flaming wings and a feather-crown around your forehead.

The light was on in Logan's office. Immediately, I headed over. I knew it was best to eliminate Logan from a relatively short list of unlikely suspects.

"Hello?" I popped my head in, only to see that the room was empty.

After a moment of making sure I was in the clear, I waltzed in and headed for his desk.

If I can go through Cheryl's files and survive, I can go through Logan's.

120

I peered at the various files, stacks of papers with numbers and charts and symbols I didn't even recognize. Research, I concluded easily.

I opened the drawers in the small cabinet behind me, looking for anything to indicate finances or investors or the government.

It didn't take me long to find something.

A letter fluttered to the front of my fingers, announcing changes in security procedures. I perused it, skimming through the notice to see if it held anything substantial.

And there it was.

"All security clearances have been updated to include new members of our security team, contracted workers from Otherworld, Inc., to work in conjunction with local law enforcement and government officials," I read aloud. "The Skarmastad Foundation welcomes this addition to our staff and we ask our current researchers and employees to … blah-blah-blah, lots of stuff. Can't keep it short, can you?"

Glancing at the date, I saw it was shortly after Raiya and I sealed away one of the minions who tried to come and take the meteorite.

It was good to know Dante hadn't been lying to me all those months ago. He had placed security personnel around the observatory after it was attacked.

But someone managed to steal the meteorite anyway.

Well, their security can't be that great if I managed to get in here without being stopped.

"I've been waiting for you to come."

I jolted upright and twisted around, with my sword out and ready for battle; the adrenaline rush was haphazardly tempered as I realized it was Logan.

"Logan." I put my sword back down by my side. "You shouldn't scare me like that."

He smiled at me, and I could see more of the resemblance to Lee, his brother and Rachel's husband. "Sorry. I was just getting a refill on my coffee." Logan held up his now-full coffee cup with a sheepish look on his face.

"Is that from Rachel's?" I asked.

"Yeah." He grinned. "So you know about my sister-in-law's coffee shop?"

"It's famous," I said with a shrug. "I know the mayor gets all his coffee from it, too. Rachel has a big order from them for City Hall."

"It's not just for City Hall," Logan said. "The Skarmastad Foundation is a big customer. It's here and in their headquarters, too."

"Headquarters?"

"You know. The Time Tower."

The address and the numbers I'd seen in the hospital dashed across my mind's eye.

That sounds about right, actually.

The Apollo City Time Tower was close to the hospital, not too far away from midtown.

Considering the matter carefully, I knew I had to have more information on the Foundation, but I had reason to suspect Dante; he'd met Mikey there before, back before Mikey found out that Raiya was Starry Knight. I'd suspected Dante was the one who told him about her before.

An uneasy feeling suddenly settled itself into my heart. If Dante knew who Starry Knight was, she was in danger. *That* was no question. He had to find us—both of us—but it likely wouldn't take much for him to find me, if he already had found her.

But then, he didn't seem to like Stefano, I recalled. If he did know who we were, would he actually turn us into the city?

If I were him, I would turn us over to SWORD.

"Are you okay?"

Logan's question forced me out of my circle of thoughts. I pushed them aside, and decided to glance them over at a later time.

"What else can you tell me about the Skarmastad Foundation?" I asked. "I know they've been paying the mayor to hire these Otherworld guys." I held up the letter I'd taken from his desk.

"Not much, to be honest, except that they've been around for nearly a century here, and that they've funded a lot of

THE STARLIGHT CHRONICLES

different projects," Logan admitted. "Why do you want to know? Do you think they know who stole the meteorite?"

"It's possible," I said vaguely, "assuming you weren't the one who did?"

"No way." Logan shook his head. "I wouldn't do that."

"I had a feeling that was the case." I folded the letter and tucked it into the pocket underneath my armor. "I'm going to take this; hope you don't mind."

"No, go ahead. Anything to help you out. You saved my life before. I'll never be able to repay you for that."

"Please don't try," I said. "It's my job." I glanced down at the floor. "And even though you were saved, others haven't been so lucky."

"Still—"

"Still nothing. If you want to pay me back, just help me figure out what's going on."

He nodded. "Come with me," he said. "I'll show you where the meteorite was when it was taken."

He led the way, down the corridors and through the halls. I recognized much of it; over the past months, with Raiya beside me, we'd come to see the different exhibits and rooms as we'd made sure the meteorite was secure.

Someone must have stolen it right after she left, I thought. *Again, assuming she wasn't the one who did steal it.*

"Where's Starry Knight?" Logan asked.

THE STARLIGHT CHRONICLES

"Huh? Oh." I shrugged. "She's taking care of some business elsewhere."

"I know she wanted me to keep the meteorite safe," Logan told me quietly. "I was worried something happened to her when she didn't come after it was stolen."

"She's fine," I said, hoping it was true. I thought about Alora's power stopping the passage of time, and I thought about Aleia's time bubble bursting. "So, tell me what happened."

"It was a few days before Christmas," Logan said, "and I wasn't supposed to be working. But I came in to make sure the monitors were working." He nodded toward the large screens at the far end of the room. "The City's been watching the radiation signatures around the city. This computer helps monitor it."

"Is it still working?" I asked.

"No," Logan admitted. "Ever since the meteorite was stolen, it's been coming up as white noise when I turn it on."

"Creepy."

"Just a little," Logan admitted.

"Do you think it was teenagers?" I asked, thinking of what Jason mentioned earlier. "I heard from, uh, Dr. Harbor, that the police thought it could've been teenagers playing a prank."

"I don't know about that." Logan shrugged. "I do think teenagers are pretty immature though, and this seems … too complicated for them. They would've have to sneak in here and get past the security, and then find a way to remove the meteorite without tripping the sensors."

"Sensors?"

"Yeah, there's a weigh sensor underneath it, so we know when it's being moved."

"And it didn't go off?"

"No. I saw that the fuse box had been messed with," Logan said. "It looks like it was, well, burned." He pointed to the small box behind the door, close to a fire extinguisher and an AED kit. I opened it, carefully, and did see, surprisingly, that "melted" would have been the better description, but "burned" was fairly accurate, too.

"That's weird," I said.

"I know the demons have been after it, but thanks to you and Starry Knight, and your other friends, they've all been thwarted," Logan said.

I studied the fuse box and looked at the sensor plate. "Any fingerprints?" I asked.

"None."

"I guess it was a long shot." I sighed. "I don't know who took it, but I'll do my best to see to it that whoever did will be brought to justice."

"Do you have any idea who could've done it?"

THE STARLIGHT CHRONICLES

"I think it's safe to say that whoever took it is probably not a demon monster," I said slowly. "They wouldn't have been so careful about the sensors. I mean, they don't seem to have a great amount of working knowledge of human life and technology, unless they're a *tenwalisk*."

But if this wasn't the work of a demon, who would have the motive to steal it?

A Sinister, most likely. Or maybe even their new leader.

I was willing to bet it was the latter.

"Well, thanks." Logan gave me a tired look. "I'd like to have it back. I hate to think I've let Starry Knight down."

I shook my head. "I promised I would look after the city while she was … taking care of her business. If anyone's let her down, it's me."

THE STARLIGHT CHRONICLES

☼<u>12</u>☼

Past and Present

The question of the new leader of the Sinisters bothered me as I huddled under my covers, tucked into bed for the night.

It had to be someone who obviously knew a lot about humans, about how we lived and what we did. But they also knew a lot about the fallen Stars.

SWORD instantly came to mind, but I shook it off. Dante might've been the world's worst dad, but he didn't seem like the double agent type. Especially since when it came to failing to carry out his work, he only seemed to slip up when it came to Mikey.

Another agent might be a more logical possibility, I thought. It was possible, after all, that actual fallen Stars were working for SWORD, too.

"Are you still awake?" Elysian groaned as he tossed and turned over on my legs. "I can practically hear you thinking."

"Yeah, I'm awake," I said. "I'm thinking about the meteorite."

"The meteorite itself is gone," Elysian muttered. "We can't do anything about it tonight."

"I know Aleia said it could be used as a source of power for some of the Sinisters' minions. Do you think it could be used for other things, too?" I asked. "I mean, why would someone want it to begin with?"

128

"It bound the Sinisters up, along with Orpheus," Elysian reminded me, "before it thrust them through Time's power."

"So it overcame Time?"

He paused, as if he'd just realized the significance behind that reality. "I guess so." Elysian sighed and rolled himself up to face me.

"Alora told me before, about Alküzor's plan to take the Celestial Kingdom away from Adonaias," I said. "Do you think he could use the meteorite to break the world free from the other realm?"

"He's trapped in the void, squashed into this world," Elysian said. "He would have to have an agent working for him to break open the barrier between this Realm and his own."

"So the meteorite would be perfect for that," I exclaimed. "If it broke through Time's power."

Elysian suddenly stiffened. "That's true," he muttered. "But he would have to have the power of the Sinisters, and Orpheus, too. It didn't just rip through Time on its own. It had help with their power."

"And Starry Knight's," I added. "Would she be in danger, too, if that was the case?"

"We're *all* in danger," Elysian snapped. "Every day that Aleia is still cut off from Alora, and every day that Elektra and Asteropy run free, the entire world is in danger."

"I get that," I shot back. "But I mean, would Starry Knight need to be killed or sealed away in order to make the meteorite a weapon capable of freeing Alküzor, since it was her power that broke through Alora's power when she went supernova?"

"I don't know," Elysian admitted. "But I do know, if Alküzor is freed, and he gets a hold of the meteorite, he could send the universe tumbling away from the other Realms and succeed in claiming it for his own."

"That's bad."

"No kidding." Elysian huffed, sending out a small wisp of smoke. "It would be like getting stuffed into a black hole."

"Hey, stop with the smoke," I objected. "Cheryl's going to think I'm smoking if you do that too often."

"You're worried about her thinking you're a smoker when you've hacked her computer and stole information off of it?" Elysian's smirk was clear in the sliver of moonlight sneaking through my curtains.

"Yes," I said, smacking him lightly across the snout. "There's no need to cause more problems than you need to. And we have a lot of problems as it is."

"That sounds smart," Elysian said. "Who gave you that advice?"

"Mrs. Smithe, actually," I admitted with a grin. "She tends to be right, even more than me."

Elysian rolled his eyes. "Well, at least you finally seem to be better about concerning yourself with your real self, rather than the fake you."

"None of me is fake."

"You put on your little shows quite a bit," Elysian pointed out.

"I can act fake, but I am not fake," I asserted. "Lawyerspeak wins again."

"I was more focused on how you've seemed to come to terms with your destiny as a fallen Star."

I pretended not to notice that he silently agreed that I had won the argument.

"Well, it's easier to believe this stuff when I have you and Starry Knight and Aleia with me." I shuddered. "I can't imagine how it was for Raiya when she found out. She told me she was seven at the time."

"Ten years is a drop in the sea, in light of Eternity." Elysian huffed. "And she seems to be better for it, especially when compared with you."

For a moment I didn't say anything, mostly because I hated how often Elysian had compared me to Raiya before. Wasn't it good enough that we were both working toward the same goal, and that we were, finally, together again, and facing destiny together?

And then there was the fact that she wasn't exactly alone. I'd neglected to tell Elysian about Grandpa Odd as a—what did he call it—an "ambassador" for the Celestial Kingdom.

That might have actually made it harder for her on some ends.

A small smile crept onto my face; for all Raiya and Grandpa Odd shared similar interests, I didn't think it would be easy to have a grandfather as a best friend.

"I guess eleven years would be closer," Elysian amended a moment later. "Her birthday is coming up."

I was surprised by his comment. "You're right," I said with a sigh. She'd told me her birthday was sometime in late January; I wasn't sure of the exact date offhand. "I hope she's back by then."

"I wouldn't worry about it," Elysian said. "Your track record with birthdays and girlfriends isn't so great. And anyway, if St. Brendan gets here soon, we might just see her at Alora's."

Before I could say anything else, a now-familiar sensation took hold of me; my breath caught in the back of my body, and my head seemed to experience a case of whiplash as time once again stopped.

"Ouch," I muttered. "I'm surprised that time stopping hurts so much."

Elysian grumbled. "We don't always agree, kid," he said, "but when time stops like it's been doing, I feel like my mind is trying to escape my body."

"That's pretty much how I feel." I was about to ask him if we should go out and see if we could find Asteropy or Elektra when I heard it—the soft, helpless cries of a child.

Adam.

"Why is my brother awake?" I asked. "He's not a fallen Star." I frowned and looked at Elysian. "Is he?"

"No," Elysian said as he shook his head. "But he was also able to resist Asteropy's power before. Perhaps this is similar to that."

"Let's get him, then," I said, "and head out to meet Aleia. Surely she'll be able to tell us something this time."

"I don't know about that," Elysian said, his voice quiet all of a sudden. "She has been avoiding even me lately."

"This isn't something we can avoid forever," I insisted. "Now, let's get Adam and get out of here."

"Okay, okay. But you're going to have to hold onto him. I don't think it would be prudent to let a four-year-old ride on my back."

I grumbled, but I knew he was right. I thought about what Raiya had said before, about Adam.

"Are you sure you want me to tell you the whole story of how I know your mother?" Raiya asked me as we settled into the shadows of the Time Tower's closed rooftop, its classic spire rising up into the cloud-covered night. It was a few days before the winter solstice, but there was no lack of warmth so long as I was with her.

She playfully punched my shoulder. "We never seem to finish the whole story."

"Yes, just tell me," I said. "I'm sure it's nothing I can't handle."

"Alright. But don't get me off topic this time."

"I won't!"

"We've started this conversation several times, but we never seem to finish it."

"Well, we'll finish it this time," I assured her. "Just tell me. Tell me before a demon shows up or something."

Raiya grinned. "I met your mother for the first time after she'd given birth to your brother," Raiya said. "At the time, I was going to see your dad and some of the other specialists at the hospital, for some time for my heart."

"Which never got formally diagnosed," I inserted. "I remember that part."

She nodded. "It's true," she admitted, "but it's also more like it's been diagnosed several times."

I smiled at her. "Clever."

THE STARLIGHT CHRONICLES

"So your dad was working when your mom came into the hospital when it was time for her to give birth." Raiya glanced off in the distance, toward the hospital, as if she was reliving the experience. "Your dad had to run, since it was close to the time when the baby would come, but I had more questions, so I followed him."

"I can believe that," I remarked. "I'm sure Cheryl waited until the last possible second."

Raiya giggled. "You're probably right about that. Many people didn't even realize she was pregnant."

"I believe that too. She regulates food in our house down to the last crumb and switches diets so often she might as well have a seasonal collection. Did I tell you she's finally off the fasting diet? And I thought there wasn't one I would hate more than the fresh meat and sugar-free shake diet."

"Anyway," Raiya said, "before you start complaining too much again, let me tell you what happened. Dr. Dinger went to go and see her, and I followed as much as I could. While I was waiting to be picked up—I was only thirteen at the time, so I needed a guardian to take me to school—your dad comes out and says that the baby was dying, and he's calling for more nurses and for help. He was pretty panicked before he rushed back into the room with your mom."

A strong rush of emotion hit me. "They never told me that part."

"Your mother can't handle losing a case," Raiya pointed out. "How do you think she felt about losing a child?"

I certainly never considered it like that before.

"I was growing into my power as a fallen Star at that time," she continued. "I wasn't as strong or sure as I am now. But I knew I had to do something. So I snuck in to see her and the baby."

"Didn't someone notice you?"

"When you act invisible," Raiya told me, "the rest of the world is willing to go along, more often than not."

"But it had to have been chaotic."

"It was. Many of the nurses were running around and calling for supplies. None of them saw me as I made my way over to the baby."

"Adam was alone?"

"They'd prepared him to go to the NICU, and your mom was completely despondent; I doubt you would have ever recognized her. Your dad was tending to her when I came in. Adam was lying in an incubator."

"So you just picked him up and healed him?"

"I wish," Raiya admitted. "It would have been easier. I told you I didn't really know how to control my power. But I did pick him up and try to do something. It didn't work completely, but he did calm down and his condition stabilized as I held him. So, after talking with your dad, I convinced him to get the baby a transfusion."

"That had to have been hard."

"I told him more or less the truth, that my blood could heal people." She sighed. "He didn't believe me, but when he saw

THE STARLIGHT CHRONICLES

Adam's readings confirmed that he would benefit from a transfusion, I offered my blood. Your dad only hesitated for a second."

She turned her gaze away from me again. "I'd forgotten, for the longest time, how blood is powerful in a Star. When Aleia reminded me, I knew it had been a mistake to be so flippant about using it."

"But you saved Adam," I said. "That's something."

"That's a great deal of something," Raiya agreed. "And I take comfort only in that. But he might struggle with side effects for years to come."

"They might be good side effects," I suggested.

"True. We'll have to see about that." She shrugged. "My blood managed to revive Adam. When your mother learned what happened, she was so happy Adam was going to be okay. She promised me if I needed any help, ever, she would be there for me."

"I hope you got it in writing," I said with a laugh. "She'll never honor it otherwise."

"I think that's part of the reason she never liked me after that," Raiya said. "I can't blame her entirely. After all, I did get your dad to cooperate on something pretty risky, while she was in a vulnerable state. Even if she didn't know all of it, she knew I was dangerous."

"She certainly seems to think that," I agreed. "She's not happy that we're dating."

THE STARLIGHT CHRONICLES

"I'm surprised we still are dating," Raiya admitted. "Especially if she is unhappy."

"We're still dating because *I'm* happy, not because my mother isn't," I assured her. I reached over and cradled her face in my palms, then drew her close to me. "And I'm so happy," I told her, "that even when you make me angry or upset, I'm still happy."

"*I* make *you* angry and upset?" She arched a brow at me, making me laugh before I leaned in and kissed her.

"You might give me pain," I murmured against her mouth, "but you're my pleasure, too."

She clutched at me, and I went back to kissing her before either of us could start another argument.

At the memory of Raiya telling me how she'd saved Adam, minutes after he was born, I tightened my grip on him as we flew through the sky. The loss of Time's power to move us forward into the next second was probably harder on him than it was on me.

Maybe this is one of the side effects Raiya was worried about before.

Adam was content to ride piggyback style, while Elysian flew through the air beside us. I appreciated Adam seemed to sense, even at his young age, that this was an important mission and he had to behave. I also appreciated that I didn't

THE STARLIGHT CHRONICLES

have to tell him *not* to rip out my feathers or pull on my armor.

"You okay, Adam?" I called back.

He said nothing, but I felt his grip on my shoulders squeeze just a little bit harder, and I took that as a good sign.

"We're almost there," I promised.

Elysian gave a loud roar as we approached the church where Aleia was staying. It was surprising to me, but when we landed in the back gardens, I realized he'd been calling ahead to let Aleia know we were coming.

"We need to get a phone plan or something," I muttered. "Texting would make a lot of this easier."

"I don't think any of the companies would consider us a legitimate business," Elysian said. "Besides, I would have trouble using the keys with my claws."

"You seem to do okay with my parents' TV remote." From behind me, I thought I heard Adam giggle.

We glanced around as we landed in a small patch of starlight. Nothing else moved for a long moment, and then Aleia stepped out to see us.

Even in the moonlight, I could tell she was distraught.

"I was hoping you would come," she said.

"What's wrong?" I asked. "Are you hurt?"

"Not physically," she said. "But my heart is aching."

"Maybe we should go downtown and see Mikey," I said, half in jest. "His medicine might be able to help."

Elysian's tail whacked me on the head. "That's nothing to joke about." He turned to Aleia, his eyes glazing over with at least a hundred percent more compassion. "How can we help?"

"Alora's power is dwindling," Aleia said. "And with my memory bubble broken, there's no way for me to help her. I need to go see her as soon as possible."

"St. Brendan is coming," Elysian said. "He can't be too far out."

"I know." She sighed, and I caught the hesitancy in her eyes.

"Are you worried about Orpheus, too?" I asked.

She pursed her lips. "Yes," she admitted. "I'm worried that he *was* lying to me before."

I shifted my feet into the ground uncomfortably, using the moment to shift Adam's weight from one side of my back to the other. I didn't know what to say to that, but I knew by now that "I told you so!" wasn't the best option.

Even if it was most likely true.

Glancing between at Elysian and Adam, I knew we were all unsure (or unable) to say what needed to be said to make her better.

But I had an idea of what would help.

"I can't help your pain," I finally said, leading with empathy, "but I know what we can do while we're stuck here. Let's go out and see if we can find Asteropy or Elektra."

"That's a good idea." Aleia made a show of straightening her tunic. "I know I shouldn't despair."

"It's okay to mourn," Elysian said. "But you can't let life keep you down."

She nodded, and I saw more resolve in her gaze. "I know," she said. And then she came over, got on her tip-toes, and planted a small kiss on Elysian's cheeks. "Thank you, Elysian."

I swore I felt the heat from his blush. "No thanks needed," he grumbled, but he suddenly had a solemn look on his face.

I knew that Elysian and Aleia had known each other before their respective falls from the Celestial Kingdom. I also knew Elysian well enough to know that he probably wondered whether or not Aleia, from whom he had stolen the special water from her star, had truly been able to forgive him.

Maybe that was what made him keep judging me, I thought. He doubts his own forgiveness, so he seeks to undermine my own redemption.

It wouldn't surprise me.

I cleared my throat. "Well, let's go."

"Wait," Aleia said, "what are you going to do with your brother? He probably shouldn't be fighting with us."

"Ugh, you're right," I groaned. "Well, let's go to Rachel's and see if Mary can watch him while we work. With any luck, if time resumes, I'll be able to sneak him back into our house before Mark or Cheryl are any wiser."

I didn't know how well the plan would work out; but when I saw the lights on in Rachel's, a sense of hope flared up inside of me.

"Mary?" I called tentatively, opening the door. I left Elysian and Aleia outside as I walked in and glanced around the café.

"Mary's upstairs."

I jerked around to see Grandpa Odd, not sitting at his usual seat by the bar, but in the back of the room. "Grandpa Odd."

He smiled in greeting and confirmation.

He's okay with the time stops, I reminded myself. *That means he knew about Mary, too.*

I didn't know whether to be happy about that or not. "I guess you know that Raiya's not here," I said slowly.

"I know my granddaughter better than anyone," he said, "and Mary, while she is charming and lovely, and dutiful as ever, is *not* my granddaughter."

"So you know where she's gone?"

"Yes." He nodded. "She's gone to see her prince about getting a new wish, so she can live freely once more in the Celestial Kingdom."

"I guess you do know," I said.

THE STARLIGHT CHRONICLES

He laughed. "I salute you, Wingdinger, sir," he said, "but I must warn you not to underestimate me."

"What's that supposed to mean?" I asked.

"Astraiya, like all Stars, has a destiny," he said, surprising me with the use of her Star name. "And she will meet it one day. I will see to that."

"Okay," I said with a shrug. *What was that about?* "In the meantime, can you tell me anything useful? Is Mary here?"

"She's coming. She was, like the rest of us, not expecting the time stop. But I do happen to know that St. Brendan will be here the next time Alora's power stalls," he said. "So you can tell Aleia to take heart."

"How do you know that?" I asked.

"I told you before," he said easily enough, "I'm here from the Celestial Kingdom myself, on assignment. That means I'm privy to certain information others are not."

"I've heard that this world can cloud your memory of the other side of Time."

"Prince Adonaias has no problem crossing the different planes of existence," Grandpa Odd pointed out.

"But he's not a fallen Star—"

"Hamilton," Mary called as she came out from the back of the kitchen. "I'm here." She nodded to Grandpa Odd. "Thanks."

As she turned to me, I nodded toward Adam. "I was wondering," I said, "since Starry Knight's not here, if you wouldn't mind watching him while we go investigate."

"No problem," Mary said with a smile. She reached over and took Adam, who instantly clung to her. "I imagine it's hard for him to experience this sort of thing."

"I don't even want to think about what will happen if we have another stop like last time," I said. "Mark mentioned to me the daycare place had a lot of issues with him on the day that Alora's power stopped."

Mary nodded. "Go," she said. "I'll take care of him."

"Thanks." I waved and headed out the door. Before I left, I turned to Grandpa Odd. "You wouldn't happen to know where Asteropy and Elektra are, would you?"

"The Sinisters are not a terribly creative bunch," he said. "As far as evil goes, it can't create anything on its own, but only uses what it is given; it has a limited creativity."

"What's that supposed to mean?" I asked.

"It means that I think it's likely you'll find them in familiar places." His eyes twinkled, and his wrinkled face seemed even older as he smiled.

"I guess I should've known that Raiya didn't learn to be cryptic and unhelpful on her own." I sighed and rolled my eyes as I headed back outside.

☼13☼
Greed

I wasn't entirely sure what Grandpa Odd meant by his "clues," if indeed he meant anything at all. He seemed like the kind of person that would trick me into wasting time and effort and energy—something I absolutely, absolutely hated. The best thing I could guess was that I should look in other places where the Sinisters had shown up.

Immediately, I ruled out any high schools; they were out for the night, so it was unlikely that anyone would be there, aside from a janitor or a night watchman. It was also unlikely that Asteropy or Elektra would go where there was little power or money involved in their daily business routines.

The last battle had been at the Time Tower, I recalled. "Maybe we should look there."

"Look where?" Elysian asked as he scooted through the sky beside me.

"The Time Tower," I said, pointing toward the clock tower that dominated Apollo City's skyline. "It's going the power component for Asteropy, and I've been wanting to check it out anyway."

"Why did you want to go there?" Aleia asked, leaning forward as she sat astride Elysian's back. "Did you find something new from our battle with them a few months ago?"

"Maybe," I said with a shrug. "The Time Tower is home to the Skarmastad Foundation. They're the ones who are making Mikey's medicine."

"Medicine?"

"They've been using Star blood," I told her. I briefly explained the connections between SWORD and the Skarmastad Foundation. Between the medicine, the radiation machines, and the meteorite—not to mention the money—I started getting more suspicious by the moment.

"What makes you think the Sinisters would be there, if SWORD is trying to stop them, same as we are?" Elysian asked. "Wouldn't they be further away?"

"I don't know," I said. "But Grandpa Odd is right; they aren't a terribly creative bunch, and if they were able to hide from us, then it might make sense for them to go where we would least expect them."

"Grandpa Odd?" Elysian repeated. "That old man you hate?"

"More or less, yes."

"He's a Star, too?"

"I guess."

Aleia spoke up. "He's not a Star," she said, "but he is from the Celestial Kingdom."

"He's Raiya's mentor," I added. "He's raised her and taught her about her power."

"And we didn't know?" Elysian asked.

"Well, I did," I objected. "You know, after the last time that Alora's power was interrupted."

"I knew there was something unusual about him when I first saw him." Elysian frowned. "Well, if he is from the Celestial Kingdom," he said, "then he might have a point about the Sinisters. We should at least check it out."

"So, let's go to the Time Tower," I said.

"Are you sure?" Aleia asked. "If there's another place—"

"We had that big battle with Orpheus and the Sinisters at the park, and that other one near the observatory," I said. "Then there was that one at City Hall where Krono tried to kill me … "

My voice trailed off as we passed over City Hall, and my wrist started to hum with small pain.

"Okay, never mind about the Time Tower," I grumbled. "There's activity down there." I nodded in the direction of City Hall and swiftly turned my wings toward my new intended destination.

Maybe both Elektra and Asteropy are here, and we can finally capture them, and then Gwen will wake up, and Mikey could be discharged from the hospital. Assuming that Dante doesn't have a backup plan to protect him by poisoning him or something.

I could only hope.

As we landed at the front of the building, I felt the slow-burning twinge of my wrist burst into full-on pain.

"Ouch," I cried, grabbing my wrist. "You know, this has got to be the stupidest way of letting me know that evil's around."

"If it's effective, it's probably not stupid," Elysian said, making me glare at him vehemently.

I graciously decided not to comment (or hit him). Instead, I knew it was better to channel my frustration into defeating the real enemy. I turned to Aleia. "Can you scout around the building? Elysian and I will check inside."

"You have better knowledge of the building's insides," Aleia said. "I haven't been in here since the last time a Sinister and her minions were in here."

"That was Elektra," I said. "So she's the one who's likely here."

"We'd better make sure she doesn't try to take your soul again," Aleia said. "It would be harder without Starry Knight here to return it."

"Why?" I asked. "She's told me before of the Starsoul, and the different parts of the soul and spirit. Why can she help me?"

"Because you love her," Aleia said simply enough. "Once a human's Soulfire is free from the Sinisters, it's easy enough to return to the body. But for you, the Starfire inside of you— the raw materials that make you who you are, bound up inside your Starsoul—would want to return to the Immortal Realm. With Starry Knight here, you are more likely to want to stay here, with her."

"I see." I frowned. "What do we do if she takes yours?"

Aleia paused for a moment. "Let's hope it doesn't come to that," she finally remarked.

Before I could reply, she gave me a rueful glance. "Or maybe we should. Then I could return to Alora and see what's going on up there."

"Don't say that." I patted her arm lightly, feeling awkward. *This is more Raiya's department,* I thought. "I know these things hurt. But you're a member of our team, and it's just not complete without you. We need you here to help." I glanced over at Elysian, who came over and rubbed his cheek against her leg affectionately, almost like a large, scaly cat of some kind.

"Don't worry," Aleia said with a small smile. "I know I have a purpose here."

"No," I argued, "you have *friends* here." I whipped out my sword. "Come on, we need to go now. There's no telling when Alora's power will resume."

"True." Aleia gave my hand a quick squeeze. "Thank you. I'll see you in a bit." She smiled as she patted Elysian on the head before she headed out.

"That was kind of you," Elysian said. "I'm surprised."

"We're all hurting, Elysian," I snapped. "Even you are, aren't you?"

He shifted uncomfortably. "I don't want to talk about it."

"You never do," I pointed out. "Maybe you should tell more people about what happened with you and Draco. It could be helpful to you. To, you know, feel better and stuff."

Technically, therapy is supposed to work, right?

"I don't need to *feel* better," he retorted. "I needed to *be* better. And it's too late for me now. Once I took the bloodwater from Aleia's star, it was over for me. I deserved to be punished and went into exile. I don't talk about it with a lot of people. In fact," he said, "Aleia and you are the only ones who know the truth down here, so far as I know."

I was surprised. "Starry Knight doesn't know? But you asked her about Draco before."

"I've never told her the full story," he contended. "But she probably has her suspicions."

"That's probably true."

Another moment passed before I pushed through the glass door, glad it was unlocked; it was indeed a relief to know I wouldn't have to break in. "Let's go. I'm going to head for my usual office space in the back, near the Mayor's office. You take the records and the departmental offices. Let's meet back at here when we're done searching."

"Right. See you in a bit," he called, already speeding off.

"Keep it down," I yelled back. "There's no need to alert them to our presence."

Elysian had flown off, heading down the halls with haste; I was a bit more cautious in my steps. My marked wrist still pulsed with pain, but it was getting easier to bear.

I heard a moan drift eerily down the hallway. "Gotcha," I muttered and headed off to start the fight, determined to stop the Sinisters or any of their demon monsters.

THE STARLIGHT CHRONICLES

Sword held up high, I struck through the door with my foot and burst in. I was ready for them.

But I was not ready to see Mayor Mills beside his desk, clutching his chest.

"Help me," he managed as he wheezed. He saw me as the door opened. "Help me, please." He gasped, groping his arm with a pained expression.

"Mayor Mills?" I rushed over to him. "What's wrong? Are you having a heart attack?" Kneeling down beside him, I took his arm, looking for a pulse. "Do you want me to call—"

The instant before his thick hand grappled for mine, I put it all together.

He was moving when Time's power had ceased; he could not be a normal human.

Stefano was also the head of the entire city government. He had power. He had class. He had money.

He was a prime target for a Sinister.

No wonder he seemed so weird before, talking about how Patricia Rookwood's soul had been ripped out. Stefano wouldn't talk like that, unless he knew of the Sinisters' powers …

"Augh!" I hollered as a new pain ran up through my body while Stefano twisted my arm.

"So, Wingdinger," he practically sang, "we meet again."

Elektra's voice suddenly came out of the depths of his body. "Did you miss me?"

I grappled with Stefano's/Elektra's grasp, quickly jerking myself free and finding a secure grip on my sword. "Yes, I did miss you, as a matter of fact," I replied. "But I won't miss you again."

"Careful." Elektra giggled. "You wouldn't want to kill the mayor, would you? As I understand it, he has enough of a case against you."

I gritted my teeth. She had a point. I would have to free Stefano from her power first.

Stefano found his voice again. "Please, help me," he said. "She promised me power if I let her in, but she's done nothing but pain me."

Elektra laughed, making it seem as though Stefano was having a conversation with himself in two different voices. "That's what you get for falling for vague promises for power from someone you can't trust."

"How is he moving?" I asked. "Asteropy wasn't able to control Patricia when Time stopped before. She wasn't even able to escape her."

"So, you've seen my sister, have you?" Elektra laughed. "I had a feeling that reporter was housing her when I heard of the incident."

She waved Stefano's hand wildly, as if to prove the extent of her power. "I can move him because he willingly let me give him power, and I've been in here long enough that his Soulfire is saturated with my essence."

"Ew." I cringed. "That's gross."

"The truth hurts," Elektra assured me. "Just like this will."
Working Stefano's body like a puppet, she flung him at me.

I dodged to the side and quickly sent a stream of power out
the window, calling for Aleia and Elysian, and possibly
SWORD.

How am I supposed to get her out of Stefano's body? I scrambled to
find an answer, wracking my mind apart, as Stefano once
more turned to face me.

I had no answers.

Regardless, Elektra had a point; I put my sword away,
letting it hang at my side.

"Hey, Mayor Mills," I called. "Can you hear me in there?"

His body jerked and stalled, almost as if it were being pulled
in two different directions.

I had to stop myself from making jokes about *The Exorcist*.
Sometimes, being a superhero is amusing—amusing in a
morbidly, absurdist sort of way, of course.

"Can you hear me?" I called again.

"He can," Elektra said, "but I'm not letting him reply. Such
a hard thing for a politician, too, isn't it?"

"Save me," Stefano cried, his voice whimpering in pain,
even as he headed toward me once more.

Elysian came flying through the door, roaring loudly. I
clasped my hands over my ears as Stefano stumbled and fell
over.

THE STARLIGHT CHRONICLES

"Get up, you oaf!" Elektra cried.

"Thanks," I yelled at Elysian. "I hope I didn't go deaf from it!"

"No problem," he said with a grin, clearly mishearing my sarcasm as volume.

I shrugged it off for the moment. I had to move as Stefano regained his standing. I was just thinking about knocking him out when he started to scream, loudly, clearly traumatized.

"What's wrong?" I yelled.

"Augh!" His eyes, full of tears, went wide, and his mouth dropped open as a powerful ball of energy formed between his palms. "I … can't … take the pain!"

The energy, burning and blazing with orange-tinted fire, exploded at me. I ducked, and Elysian moved quickly to block the rest of its wave from me.

I watched as his skin licked it up and seemed to redistribute it across his scales. "Cool," I said. "Thanks."

"I got your back, boss," he said.

Stefano collapsed onto the floor, and Elektra was fuming. I could see her power wriggling around inside of him, almost like she was trying to chase down his non-existent willpower.

"I need to get her out of him," I told Elysian. "How are we going to do that? She told me that she's overtaken him."

"This is similar to Mikey's situation, by the looks of it," he said. "How did you heal him?"

"I used my power," I said.

"That's what you'll have to do now," Aleia said, stepping in behind Elysian. She pulled out her twin daggers. "Elysian and I will try to pin him down," she said. "And then you'll have an opening."

"Okay." I nodded. "I think I can do that."

I shifted off to the side and let Elysian position his long body around Stefano as we waited for our best chance to strike.

"You'll have to be careful," Aleia called. "Elektra's the one who has control this time, not one of her minions."

As she met my gaze, I knew she was thinking about our earlier conversation.

Before I could assure her that Elektra was no match for me and the Sealing Sword, Stefano managed to stand up. Another ball of energy began forming between his palms. I took a tentative step back.

He wasn't screaming this time; his human consciousness had fainted from the pain. Elektra was in full control of his body's movements.

"Take this!" she screamed, once more flinging her power free.

"Duck," Aleia called, jumping up and slicing her dagger down the middle of the energy bomb. It separated and bounced, ricocheting off into different directions.

The power of the explosion sent all of us reeling.

THE STARLIGHT CHRONICLES

I grimaced as walls were punched right through and massive holes appeared. I'd known from the start of this battle that taxes were likely going to go up as a result, but I sincerely hoped that City Hall's insurance would cover most of the bill for the damage.

"Go," Elysian called, shaking me out of my thoughts.

"Going," I remarked, running hard toward my target. Aleia managed to pin Stefano down to the floor using her daggers, while Elysian tangled himself around his limbs.

I grabbed his hand and pressed forward with my power, seeking a way inside the Realm of the Heart, where Stefano really resided, trapped by Elektra's power.

This time, I thought I heard her scream as I passed onto the plane of a different existence.

It didn't take me long to realize, as I was standing around in what was essentially his heart, that I didn't know Stefano very well.

It took me even less time to figure out I actually didn't like him very much.

Stefano was a robust man, easily capable of coming off as a man with purpose. I'd thought he was a classy man—a man of the people, and a man dedicated to defusing hate, settling debts, and working with people for the better.

156

Turns out most of those phrases are vague enough for superficial judgments.

Muck and slime swathed the otherwise regal setting before me. There was a throne-like chair sat in the middle of the room, flanked with drapery. Beside it, chained, was a ghost of a figure in the corner; it looked like an old man, scraping the carpet with worn, brittle fingers. The closer I got, the more I realized the man looked like Cecil, the county clerk who doubled as a greeter for our office; the biggest difference was this man was frail enough to be a skeleton in addition to a ghost, while the Cecil I knew was much more robust and rounded.

"Cecil?" I asked, coming up next to the man. "Is that you?"

The ghost-man didn't hear me; he just kept scraping away at the carpet.

"He's got Cecil under his thumb quite nicely," Elektra said. "You might as well give up on trying to talk to him. He's not able to hear you, in this world or the other."

I whirled around to see her sitting on the throne, with Stefano's body lying face down and flat before the chair, and propping up her legs like a human ottoman.

"What do you mean?" I asked, trying to keep Elektra busy.

"He's been blackmailing Cecil for years," Elektra said, thumping her foot down on Stefano. "Why do you think he's never quit and never moved up the ladder?"

"What kind of blackmail?" I asked.

"Let's just say he's the son of someone with a less than spotless reputation," Elektra said, her smile appropriately sinister. "Not the kind of person you'd want in charge of government, that's for sure. Cecil tried to hide it, but Stefano found him out."

"It's not his fault who his parents are," I objected, instantly incensed.

"No, but we all have little caveats to achieving our dreams," she spat back, her tone bitter.

For a moment, the briefest moment imaginable, I wondered what argument had won her over to Orpheus' cause.

Before I could ask, she shrugged off her offended demeanor. "He's just one of Stefano's favorite victims. Over the years, Stefano's collected quite a few."

I made a mental note to have someone secretly check into that when I got out of his heart.

I was disgusted to hear of Stefano's practices. It put everything he did in this corrupt, calculated light; settling with the protestors earlier in the year gave him a reputation with the public as a peacemaker, while the protestors would be indebted to him and his policies. Running the Flying Angels case put him in a position to influence the courts and the media. Even going around and convincing Rachel to supply the city's offices with her coffee suddenly seemed like a menacing move, though I didn't know how he was using it to his advantage.

"No wonder this place is covered in slime," I muttered, glancing around again. I wasn't that worried when I saw Stefano had his face planted in it.

Elektra laughed. "Yes, it is fitting," she said, relaxing back in her chair.

I whipped out my sword and pointed it at her, feeling a rewarding rush of pleasure at the finer movements of my form (Aleia and Raiya had been working with me to hone my fighting skills over the past months). "Even so," I said, "his life has value."

As much as I'm having a hard time believing it at the moment.

"And I won't let you keep him under your power," I finished.

I was perturbed when Elektra yawned. "I could suck him dry at any moment," she told me.

"Then why are you … ?" My voice trailed off.

Elektra leered down at me. "I haven't been able to forget the last time I had you at my mercy."

"If you think," I muttered, "I'm going to let you get to me, you've got another thing coming."

"We'll see," she said. "You might not be the toughest fighter of your little band, but for some reason you have the brightest soul. Orpheus was a fool to want to kill you."

I scowled at her.

THE STARLIGHT CHRONICLES

Stefano's head peeked up from his mud casing. "Help me," he sputtered. "Help me, please."

My attention snapped back to him. "Mayor Mills, you need to—"

I should have known better.

Elektra shrieked in anticipation as she lunged at me. I hurried to roll aside from her attack, but she still managed to claw me.

Turning, I lashed out a feint with my sword, before launching out a roundhouse kick. She stumbled, surprised, and I was able to regain the upper hand.

"Help me," Stefano cried out again.

"Just shut up for a moment," I said, pushing Elektra away again.

"She's killing me!"

Exasperated, with only seconds of free time, I turned to face him. "Then maybe you shouldn't have let her use your soul for fuel," I snapped. I turned back to where Elektra was once more taking a fighting stance.

An idea suddenly popped into my head.

Maybe I can cut off her supply if I can get him cut off from her.

I ducked Elektra's attack and slid over to where Stefano's body was stashed inside his sewage-filled mind. "Hey!" I called, grabbing his head and trying to pull him up. "Hey, get up."

THE STARLIGHT CHRONICLES

Elektra cackled. "You won't convince him to leave me."

"I can't," Stefano said. "She's promised me what I can't resist—power."

"So, she's giving you power, and you can't use it to break free from her? Yes, that seems absolutely logical." I wasn't sure if Stefano was aware enough to recognize the disdain was in my tone or not, but it made me feel better.

Another attack launched at me. Calling on my own power, I tried to use it to protect us.

A thought occurred to me. *If Elektra were to attack Stefano, she might weaken him enough that her own power would dissolve.*

But that would allow Stefano to get hurt. And generally speaking, that was supposed to be a bad thing.

For a long moment, I considered it anyway.

Eventually, and inevitably, I discarded the idea. I was supposed to capture the Sinisters, yes, but I doubted that it was to be done at the expense of others.

Even when someone like Stefano deserved it.

"I will defeat you!" Elektra unleashed a storm of energy, and I went on the defensive, still somewhat disgusted to be protecting a man who, if our roles were reversed, would likely not hesitate to throw me to the wolves.

A memory popped into my head—Stefano listening to the protestors outside of City Hall.

I cringed. *Is he really that bad of a guy?*

Yes, he is.

But I'm not that good, either.

I thought about how I'd "listen" to some of my friends, or humor some of the less popular kids while I was in school. If our roles were reversed, I realized, I would be just as undeserving as Stefano when it came to being saved.

At best, I was only slightly better. But that was not comforting—not at all, not in the least.

"You can't outlast me," Elektra said.

I knocked over Stefano's throne, using it as a barrier between Elektra and the two of us as she inched closer.

Okay, so what would I do to save myself in this situation?

"Come on, come on, think!" I yelled at myself.

I couldn't break her power over him. I couldn't make him break it. I couldn't seal her away without worrying he would get sucked in, and that would be less than ideal if he did.

The last time I had this issue, I thought, *my own power forced back the fenfleal demon inside of Logan.* Would it be possible to do that again?

"It's worth a shot," I said with a groan. *This is going to hurt some.*

I was never good with fear, but I had to have faith that it would be okay. I could survive this. *Courage, please*, I prayed.

As I leapt to my feet, I kicked away from Stefano and pulled out my sword. "This is it!" I yelled as I charged forward.

Elektra took the bait.

She reached for me, clipping her arm on my sword but never faltering as she grabbed for my heart once more.

At the sudden and forceful onslaught of power, I nearly collapsed. My sword fell from my hand as I grabbed hers with both of mine and held her there.

"Too painful for you, Wingdinger?" she asked, goading me.

I had to grin through my pain. "Funny, I was just about to ask you the same question." And then, grasping her even more tightly, my own power—the power of my heart, mind, and soul—all rushed at her, sweeping her under a tidal wave of light.

Now it was Elektra's turn to scream, as the blood-colored flame inside of me sprouted forth, rushing into her. I watched as her power diminished and crumbled. Her orange-tinted skin turned into a glaring red and dulled to ash-black as I cried out, terrified to see the extent of my own capabilities.

I felt the moment that Stefano was freed from her control. I saw into Elektra's mind as she gave away her power in love and kindness in her previous form as the Starry Virtue of Generosity. I knew of her doubt and fear as she looked away from the Celestial Kingdom toward a fallen Earth. I mourned the second she agreed with Orpheus, that such things needed power in order to be done.

163

And when Elektra felt her own remorse, I no longer felt my own power causing her pain; rather, it was her own knowledge of her choices that started to cause her to implode.

I stepped free from her and saw her tears of regret. "I'm sorry," I said, not sure what exactly what I was sorry for. Maybe it was just because I didn't want her to cause pain to others anymore, and it had to end this way because she couldn't stop. Or maybe it was because she gave up her power to do any good when she tried to take a shortcut.

Stilled, Elektra said nothing else—nor did she speak ever again. I picked up my sword and slashed through her. She allowed me to, with no resistance.

I breathed in and out, hard and silent, as I watched her own soul wrap around her and send her into a crystalized version of a black hole.

"Is she gone?" Stefano's voice broke through the quiet of the moment.

"Yes," I said, grabbing a hold of the blackened orange crystal before me and tucking it into the pocket at my shoulder.

All the world would be a better place if we just admitted we're terrible at not being terrible.

I thought it was odd, for just that moment, that I'd been christened the Star of Mercy, yet sent to capture the Sinisters. What was I doing to offer mercy to those who, if they'd only felt the sadness their actions caused, would change?

And then I looked at Stefano, and I knew why. Mercy could only be granted to those who actually felt remorse for their actions, and when harm was stopped, it was a gift to those who were under the tyranny of the unmerciful.

As Stefano stood up and righted his throne, his pride and pomp returning, I had to wonder, as I returned to the world of reality around us, if I'd saved the right person.

THE STARLIGHT CHRONICLES

☼14☼
Across Dreams

I felt better about Stefano when my eyes opened and adjusted to the environment with which I was most familiar. Before, he had been restless and shaking; when I glanced at him, he seemed to have calmed down quite a lot. Upon reentry into reality, I saw Elysian and Aleia standing over me as I held onto Stefano's arm. I dropped it unceremoniously.

"Are you okay?" Aleia asked. "We were concerned."

"I'm fine," I said, my voice raw against the gradient of the atmosphere. What was it about this plane of existence that just seemed so oppressive sometimes?

"What happened?" Elysian asked. "Did you capture Elektra?"

"You don't see her here still, do you?" I retorted.

"Time has yet to resume," Aleia said. "I imagine we've been here several moments, but the world will pass over it."

"That might be a good thing," I said, gesturing down to the sweaty but still man beside me. "Mayor Mills is silent, thanks to Elektra's defeat." I reached into my pocket, where Elektra's crystal now resided, and pulled it out.

"You did get it," Aleia said. "Great work."

"It wasn't easy," I said, recalling the pain. "She actually seemed sorry for her actions when I bested her."

"She might have just been sorry for getting caught," Aleia said, glancing pointedly over at Elysian. "A lot of people struggle with that."

Elysian frowned at her, before sniffing resentfully at her insinuations.

"You two should stuff it," Elysian argued.

"I was just pointing out that it's a common problem," Aleia murmured.

"I can well imagine that," I said, thinking of the time Mrs. Smithe had given me a detention for playing my Game Pac in class. Glancing at Elysian, I added, "The first part, I mean, not the part about Elysian having issues."

It suddenly hit me that because of my detention, I was able to meet Raiya. *Sort of,* I mentally corrected myself. She was there. I'd seen her, in passing, for the first time, even though I'd missed her and all she meant for my life at the time.

"I miss her now," I admitted aloud.

"You mean Raiya?" Aleia said, ducking free of Elysian's mutterings, as she turned to me.

"Of course," I said. I playfully tossed Elektra's crystal up into the air and caught it. "I wish I could tell her we only need Asteropy now. She would be happy to hear that."

"You know she's in your heart," Aleia said, taking my hand and placing it over my chest, right up to where I could feel my heart beat.

THE STARLIGHT CHRONICLES

My fingertips grazed the area where Elektra had attacked me moments earlier. It was still raw with traces of lingering pain. "It's hardly the same," I said. "She's been gone for close to a month now."

"We'll see her soon," Elysian said. "When we go up with St. Brendan."

"I know." I sighed. "It's just that this is a victory for us, for our mission. We're supposed to capture the Sinisters, and once we do that we'll be done with all this superhero stuff."

Aleia gave me a quizzical expression. "Are you that eager to be done with our work?" she said.

"Shouldn't I be?" I asked. "It's not like the Sinisters are doing anyone any favors, rampaging around the town, trying to get people's souls and stuff. And there's got to be more to this life than just chasing the bad guys around and saving the world."

"You won't save the world," Aleia told me, her voice uncharacteristically blunt. "You will help the world, it is true, but capturing these beings so intent on destruction and demoralization is not your final calling. There are other battles that you will face, Hamilton—battles of the heart and inside the human soul."

She nodded toward me. "Even in your own heart."

I had a feeling Aleia was warning me that the battles I wanted to run away from were going to be mere warm-ups for the ones I wanted to run toward.

I didn't really know what to say to *that*.

THE STARLIGHT CHRONICLES

Fortunately for me, I didn't have to worry about a response.

Time's power resumed, and I felt my body and my inner self struggle to slide back into its same rhythm.

"Ow," I muttered, making sure my knees didn't buckle and my balance wasn't lost. "That's going to get old." I brightened a moment later. "Good thing St. Brendan will be here the next time Alora's power stalls."

"Where did you hear that?" Elysian asked, shaking his own scaly skin at the bristling effect of Time's power.

"Grandpa Odd told me," I said.

"And you believe him?"

"He's Raiya's mentor, in addition to being her grandfather. I guess he would know some things like that."

Elysian snorted, and we must have looked like we were going to prepare for another one of our arguments because Aleia stepped between us.

"Let's hope that it is true," she said, "since there's no way to know if he will come sooner. And if we leave when Time is stopped, we might be able to get to Alora so I can fix the time stream for us, so no one will miss us while we're gone."

"That would be an advantage," I said. I still had to take my detention for vanishing from school in the middle day from before, and I didn't really want to earn any more.

THE STARLIGHT CHRONICLES

"Aw … " Stefano moaned loudly as his eyes blinked open. His hands grappled for something to latch onto as he began to shake. "What's going on? Where am I?"

"Mayor Mills?" I asked tentatively.

His hand found my arm. "You! You're one of those superheroes," he said.

"Yes."

"Help me, help me. One of the monsters. She was … attacking me … didn't realize it was … I need you to help me, please … "

I glowered at him. "If I help you, will you stop blackmailing Cecil?"

Stefano's eyes went wide. "How do you know about that?" he sputtered, before getting angry and "correcting" himself. "I mean, that's a terrible thing to say, young man, especially when you don't have proof … "

I sighed. "I suppose we have to help him anyway," I said to Aleia, who nodded.

"I'm afraid so," she agreed.

"I want my lawyer," Stefano said. He grabbed his chest with his arm, a pained expression on his face.

Classic heart attack signs, I thought grimly.

"You *need* a hospital," I corrected. "You're shaking and you're having chest pains. You need to go to a doctor."

THE STARLIGHT CHRONICLES

"I confess nothing," he insisted.

I was strongly tempted to slap him before I turned to Elysian. "Elysian, can you fly with him on your back?"

Elysian made a face, but he moved to help Aleia and me as we lifted him up. Aleia held onto him from behind, while I promised to fly beside them and steady him.

It wasn't long before we dropped him off at the hospital, but it felt like forever before I retrieved a screaming Adam from Mary and Grandpa Odd, found my way to my room, and flopped down on my bed to find sleep.

It had been a long time since I had dreams of another realm.

I suspected it had to do with the fact that I was more willing to accept my destiny, to believe that what was happening with my life was a good thing, and to act on it when circumstances demanded.

But even though it had been some time since the last time my mind was transported to another world, I immediately recognized the instant mix of fear and frustration that encapsulated me.

So, where am I going now? Maybe back to Raiya's star so I can watch it supernova again? Or am I off to see Orpheus, or Asteropy, or the new leader of the Sinisters?

I was, in all fairness, used to getting the worst and used to disappointment, even at the best.

So I was surprised to see glimpses of the world beyond this one—the beauty and majesty of the heavens, the seas of space-time; it was the cosmic home of the Stars. The place had passed me by as I rode with St. Brendan on the *Meallán.*

I looked down to see my superhero self; I had transformed and I was flying through the realm beyond Time.

From the shining beauty of the Field of Lights, the quiet burning of bright Stars, the Reborns, to the compelling complexity of the unliving, the scars of the supernovas, and the pervasive design of the fabric of time—all of it rang with astounding clarity in my dream.

I would have liked to believe that nothing was so beautiful as the sight of Starry Knight as she sailed on in the starlight. But I knew I would be lying.

Elysian once said that he found the ride to Alora's Star depressing, because he knew that in all the goodness of his surroundings he failed to live up to that standard.

It was clear as day to me, as I looked on Starry Knight, that he probably had a point.

Raiya, even in her transformed outfit, with her determined focus, looked tired and worn. The light in her eyes, the vibrancy of springtime violets, seemed dulled and dim against the sparkling gems in the surrounding atmosphere.

I still wanted to be with her.

Maybe I am with her, I thought. *This could be a nice dream, couldn't it?* Not everything that happened in my dreams happened in real life.

A disquieting sensation shot through me. I recognized where we were.

Raiya set her boots down on the ground at one of the bases of Aleia's star. She seemed nervous, almost; I watched in amusement as she squared her shoulders and folded her wings back. She didn't seem to see me as I stepped down behind her.

I looked up at the tree, the one that grew from the center, with the roots wrapped around the River of Life, with its creepy water, red on sight, but red and clear when picked up. There were crystals running through it, full of memory bubbles.

I wonder where St. Brendan is? I glanced around, looking for any sign of the *Meallán* or any possible cosmic surfers out on the horizons beyond me.

Turning back, I was surprised to see Raiya was already disappearing into the heart of the Aleia's star.

"Hey!" I called. "Wait for me."

I hurried up to her.

Everything was the same as before; the waterfall running from the tree, and all around, like a strange, wooden heart of sorts. I could even see the same rocks as before, with Folly and Foolishness, the two unliving, cursed to remain sealed by Aleia's blood.

They were muttering to themselves as I walked by, making comments as they watched, along with me, as Starry Knight made her way to the nearby stream.

"It's about time. I was beginning to wonder." Folly chuckled.

"It doesn't matter," Foolishness replied. "We're still trapped here."

"Not for long. Once the Star of Memory is taken care of, we will be free, as Draco promised."

I stopped. "What did you say?" I asked.

Neither of them seemed to notice I was there.

"What're you planning?" I asked, swiping at them. My hand went right through.

I glanced down at my hands and saw they were transparent, like a ghost; was that what I was? Could they see me?

Could Raiya even see me?

"Raiya!" I called.

I turned back to see her—with a handful of water.

"No!" I stomped forward. "Stop!"

She didn't seem to hear me.

Elysian and Aleia had warned me about drinking from the River of Life without permission. It would grant immortal life, but it was a cursed life—immortality Raiya might have wanted, since her whole point in coming here was to regain her standing as a Star.

"Stop, Raiya!" I called again.

This time she stilled. "Almeisan?" Her eyes went wide as she turned around and finally saw me.

"Yes, it's me," I said, stepping forward. My feet disappeared into the river as I stepped out to meet her, even though I felt nothing of the water.

Her mouth dropped open. "You're here?"

"Yes," I said, exasperated. "And good thing, too. You were about to condemn yourself. Please don't scare me like that."

"What are you talking about?" Raiya asked. "I was told that if I drank some of the water from the River of Life, I would get a new wish."

"Did Alora tell you that?" I shook my head. "Elysian told me that if you drink this water, you'll get immortal life, but you'll be damned."

"I … I was told this is the only way to get what I want," she said carefully. "A way to live forever without being damned by Adonaias."

"Well, that's true, in some ways," I said. "But this way, you're just damning yourself, rather than owning up to your choices."

She just gaped at me, her eyes fearful and confused.

175

"Please, come out of the water." I reached out to take hold of her arm. Shock struck me a second later. I couldn't touch her.

"How do I know you're real?" she asked, suddenly suspicious. "And that this isn't some kind of trick?"

"Are you kidding me? You're going to distrust me? After all the times *you've* withheld information from *me*?"

"Prove to me it's you."

"Well, I know that your Star name is Astraiya," I said, listing off some of the things I knew about her. I had to stop her from drinking the bloody water at all costs. "You make the best mocha in town, Rachel is your best friend, and you promised your ornery grandfather that you wouldn't tell me that he's from the Celestial Kingdom, too."

"What? I never told you that."

"Well, that's part of the point. You didn't tell me, but *he* did, after Time's power stopped and stalled time on Earth," I told her. "I caught him at a strange moment, I guess you could say."

"Time's power stopped?"

"You didn't know?"

"No. That seems pretty serious." Raiya thought about it. "You could still be an illusion, designed to test me."

"Trust has always been a terrible test for you," I snapped. "Especially when it comes to trusting me." I threw up my hands, frustrated. "Ugh, I can't believe I missed you! You're so irritating sometimes."

But even as I said it, I knew I was lying. My eyes fell to her lips, even as I felt nothing but annoyed by her perpetual doubt.

I was about to rant some more when she smiled and laughed.

"Okay, I know it's you," Raiya said, still laughing. She reached out for me this time; I felt a sinking feeling of disappointment as her body passed through mine. "I wonder why I can't feel you?"

"I'm dreaming," I told her. "I'm lucky that I can talk with you. I've never had dreams where I was physically present with others before, like this."

"I guess you're not actually here," Raiya conceded. "But I'm glad we can talk. I've missed you, too."

"You must've missed me, clearly," I said, gesturing toward the river. "You've forgotten all I've taught you about semantics and political language, by the looks of it, and you were almost lost because of it."

"You can't blame me for being somewhat careless," Raiya said. "I'm trying to save myself here."

"And that right there just goes to show you just how careless you were," I replied. "You *can't* save yourself. You know it, I know it, even Elysian knew it! He knew that he was fallen the moment he took this water to Draco."

"Draco?"

"His brother," I said with a shrug. "He doesn't like to talk about what happened."

"I thought Draco was unable to do much because he was captured," Raiya said. "Isn't he the one around Alora's star?"

"Well, that's his skin," I said. "Elysian told me he's actually on Earth now, somewhere. He thinks that Draco is the one who took over leading the Sinisters after I fried Orpheus, because he knows how to escape detection from Alora."

A stricken expression suddenly came over Raiya's face. "I see."

"What?" I asked. "What is it? Tell me."

"He might be right," Raiya said, as her face fell into her hands. She slumped over onto the ground and fell onto her knees.

I reached for her again, still unable to touch her. Helplessness overtook me. How could I comfort her if I couldn't even touch her?

"Tell me," I said. "Tell me."

"I don't know for sure," Raiya admitted. Her voice was still sad. "And I don't want to be betrayed."

"I'm not trying to betray you," I insisted.

"I didn't mean you," she promised. "I'll need proof."

"Can I help you at all?" I asked. "We—Aleia, Elysian, and me—are all waiting on St. Brendan right now. We lost contact with Alora a while ago."

"Aleia can't communicate with her?"

"Her time crystal ball thing was … well, it dissolved," I said, still not entirely sure what had happened. "Can you tell me what happened when you arrived at Alora's?"

"Orpheus and I arrived, and I gave Alora the Sinisters."

"Did you give her the meteorite, too?" I asked.

"What?" She frowned. "No. We don't have it. Isn't it back at Lakeview?"

"It was stolen," I told her. "Logan was quite upset about it."

Despite her shock, she gave me a half-hearted smile. "He would be," she said. "Do they know who did it?"

"No." I looked down at my palms. "I thought maybe you took it, actually."

"Why would I take the meteorite?" She wrinkled her nose in disdain. "I don't need the reminder of my failure before my fall. I knew I had to protect it, in case other … "

I nodded as realization dawned in her eyes. "In case other demons or monsters wanted to try to use it to hurt others," I finished.

"That's probably what happened," Raiya said. "Someone took it with the intent to use it." She sighed. "This is so confusing sometimes."

I tried to take her hand, before I remembered I couldn't touch her. "There's a lot going on."

I was gratified by her small smile. "I'll say," she said.

A moment passed between us, and it was one of those magical moments when you don't need to say the words to let the other person know that you know what they want you to know. Looking at her, I knew we would get through this, together even though we were apart, and I felt much better.

"Tell me what else has happened," Raiya said. "I know a lot of time must have passed."

"It's been about a month," I said. "Do you know of a Mary from up here? She said she came to hold your place for you down there while you were up here."

"I know of Mary," Raiya said, nodding. "I never imagined she'd be taking my place one day."

"She's nice," I said, "but no one can tell it's her and not you."

"That'll be helpful for school," Raiya said. She smiled. "I imagine a lot of our friends wouldn't mind if Mary stepped in for them for a while."

I chuckled at the thought. "She'd have a long waiting list," I said. "The guys would run over each other trying to get to her first."

"How's the city?" Raiya asked a few moments later. "Everything okay?"

"It's alright," I said. "I have found a few mysteries to amuse myself with while you're gone."

"How's Mikey?" she asked. "Did he tell you who told you about us before?"

"You know, I forgot about that," I admitted. "I was just really caught up in wanting to spend time with you, and then everything else."

"It sounds like it's been an exciting couple of weeks, with all the time stops and the meteorite getting stolen," Raiya said. "And I can understand about wanting to spend as much time together as we could." She shook her head. "Maybe it's better if we're not together. We might get more work done."

"Like the Weaving Girl and the Herding Boy tale?" I asked. I frowned. "No thanks. I'd rather not see you just one night a year."

She leaned over to kiss me, and we were once again disappointed to find we were unable to feel the warmth we each had to offer the other.

"There's been other stuff, too," I said. "I'm sure Mary can catch you up with school, but we did manage to seal Elektra away."

"You did?"

"Yeah." I smiled. "I'll bring her crystal up with me when we get to Alora's."

THE STARLIGHT CHRONICLES

"I'll start heading back over there," Raiya said. "I'll trust you for now about the water."

"Didn't Alora warn you about that?" I asked. "I know she doesn't always tell you everything up front, but that seems wrong."

"I didn't talk to her much," Raiya admitted. "Orpheus requested meeting with her in private after I gave her the crystals."

The light around us seemed to darken. "I'll bet he's behind the trouble we're having."

Raiya shuddered. "I better head over there. I'll see you when you get here."

"Hopefully it's soon," I said. "I miss you."

I couldn't help it; I reached for her again.

Ghosts and dreams and logic and all of reality fell short of explanation as I leaned into kiss her and finally managed to feel her; the warmth of her lips meeting mine sank into me, and it was the sweetest moment of my life.

It was almost like a parting gift as I felt my physical body struggle awake, jostled from my dreams as I returned to my world.

☼<u>15</u>☼

Across Memories

A new determination spurred on inside of me as I headed out of my last class.

I was so determined, I didn't even have to stop for coffee; I did because it was on the way and out of habit, but I didn't *need* to. That's the important part.

I did make it a quick stop. I got in and out, not even really paying attention to Rachel or Mary, or even Grandpa Odd. I still wasn't comfortable with him, even if he did help me out by helping Mary watch Adam the other night.

After that, I headed for the hospital. I knew it was going to be a less than pleasant conversation with Mikey.

Maybe I should have brought Mary, I thought. A moment later, I decided it was better that I didn't; I didn't really want to put her in that situation.

I didn't even want to be in that situation.

This notion became extremely prominent the moment I walked into Mikey's room and he groaned.

"Where's my call button?" he complained.

"Nice to see you too," I grumbled.

"Shut up."

"Come on, Mikey," I said. "I did apologize."

"You're not suffering like I am," he insisted. "You don't deserve any forgiveness."

"If I deserved it, it wouldn't really be forgiveness, would it?" I sighed.

"I don't need your smart attitude, either," Mikey said.

"You know, I didn't treat you like this when I was in the hospital before." I leaned against the window.

"You're glad that I'm all mangled up?"

"No," I replied tersely. "Why would you even ask that? Were you happy to see me all mangled up before?"

"Kind of." Mikey smiled, and I almost smiled back.

I paused for a beat, and then moved onto the reason I came to see him. "Who told you about me and Starry Knight, that night you came to the observatory?"

Mikey snorted. "Why do you need to know that?"

"I need to know because the Sinisters have a new leader. Elysian and I are not sure who it is, but if it wasn't Dante or SWORD, we might have a problem."

"I still don't—"

"I need your help," I said. It was time to do something I never wanted to do, if I could help it. It was time to be open. "If SWORD knows who we are, or if the new leader of the Sinisters knows who we are, then Raiya could be in danger. I know we haven't been close lately—"

THE STARLIGHT CHRONICLES

"Understatement of the year," Mikey interrupted.

"Fine, yes, it is." I clenched my fists. "Look, Mikey, I'm in love with her."

I saw him do a quick double-take before scowling at me. But he said nothing, and in all honesty, I could understand his hesitancy to believe me.

"I mean it," I continued, pushing onward. "I love her, and I'm worried for her. You know how she is. She's determined and strong, and if something is out there, she's more than willing to face it. With or without me." I shook my head. "I can't protect her without your help."

Dead silence lingered between us for a long moment.

"You can't protect her even with my help," Mikey finally said. "I don't remember who told me."

I frowned. "How can you not remember?"

"I mean, I can't remember. I remember I was at Rachel's that night, and then all of a sudden I was walking to the observatory." He shrugged. "Maybe I was headed there on instinct?"

Doubtful. I knew Mikey, and it did us no favor to say his instincts were well honed.

I was not trusting enough. Calling up my power, I checked his emotions; I was surprised to see genuine confusion leaping up from the usual mix of depression, apathy, and frustration.

Okay, so he's not lying. Too bad. I guess.

185

A new idea formed inside of my mind. "Can I see?" I asked, holding my hand out to him.

"See what?"

"Uh … can I see into your heart?" I asked, having a hard time keeping my voice sounding normal. (It's not a question you go around asking people.)

I was prepared for him to say no, so I was further surprised when he shrugged. "I guess so. I know I'm telling the truth." He paused for a moment, and then said, "And if it will help you protect Starry Knight, I suppose it's the right thing to do."

A rush of gratitude settled between us. "Thank you," I said quietly.

"Don't get mopey about it," Mikey muttered. "Just hurry up. I don't want the nurses to see me doing this."

He reached out for my hand and grasped it.

"Just try to think about that night," I said, allowing my power to reach into his heart.

He sighed loudly, but he did it.

A second later, I could feel the innocence of his heart, the happy daydreams of Starry Knight, and the excitement of seeing her again.

Pictures began to form around the experiences. I was in Rachel's when a shadow stepped forward.

I frowned; a shadowed figure, wearing a dark cloak. Just as Asteropy said before. Red eyes glared out from underneath the darkened hood, and I didn't need to look too closely to see how they resembled the shape and size of Elysian's; in the dim lighting, I could just make out a scaly pattern on the hand that reached out to Mikey.

Draco.

I gasped in pain, as the strange figure unleashed a string of power to fold Mikey's mind inside itself, twisting time, memory, and perception.

I dropped his hand and broke the connection.

"Woah, that was weird," I said.

"Did you see who it was?" Mikey asked.

He still didn't see the guy in the cloak?

Well, I thought, *in all fairness, it wasn't the first time that the Sinisters or Orpheus had managed to fool others I knew.* During the first "real" attack I experienced, Maia attacked us dressed up as a police officer, and I was the only one between me, Mikey, and Gwen to know otherwise.

"I saw," I said finally, "but I don't know …"

I don't know how he managed to be in a human-like form.

Elysian told me before that changeling dragons were rare. They had the power to transform into a variety of reptilian forms; I didn't know if they were really able to turn into humans, too.

I shuddered. Part of me *didn't* want to know.

"So you got nothing?" Mikey asked.

"No, I got something," I assured him, seeing his disappointment. "It's enough to give me something to look for."

"Well, that's good, I guess—augh!" Mikey doubled over, grabbing his forehead in pain.

"Mikey?"

"It hurts!" Mikey cried. "It hurts."

"What's wrong?"

"Get the nurses," he stammered. "Ugh, what did you do to me? It hurts!"

"Nothing," I swore, clamoring around for the call button. "Nothing, I promise!"

Two nurses came in and hurried forward, as Mikey continued to twitch and yelp in pain.

What happened!? I watched, helpless, as the nurses injected Mikey with something, and then he relaxed.

"You'll be fine in a few moments," the one said. "The medicine has to kick in again."

The other one turned to me. "That's the quickest we've ever gotten to him when that happens. It's good you were here, but you should really let him rest now."

I just stared at her, blankly, until the two of them shuffled me out of the room. I'd never seen Mikey like that.

Did I do something that hurt him?

I didn't do anything, I realized. Draco did.

Maybe Dante wasn't wrong in trying to use that medicine to try to help him.

The nurses shoved me out the door a few moments later, all while I was calling out to Mikey to tell them to let me stay.

After realizing my protests weren't working, I dug my hands in my pockets angrily. Raiya had said it was likely Mikey had a broken heart, but it was clear to me after that he had a broken mind. And not the insult kind, the sort I would say to him if we were normal kids in high school.

"Come on, Cheryl—I mean, Mom," I said, nearly yelling into the phone. "This is just something that can't wait. I have to take off work today."

"Stefano's still in the hospital," Cheryl reminded me brusquely. "He's counting on us to keep the city running while he's ill."

"Get Cecil to help," I said, remembering how he had ambition. "He's worked at City Hall way longer then me anyway."

"I don't see why you have to study for your SATs so desperately," Cheryl said. "They're not until close to April, anyway. Didn't you tell me that you had plenty of time to study for the test before?"

I almost groaned. Why did my excuses have to be so lame sounding, especially when I had to deal with my mother? My uber-controlling, unrealistically expectant mother?

Cheryl could watch the world burn around her and only blink at the carnage, so long as she had her office to run.

"January's almost over," I reminded her. "And I've had a hard time juggling work and school and, um, all the swim team stuff … " (which, I suddenly realized I'd missed their last two meets) " … so you'll have to excuse me today, especially if you want me to qualify for dual enrollment next year."

I knew that argument would win her over, especially since I'd been stupid enough to hesitate when she told me about it.

"Fine," she finally replied. "I have to consider your education first in this matter. But I want to see perfect scores when they come in."

"Deal," I said. Before she could say anything else to annoy me, I hung up and started to run.

I headed for Aleia's church, knowing that she was in all likelihood there. I needed to tell her what I'd found, and it wasn't pleasant.

THE STARLIGHT CHRONICLES

Draco was here, and he knew who *I* was, anyway, and likely Starry Knight, too. He'd poisoned Mikey's mind, and he was directing the Sinisters, and in all likeliness, Orpheus, too.

There was also the matter of SWORD. They were supplying "security" to the city, and they were being paid by the Skarmastad Foundation, who just had the meteorite stolen from them, and they had a bunch of radiation monitors on the city for enemy activity.

To top it all off, I hadn't seen Asteropy since she left Patricia Rookwood's body in an undignified pile in the middle of the street.

"I wish I'd told Mikey we were close to getting Asteropy," I muttered to myself.

I stopped at the church gate as the first raindrops of a storm began to fall.

Aleia was where she always seemed to be when I came, sitting on a small bench on the winding garden path.

"Are you okay?" I asked, then I sat down next to her. There was a forlorn look on her face as she stared off into the distance. "You seem sad."

"I do believe it is possible to be both joyful and sad at the same time," she said primly as she folded her hands together in her lap.

"Maybe," I replied, "but I'm pretty sure we call that being bipolar here."

She snickered. "You're funny. And kind."

"I try," I said. "Tell me what's wrong."

"I feel terrible about this whole mess," she admitted. "I knew I would find Orpheus here. I thought maybe he could change, that he could repent. After you purified him with your fire, I was especially excited. Perhaps too excited."

"I know love makes people do funny things."

"This is the farthest thing from funny as I can possibly imagine. What if he's hurting Alora? Or Raiya?"

"I'll kill him with my bare hands, that's what." I watched as she flinched, and then added, "I see what you mean. It's not very funny."

We sat there in silence as the rain continued to pour down on us.

Finally, I spoke. "I don't know what he's done, if he's done anything at all," I said. "And we can't know. Maybe it's possible that it's something Draco or Alküzor are doing."

"Draco?" Aleia repeated.

"Yeah." I leaned against the back of bench. "I went to go visit Mikey today. Remember when he found me and Starry Knight in the observatory?"

"I can probably pull up the blog from that night," Aleia said, making me blush.

"No need. I asked him who told him. Originally, I thought it was Dante or SWORD. They had the radiation monitor, you know, and I thought maybe they knew we were there.

But Mikey seems too specific of a target; it was a personal choice."

"He was the one who was writing the blog," Aleia pointed out. "Maybe he was singled out for that."

"I thought about that too," I said. "And for a while, I agreed with that. But it doesn't make sense. If they wanted a journalist on it, they could have sent anyone from the news. Even Patricia Rookwood."

"I see."

"So when I asked him, he let me check his heart and it took me back to the memory of when he was told to go to the observatory," I said.

I quickly related everything after that; how the cloaked figure shared traits with Elysian, even if I couldn't see his face.

"It makes further sense to me," I said, "because I think I ran into him before at Rachel's, back when we captured Celaena. I just didn't see him completely; I thought it was Orpheus at the time."

"So Draco has been here all this time," Aleia said, her voice full of disbelief. "Incredible."

"Alora told me that he has been able to slip under her radar before. And he's likely taught the others how to do so." I reached over and patted her shoulder. "So if Orpheus fooled us, he fooled us all."

Aleia gave me a tiny smile. "It's a small comfort," she said, "but no less damaging."

"We'll see how damaging," I said. "You were the one who told me I have to have hope. And if nothing else, we'll be able to stop him."

"Raiya was right about you," Aleia remarked. "She says you've changed a lot."

"I don't think I've changed so much as I've been changed," I said honestly. "I never thought I would have this kind of life."

I laughed suddenly. "My SATs are coming up, and I'm not concerned with them at all. I mean, I normally wouldn't be, but I barely even think of them. I have too much other stuff on my mind."

"What else are you worried about?" she asked.

For a moment, I didn't answer her. But she was my friend, and she was one of the few people I could be honest with about everything. So I gave in and told her about my dream, where I was able to meet with Raiya for a short time.

"That's amazing," Aleia said, "that you were able to see her."

"I'm surprised I was able to stop her," I admitted. "Sometimes I worry about her."

"I can understand."

"I mean, she was comfortable with sacrificing herself for her mission before. I'm worried she'll still feel that way. And I'm more worried that … "

"That what?"

"That it's what Adonaias wants," I finished, my voice barely a whisper. "When Maia attacked us, down by the marina, I heard him as I reached for her in the water. He said he was waiting for her."

"She went up to Alora hoping for a new wish," Aleia said. "She's pretty stubborn."

"What do you mean?"

"She wants to be back with him, too, of course," Aleia explained. "Even though she loves you. She thinks a new wish will grant her what she wants. But she really should just ask him."

"What if he doesn't want to talk to her?" I asked. "I mean, sometimes I talk with him, but not a whole lot, and it's usually when I'm … afraid or something."

"Maybe you mean more along the lines of vulnerable," Aleia suggested. "Raiya has always been tough, and proud, and strong. And she should be. She is a powerful, adept Star, with full knowledge of right and wrong. But it seems that her pride is getting in the way of asking for help. She has always seen work as a way to get what she wants, and this is, unfortunately, not an exception."

"She did say she was hoping the Sinisters' return would grant her that," I said.

"Self-reliance is a good skill to learn," Aleia said slowly, "but it is not meant to be taken to the extremes. Alküzor is proof of that. He is alone in his own world, only able to take from this one."

"I definitely don't want her to end up like him," I said.

"I don't think she will," Aleia said. "She loves you. He only loved himself."

I felt the heat in my cheeks rise. "I'm thinking of asking her to marry me."

Aleia's eyebrows rose in surprise.

"I know," I blathered on, scratching my head nervously. "I'm a little caught off guard myself. And I don't know what she would say. I mean, given everything that's been going on, and there is the fact we're only seventeen and all, but—"

"I think she would love it," Aleia said quietly.

I grinned. Before I could reply, I felt the now-familiar sensation of my body flinging forward as my inner world came crashing against the solid ends of myself.

Time stopped, once more.

I gritted my teeth together. "I hate that."

"Look," Aleia said, pointing at all the millions of raindrops caught in mid-fall. The brilliance of it added to the overall magic of the night. "Time's power is amazing, even when it is not in motion."

THE STARLIGHT CHRONICLES

"St. Brendan is supposed to be coming," I said, pointing to the incoming fog. "He must be close. This happened the last time he came."

Elysian came swooping out of the sky, spluttering as he tried to navigate through the rainy night. "Good, I was hoping you'd be here," he said.

"Why? Did you see Asteropy?" I asked.

"No," he said as he shook his gigantic head. "We've got to get to the harbor. Aleia can fly on me."

"I could've taken her, too," I said. Before we could argue, I shook my head. "It's just as well that you're here though. I need to make sure Adam is safe with Mary before we go."

"That's right," Aleia said. "He's supposed to be at his daycare. I was supposed to pick him up."

"I'll get him," I said. "And I'll take him to Mary. I know she's at Rachel's."

"Be careful," Aleia said. "If Draco is watching us, he'll be able to move through the time stops, too."

"I'll watch for him—"

"Draco's here?" Elysian's narrowed eyes found mine. "And you said I was paranoid."

"Not exactly," I said. "Just that it was more likely someone from SWORD who was bothering us."

"SWORD is supposed to be on your side."

THE STARLIGHT CHRONICLES

"Well, you'd think your brother would be on yours," I said.

Elysian snorted out a long stream of smoke. "Don't go any further," he said dangerously.

"Honestly, you two," Aleia said with a motherly sigh. "Elysian will take me to the marina. Hamilton, we'll see you there. Please try to hurry; the faster we can get there, the faster we'll get our answers."

☼16☼
Across Time

"Woo-hoo!" Adam cheered as he rode on my back.

I was glad to see that he'd given up on screaming; when we first took off, I had a feeling the petrified rain came as an unwelcome surprise to him.

But it was not a permanent surprise. He giggled as we flew through the night, heading over to Rachel's.

I wondered at the picture he made for a moment, as he propped himself up on my back, grasping for the rain and catching the clouds.

Oh, the innocence of childhood. I wasn't sure if I ever recalled feeling as free as Adam looked. But I smiled, because I knew that was one of the things I loved about him.

We arrived at Rachel's in record time; Mary greeted us at the door.

"I was wondering if you were coming," she said, handing me a small cup of coffee as Adam took her hand.

"Thanks," I said. "You've been a good stand-in for Raiya; she would've given me a cup, too." *Although it would have been a large.*

Mary smiled. "I'll likely be here when you get back," she said, "but since Raiya will returning, there's no need for me to stay. I'll remember you fondly."

"You're going to leave?"

199

"Once Raiya is back." Mary nodded toward the house. "Grandpa Odd is here, if you're worried I'll leave before you get back."

"Now I'm worried," I said her, only half-jokingly. But I did take hold of her hand and grasped it, knowing it was unlikely that I could convey all my gratitude to her through such a quick contact. "Thank you for all your help," I said, sincerely and certainly. "I miss Raiya, but I'm glad someone as kind as you was able to come and help us out. If I don't see you again, it's been fun."

"It's been a pleasure," she said, giving me a wink.

"Adam," I said, turning to my little brother, "make sure you give Miss Mary here a warm farewell."

Adam cooed in agreement, hugging Mary's leg.

I laughed. "Thanks again for the coffee," I said.

"Until we meet again," Mary said as she waved good-bye, Adam already climbing up into her arms.

I might've loved my brother, but the moment I knew he was in good hands, I rejoiced; I was off to see Raiya again.

Of course, I had to help Alora and find out what was going on up there, and possibly comfort Aleia.

But just like before, Raiya managed to push back the unpleasantness. Seeing her again was worth all the suffering.

I grinned as I spotted the *Meallán* coming into port at the marina. I pushed myself to fly faster. In the distance, I could make out Elysian's misty shadow as he flew Aleia up to board the whimsical boat filling up the bay.

"Wingdinger!" The enlightened outline of St. Brendan the Navigator came into sight as he called out from the top deck of his ship.

I grinned as he waved; I was about to call back when I saw he was signaling to me to hurry. The anchor was raising, and the ship was already turning to head back out to sea on the ocean of awaiting starlight.

I knew I had to push to make it. My wings fired up at the challenge, burning so much I could've sworn there was a trail of flames following me.

"Whew!" I said, grabbing onto the railing as I hauled myself up onto the deck.

"Good job, lad," St. Brendan said. "I'm afraid it's not much of a stop here we have."

"I'll take it regardless," I said, grasping his hand in mine in welcome. "Nice to see you again."

"Same to you," he replied, his smile as quick as ever, though it did not reach to into his eyes. "I'm afraid there's trouble back at milady's star."

"We had a feeling," Elysian said drily as he came up behind us. "We haven't been able to get in touch with Alora."

"Something happened with my memory bubble," Aleia explained, dismounting from Elysian's back. "Thank you for coming so quickly."

THE STARLIGHT CHRONICLES

"You know as well as I the earth lives in perilous times," he said.

"It's quite a different experience living through it," Aleia assured him.

"Aye," St. Brendan agreed. He ran a hand through his black hair and turned toward the world. "I know that quite well."

"What's happening at Alora's?" I asked, deciding it was best to redirect the focus of the conversation. As much as I liked both Aleia and St. Brendan, I wanted answers.

He shook his head. "She's been attacked," he told us. "I came only because I knew you could help."

"What happened?"

"When Lady Justice came up with Orpheus, he seemed a nice enough fellow, looking for a second chance," St. Brendan said.

"He didn't hurt Starry Knight, did he?" I asked. I shook my head a second later. "Sorry, keep going. Didn't mean to interrupt."

"Lady Time welcomed him and took him into her castle, along with your lady," he said, nodding to me. "Lady Justice was content to wait for Orpheus to return. She grew restless and then headed out on her own, saying she wanted to go out for a spell. It's not too unusual, seeing as this was her home."

"Alora wouldn't object at waiting for her," Aleia said. "I know she is not exactly friendly with Starry Knight."

THE STARLIGHT CHRONICLES

"I remember," I said. "Raiya told me she was the one who made the hole in Time's power when she went supernova."

"Lady Time has always said she will let the matter rest when she gets back what is missing," St. Brendan said.

"What's missing?" I asked. "If there's a hole in Time's power, there's a hole."

"Time's power is more like a fabric. There's a piece that is missing, and Lady Time suspects that your lady still has it."

"Why would she have it?" I asked. "And how? That's not something that seems like it can be reborn into humanity very easily."

"Well, there are some speculations—"

"You know what, I'm sorry I asked," I said. "Tell us what you can about Alora and the attack."

"I saw the chamber door to her castle close, and a rush of power detonated from inside; it is unusual, so I set out to investigate. Lady Time told me to go and get you, saying her time pool had been poisoned."

"That's not good," Aleia whispered. Her head fell into her hands. "How could I have been so blind?"

"He managed to escape my scrutiny as well, Lady Memory," St. Brendan said apologetically. "Evil is better at hiding than we think."

I put my arm around Aleia's shoulders. "I'm sorry too," I said.

"Don't be," Aleia said. "Everyone has choices to make. You had yours, after all, and Raiya had hers. I was hoping that Orpheus would make that choice, too, especially after he was able to cut ties with the darkness around him. I should have known he still had some inside of him, and he would be tempted by it."

Elysian sighed. "I should have told you before," he said scaring me. For the first time in his life that I could remember, he looked genuinely contrite. "I knew about the power to hide from Time, but I didn't think anyone else did."

"Draco must have taught him," I mused.

"Draco?" Elysian eyed me. "You mean you believe me about him now?"

"Well, I sort of got proof," I said. "He was the one who told Mikey to go to the observatory, where I was with Starry Knight that one night."

"Mikey knew it was Draco?"

I explained to Elysian what had happened when I went to visit Mikey in the hospital.

"That demon," Elysian spat. "I should've known." He flicked his tail angrily, striking the cabin doors nearby.

"Please, sir," St. Brendan said, "not on my ship. You'd best save your anger for the battle ahead." He nodded toward Alora's castle, which had a blood-colored aura around it.

"What's that?" I gasped.

THE STARLIGHT CHRONICLES

"The blood of a Star," Elysian murmured. "If Draco's in on this plan, we'll have to be very careful."

"I don't think he's here," I said. "I mean, surely someone would've—"

"Would've noticed?" Aleia finished. "We can't be sure of that."

"Why would Draco want to come here anyway?" I asked.

"For his skin," Elysian told me. "Dragon skin is very, very powerful. If it weren't for the fact he did drink from the River of Life, he should have died once he got to Earth."

"The dragon's got the right of it," St. Brendan said. "There's a good reason why it's tangled up in Time's power, near her castle. It took a good deal of power for her to keep it there."

I squinted up at the castle, looking for the moat of dragon skin I'd seen before. It was bathed in a cloud of black, and it was starting to sink toward the castle. "That doesn't look good," I said, pointing. "But at least it seems we have the right of what's going on."

Aleia gasped. "It's coming down!"

"Can't you make this ship go faster?" I asked St. Brendan. "We need to get there."

"She's going as fast as she can, lad," he told me. "I've got to bring her around slow, so I can cast my anchor."

I had an idea.

THE STARLIGHT CHRONICLES

I pulled out my sword, preparing for battle. "Elysian, get Aleia ready. St. Brendan, get the ship going at full-throttle; we're going to make our own exit."

"Are you sure?" Aleia asked.

"I'm up for it," Elysian said. "Anything to stop Draco's plans."

I turned to St. Brendan. "Well? You were the one who taught me how to surf on the solar winds. Surely this can't be much different."

"You always were a bit mad," St. Brendan said slowly, but he saluted me and headed toward the command bridge. "I'll see to the preparations at once. Just a bit of a warning—it'll be a hard stop once you land."

"It's already going to be a less than pleasant visit," I said. "A bumpy landing isn't going to deter me at this point."

☼<u>17</u>☼
Battle for Time

St. Brendan's warning had fallen on deaf, naïve ears.

Having surfed with him before, and having soared around the skies with Elysian, I imagined I was fully prepared to take a daring leap from the deck of a ship going breakneck speed.

I was wrong.

Close to Alora's home, there was no solar wind to catch me, there was little help in keeping a steady flight path, and there was no certainty in the landing site.

It took me approximately half a second *after* I'd leaped off the ship to realize this.

My adrenaline junkie days are officially coming to a close after this, I silently promised, repenting of my cocky, prickish pride.

The ground seemed to rush up to me, more than I rushed into it; I could hear an audible *slam!* as I crashed to a stop, my front armor taking the brunt of the beating.

"Ouch," I murmured, trying not to whimper in pain.

Elysian's cackle of smug superiority washed down on me a moment later as he landed behind me, only buckling his knees as he touched down. "You know," he said, "I have plenty of room on my back for two."

"You can't expect Humdinger here to ask for help, even if it means avoiding pain."

My head jerked up at the sound of her voice. "Raiya."

There she was, standing outside of Alora's shining castle, leaning against the entrance like she'd been waiting for me there all along. The light teased out the red undertones in her hair as it streamed behind her, pulled back in its usual half-bun.

Her violet eyes met mine, and I swear, at that moment, I could hear music swelling inside my ears. After peeling myself off of the ground, I hurried forward and immediately swept her up in an embrace.

"If I didn't run into pain willingly," I countered, "we never would've gotten together." My hands framed her face as I leaned in and kissed her.

"Ugh," Elysian groaned. "This again?!"

I waved him off as I reunited, at last, with Raiya. "Was that really you in my dream before?" I asked her quietly.

"Yes," she breathed. "But this is a dream come true."

"So you didn't drink the water from the River of Life?" I stiffened as I asked the question; it was not merely a matter of condemnation at that moment, but a statement of my word and its worth.

"No." Raiya shook her head. "I knew it was you, and I knew I had to trust you."

"Thank goodness," I murmured, before pulling her close again.

"Ugh, it's bad enough we've got to fight up here," Elysian muttered. "Can you please stop? I think you're making me sick."

I stepped away from Raiya reluctantly, but my gaze remained steady. "My pleasure."

Her hand intertwined with mine. A rush of emotions, all ranging from welcome to worry, and a silent plea for patience rushed at me; as much as I wanted to be with her and spend time with her, we had work to do, and we both knew it.

With her free hand, Raiya waved toward Aleia as she climbed down from Elysian's back. "Aleia, thank goodness you've come."

"Is it so bad?" Aleia asked as she pulled out the daggers she kept at her side.

Sadness came over Raiya's expression. "I can't get through," Raiya told her, pointing behind to the door. "Alora's sealed inside."

"Is it possible she's sealed it herself?" Elysian asked. "If we are dealing with Alküzor's treachery, there's no telling what lengths Alora would have to go to in order to keep the rest of the realm safe."

Aleia placed a hand on the door; I could see the glow of an aura, bloody and dark. "This is bad," she said. "Alora's power is behind it, but it doesn't quite feel like her power."

"How do we get in?" I asked.

"I can open it," Aleia said. "But we have to move in quickly, and I'll have to seal it behind us."

We all exchanged looks; it would be dangerous, and there would be no way out. Eventually, we all silently agreed to proceed.

"Alright, here we go," Aleia said, pushing her hands on the door.

Instantly, we were granted entrance. The door banged shut behind us, encompassing us in the atrium of Time's castle.

"Gross," I muttered as my boots sank into a stream of blackened ooze. "What is this stuff?"

Aleia gasped. "Alora!" she called, running forward.

When I came to see Alora before, she was this bright and shining beauty, with dark hair and the same crystal green eyes as Aleia.

I looked down at her on the floor of her home, her body still and her eyes closed. Her robes, once white, shined red with poured-out passion.

Before we could get to her, a menacing laughter called out. The shadows cleared, revealing Orpheus as he stood behind her, his once-white robes now covered in the same red and black substance surrounding us. I gripped my sword at the hilt.

"Alora!" Aleia cried out again.

THE STARLIGHT CHRONICLES

"How nice of you to stop by," Orpheus said. "I wondered if Lady Time had managed to contact you. She struggled quite a bit as we fought."

"What did you do to her?" Raiya asked. "She's not your enemy."

"Time is more of an enemy than you realize," Orpheus said, his voice hard. "She contains the power of death within her Star. I have been trying to convince her to give up, using the power of the Sinisters you have conveniently collected for me."

He held up his hand to reveal the cache of jewels that had once been the sealed Sinisters. He pulled out the crystals of the five fallen Sinisters—the green one from Alcyonë, Maia's blue one, the one holding Meropae glowed pink, and the purple one that housed Celaena.

"They need power to escape the jewels," Orpheus said, "and I could freely give it to them. But I have been given a new task, one I am more suited to than babysitting a bunch of self-destructive, Time-cursed soul collectors."

He glanced at me. "I see you have another one for me, too. Pity. I was hoping to take the full collection when you came here."

"You're crazy if you think I'm going to just give it to you," I snapped.

He smirked. "You're forgetting I have the upper hand here," he said, gesturing down to Alora. A crackle of dark lightning settled into his palm.

I shifted uncomfortably.

"What is your new mission?" Raiya asked. "If it's to win my love again, I can assure you that's not going to happen."

"You were always smart, Lady Justice," Orpheus replied, his voice echoing all around us as he began to circle Alora, revealing a darkened hallway behind him. I recognized it immediately; it led to the time pool. "But your weakness is the same as all the rest of the Prince's forces."

"Love is not a weakness," Raiya scoffed. "It is the greatest strength."

"There's no point in pontificating. I once understood what it meant to forsake all for love, including my values and my dignity. I've come to see, unfettered and divorced from its original context, that it has its drawbacks."

I almost felt sorry for him as he said that. Almost.

"Now I know it serves as the perfect leverage." He glanced over at Aleia. "And the perfect cover, too. Don't you think so, Aletheia?"

Glancing over, I saw fresh tears running down Aleia's cheeks. She was so happy to see Orpheus go to St. Brendan, willingly, in order that she might be granted a second chance with him.

And he'd lied to her. In "forsaking his values and dignity," he abused and manipulated hers.

"Why?" I asked. "Why did you lie to us?"

"Don't be a fool," Orpheus said, his tone growing more scornful as he turned his attention to me. "I've freely admitted to you that I was in service to Alküzor. I'm here at his bidding. And if that takes some scheming and some lying, so be it."

"You played us," I said. "All of us."

"It was easy. Aleia was the key. After she was adamant about my wish for mercy, getting Starry Knight to agree and managing to convince others of my sincerity along the way were all I had to do." He laughed. "And as I said, it was easy to do it, all because of your weakness. Thanks to you, I have all I need to fulfill my bargain with Alküzor."

"What do the Sinisters have to do with this?" I asked. "They're sealed away. Asteropy's the only one left."

"Their shadows remain," Orpheus said. "While Time and Memory have both cursed them, I couldn't use them on earth to free Alküzor; but, even with one missing, I have enough power to free him from Time."

Elysian roared angrily. "He's trying to free the River Guardian's skin."

Orpheus looked surprised. "Yes," he agreed. "Once it is free, I'll be able to free Draco entirely from his mortal life, and he will be the one to set Alküzor free."

Aleia spoke up. "You must not do it. You'll pay for your crimes with your life."

"I'm not worried about that," Orpheus said. "After all, don't you think some part of me, the eternal part of me,

213

doesn't want this part of my life to end?" His remaining eye went soft. "This is all I can do. So I will do it."

Raiya frowned. "That's hardly your only option."

He glared at her. "Well, you would know," he said, "because you're in the same situation as me, aren't you? Too proud to go crawling back to the Prince, at the mercy of your fallen condition, and too caught up in your former self to know there's no hope for you in the end?"

I was about to join her in a counterattack at his rude remarks, but she made no response. Turning to her, I saw Raiya looked stricken. "Don't let him get to you," I said, wanting to protect her, wanting to comfort her. "There is always hope."

"Enough talk," Elysian snapped. "Let's fight."

"I don't think so," Orpheus said. "If you so much as move an inch, I'll destroy Lady Time. Give me the crystal you have, and I'll let her live. For now."

"There's no way to make sure you'll hold up your end of the bargain," I said. "We'd be stupid to trust you."

"Stop." Raiya stepped forward, making Orpheus leer at her. "If this is what you want, your word must bind you," she told him. "Shake my hand, and we have a deal."

"Agreed," he said. He glanced at me, his gaze narrowed in hatred. "It would be my pleasure, my lady."

"No!" Angry at his mocking words, I grabbed Raiya's hand. "This is insane," I said. "We can't just give him what he wants."

"We need to protect Alora," she hissed back. "His word will bind him, same as it does you. If he does not follow through with his promise, I can destroy him with my power."

"But—"

"Almeisan," she whispered, surprising me with the use of my Star name. "You must trust me."

So much of what was between us relied on a shaky foundation of trust. She'd deceived me before, and I had let her down.

But as I looked at her, in that moment—that still, everlasting moment, frozen by Time's power—I knew I didn't have to just trust in her. I had to believe in truth and justice and all the power they had.

"Alright," I murmured. "But be careful." I pulled out the orange-colored crystal from my armor and placed it gently in the palm of her hand.

Raiya marched forward with Elektra's crystal. My breath caught in my throat as she reached out to shake Orpheus' hand. He grasped her, and energy burned between them.

"It is done," Raiya said. "There. I have your word." She handed him Elektra's crystal.

He grinned down at it, a power-hungry look in his eye.

"This is it," he said, his voice husky and low, as though consumed by his desire for power.

"Get back," I called out to Raiya.

It took him less than a second to send out a shockwave of energy. A rainbow of power shot out from his palm, slamming Raiya against the far wall and sending the rest of us to the floor.

"Ugh," I groaned, demanding my arms lift me up as Orpheus scrambled down the hall and out of sight.

"We should've added a 'do not attack' condition to the deal," Elysian grumbled.

I *almost* laughed.

Aleia scurried over to Alora. "Alora," she called, picking up her sister and carefully cradling her against her battle dress.

I felt a catch in my throat. "Is she … ?"

I didn't want to say it.

"She's weakened, but alive," Aleia said. "We have to help her … "

Raiya moaned behind me; seeing how Aleia was taking charge of Alora, I headed over to help Raiya up.

She rubbed her head as she stood up. "That hurt," she muttered. "I knew he would do something like that."

"Why didn't you stop him then?" I asked.

"My momentary pain is a small price to pay for her life," Raiya told me. She rubbed her eyes clear. "I expected him to attack, and I knew if he did he would feel like he had the upper hand. I didn't expect it to be such a big attack, though."

"We have to go after Orpheus. We can't let him free Draco." Elysian paced impatiently behind us. "Let's get him, the slime ball."

"Go," I said. "You and Starry Knight can go and slow him down. I'm going to help Alora, and then I'll be out to help you."

"Right," Raiya said as I helped her up.

I squeezed her hand reassuringly as I sent her onward. "See you in a bit."

"Come on, Elysian," she called. "Let's go."

They flew down the hall and out of sight.

I turned to Aleia. "What do we need to do for Alora?"

"If we can get her into the time pool," Aleia said, "she might be able to rejuvenate. It is the central hub of her power."

"Sounds like a good plan," I said. "I know her time pool is just down there." I gestured toward the hallway that Raiya and Elysian had just passed through. "Here, let me help you carry her—"

THE STARLIGHT CHRONICLES

Aleia shook her head, cutting me off. "No, I've got her," she said as she reached down and pulled her sister up, leaning Alora against her chest and gripping onto her.

Sometimes, as I worked at the superhero business, I felt more like I was just playing around. For me, it's kind of like being an adult. It seemed like this great thing as a kid, but as an adult, I feel more like I am just winging it.

I felt unworthy of my power at times such as this one, when I've been transported to Time's star and I'm fighting against an enemy bent on chaos and destruction. It was true I was surprised by my own strength at times, but I was more often surprised by the strength of my co-defenders.

"I'll help you," I said, taking hold of Alora's other arm.

"I've got her, Aleia repeated. "Go and help Starry Knight and Elysian. Your sword is the best weapon we have for defeating him."

"I have a brother," I reminded her. "And I don't know if I would be able to do this kind of thing by myself."

Aleia smiled kindly at me as she began walking down the hall. "Sometimes, we don't know we are capable of doing something until we have to."

"That's the truth," I snorted.

"Please," Aleia said. "Please, go and help Starry Knight and Elysian. I'm sure Alora will be fine."

"And if she's not?" I asked. "What then?"

"Everything will be alright," Aleia said, the conviction in her voice enough to condemn me for my doubt.

"Okay," I finally replied. "If you're sure."

"Yes, I am. You must stop him before he releases Draco. While he is not here himself, his dragon skin is determined to have power and reunite with its master."

"Got it," I said. "Take care."

I was still hesitant to leave them, but I shrugged it off. Aleia was right, after all. I knew we had to stop Orpheus.

My wings beat furiously as they took flight, hurrying to catch up after the rest of my crew.

It didn't take me long to find them. I found them in the Gardens of Time, which reminded me of the ones near Aleia's church where we would go and see her. It was such a shame to see it getting torn up as Elysian and Raiya managed to corner Orpheus.

As I made my way over, Raiya slashed upward with her bow, barely managing to miss Orpheus as he careened out of her path. Elysian came down from above, but Orpheus twisted, lashing out and grabbing onto Raiya's arm.

I called out, but my greeting was cut short by Elysian; he roared as he went skidding across the once-flawless gardens.

Orpheus tightened his grip on Raiya. "This is all your fault!" Orpheus cried, his voice sad and angry and desperate all at once. "If you had only chosen me, none of this would have happened."

THE STARLIGHT CHRONICLES

Raiya buckled at his accusation; she faltered long enough that he managed to land a heavy blow to her torso.

"Raiya!" I yelled again. "Don't listen to him."

Charging forward, angry beyond words, I took careful aim and plunged forward.

The light of the Sinister's crystals burst free as Orpheus easily blocked me. He jerked Raiya closer to him and laughed at her pain as I ricocheted off his shield of power.

I managed to tuck and roll, finding my feet easily once I landed. "Let her go," I called.

"She should've been mine," Orpheus said. "I've got her now."

"No," Raiya said quietly, "I've got you."

A bright line of light shimmered, and she unleashed an arrow, burying it deep into his heart.

Orpheus went rigid with shock and pain. He fell over, and I felt the strange compulsion to stay still.

"Watch out," Elysian said to Raiya. Elysian swooshed over, nudging her onto his back while we watched Orpheus collapse.

A shadow of power slid out from him a moment later, forming a pair of slithering eyes decorated by a familiar scaly pattern.

"What is that?" I asked.

"Remember the poison from Aleia's memory bubble?" Elysian asked. "It was Draco's power. Orpheus used Draco's power to hide away from Alora."

"He had it in his soul?" Raiya asked. "How could we not see it?"

"Draco's an expert at hiding, I well imagine," I said. "He's been doing it for a long time. Alora told me before she couldn't see him."

"I guess that makes sense." Something about the way she said it made me wary.

But we had other things to worry about at the time. I nodded toward the remnant. "So, what should we do with it?" I asked, as the little ball of shadow continued to hover over Orpheus.

"Seal it away," Elysian answered.

"Won't that be dangerous?" I asked. "Grandpa Odd told me before not to seal away the time bubble because it was too risky."

"Well, he was wrong," Elysian said. "You can seal it away."

"Alright, if you're sure." I pulled out my sword.

Before I could bring it down on the shadowy half-creature, the eyes gleamed, shining out a brighter red than I had ever seen.

"Augh!" I grimaced at the sharp light, squeezing my eyes shut at its demonic brightness.

THE STARLIGHT CHRONICLES

In the second I faltered, I heard what was left of Orpheus begin to laugh.

"The time has come for my end," he said, his voice a perfect blend of calm and crazy.

"No." Raiya gasped, as he headed toward Draco's skin.

But it was too late.

There was a burst of power thrusted down into the ground all around us, as Orpheus' essence, along with the Sinisters' crystals, broke through Time's barrier, only to be absorbed into the mouth of the dragon's skin.

"Look out," Elysian shouted, curling around us as a burst of power crackled down from above. I threw my arms around Raiya, wrapping my wings around us; Elysian roared, sending out a beam of his celestial fire as we momentarily lost our sense of direction.

After the debris cleared some, there was a loud chain of explosions as the white, floaty dragon skin of Elysian's brother broke free from his prison.

☼18☼

Time and Memory

We watched, silent and unmoving, as the dragon skin's vacant eyes gleamed with a rainbow-colored spectrum and began to push out of its gauzy barrier.

There was a cracking sound, slow and creeping, as the dragon skin broke free from Time's power; I heard it and felt as though the foundation of the world was suddenly compromised.

Which, I reminded myself, it probably was. Draco was free, and that meant he would be able to free Alküzor, and that meant that the world was doomed.

Unless we stop him.

Draco's skin thrashed about, sending different parts of Time's clear, golden castle into rubbled shards. Elysian sent a stream of fire toward Draco, but the body, empty of its master's conscience, still had the good sense to duck.

"Stop," I called, moving to block it.

Raiya fell into step behind me. "See if you can hit it with your power," she said. "Aim for the eyes."

We both tried to stop it, but it bowled us over as it sped past, affecting our aim, as it remained unaffected by our power.

Draco's ghostly skin gave one final roar as it whirled its way out of the sky, heading under the horizon.

223

I winced at the sound; while Elysian's rumbles were loud and low, Draco's were scratchy and sullen.

Elysian snarled. "We need to follow him," he said. "He'll be headed down to the earth."

"That's where the rest of him is," I remarked.

"We need to make sure Aleia and Alora are alright first," Raiya said.

"We need to stop him," Elysian argued. "And as soon as possible. There's a reason that he was trapped up here and kept under Alora's watch. He's clever—very, very clever— and he's focused. He is nothing like the Sinisters. They were convinced to defect; he had no such qualms when it came to leaving."

"Elysian would be the one to know," I said.

Raiya pursed her lips. "If we can go back to Aleia's star, we can go down the Rabbit Hole," she said. "That'll get us there faster. We might be able to stop his body before it gets back to the rest of him."

Elysian and I exchanged glances.

Finally, he wrinkled his long nose. "Fine," he said. "That's a good plan."

"I thought I was the one who had to begrudgingly give Starry Knight praise," I said, chuckling a bit at Elysian's demeanor.

"The Sinisters were child's play compared to Draco," Elysian insisted. "This is no time to be funny."

THE STARLIGHT CHRONICLES

"Let's just get back inside," Raiya said, interrupting. "We're going to just end up wasting time if we're allowed to argue."

I nodded and hurried after them, glancing around at the damage.

In addition to dents and destruction around the castle, the moat area looked like it was bleeding white blood. I faltered somewhat, stunned that this had been allowed to happen. It was clear that Alora had command of an impressive power and a significant duty. Why had she been allowed to be hurt and betrayed?

I felt like some of this was on Adonaias as much as Orpheus and Alküzor.

"You okay?" Raiya asked, coming along beside.

"Just looking at the damage," I said. "This is not good."

"No, it's not." She sighed. "But that doesn't mean something good can't come from it."

"That seems rather silly," I scoffed.

"True love seemed silly to you, before it happened to you," she reminded me curtly.

I took her hand and gripped it, trying to reassure myself as much as I was hoping to reassure her. "Alright, you've got me there. But this still looks bad."

"That's why we have to do something."

"What are we going to do?" I asked. "Draco's only going to get more powerful."

THE STARLIGHT CHRONICLES

Raiya shook her head. "We can figure it out one step at a time. The first step is to make sure Alora is alright. And then we can go down to Earth again."

While I still had my doubts, I didn't want to dwell on them. Sometimes there are questions that demand answers, and then there are other questions that will just plague you.

We entered into the atrium of the castle, and I saw Alora was inside her time pool, much as I had been once. Her gown had changed from a pure white to a shining red, but other than that she was the same as the first time I met her. Her green eyes were once more alive with energy, though it looked as though the rest of her was struggling to make a comeback.

"Hello, Wingdinger," she said. Her face slightly tightened at the sight of my friends. "Starry Knight, Elysian; it's good to see you again, too."

I had to hide my smile; I knew that Alora and Raiya had their problems. "Likewise," I said.

"I understand I have you to thank for my rescue," Alora continued.

Before I could assure Alora there was no thanks necessary, Raiya spoke up. "It was my fault that you were attacked in the first place. I shouldn't have left you alone with Orpheus."

"Orpheus deceived us all," Alora told her. "He tricked us, and he took advantage of our nature."

"He is gone now," Elysian said quietly.

THE STARLIGHT CHRONICLES

"I'm sorry, Aleia." Raiya stepped forward. "I know that your trouble was caused by me, in part."

Aleia shook her head. "He has finally paid his debt with his life's blood, but he was truly gone a long time ago."

"It's still sad," Raiya insisted.

"Mourning will have to come later," Elysian said brusquely. (Seriously, *I* even almost hit him for his insensitivity.)

"Alora, how are you feeling? Will you recover?" I asked.

Aleia and Alora exchanged uncertain glances. I suddenly wished I hadn't said anything.

"I need to stay in here," Alora finally said, gesturing toward her time pool. "When Orpheus attacked, he managed to quite a bit of damage. I lost control of my power. It is still hemorrhaging out of me. If it is not contained, others will suffer."

"The time stops were disrupting the world," I remarked.

"I'll need to stay in here, in my time pool, to keep me from succumbing to Orpheus' influence."

"What do you mean?" Elysian asked.

"You know as well as I do that life is complicated, even in a fallen world, even in a fallen realm. When things don't do what they are made to do, problems occur." She sighed. "My integrity has been compromised. I need to be contained in order to prevent such a thing from happening again."

"But your containment on Draco's body didn't hold up," I argued. "Staying in there doesn't mean that you won't run into problems."

"Staying in here means I will have protection in place and help managing it," Alora told me. "I have known for a long time that my role would be a temporary one. This is the beginning of the end for me."

"You're going to die?" I gasped.

"Time, by its own nature, has its own limitations," Alora reminded me. But then she smiled. "But no, I won't die; I will be made new."

"In the meantime, she won't be alone to fend for herself," Aleia said, stepping forward. "I'm going to stay here and help her while we wait for Adonaias to come."

"You're leaving us?" Raiya asked. This time, she was the one whose mouth dropped open in shock.

"Time and Memory work together," Aleia reminded her. "It is our duty and pleasure. Besides," she said kindly, "I've done for you all that I can. It is up to you to stop Draco and Alküzor, and capture the last Sinister."

She grinned as she glanced over at me and Elysian. "You already have a good team."

"You're the reason we are a *functional* team," Raiya insisted.

"Then honor my request, and maintain your friendship and sacred vows." Aleia placed her palm on the time pool, as

THE STARLIGHT CHRONICLES

Alora reached for hers. "This is not a sad good-bye. We will meet again."

"And we will still be able to help," Alora said. She held up her scepter, its pointy top glowing brightly. "I'll be able to keep time still while you travel back home. Once you're there and safe, I will allow it to resume."

Elysian, Raiya, and I all looked at each other; I felt as if we were all secretly wondering if we would be able to go on the same as we had before, or if we were destined to fail.

Either way, we would have to worry about it later, I decided.

"Alright," I said. "I know what it's like to have a sibling in need."

Elysian nodded. "I will miss you," he said to Aleia as he nuzzled her shoulder.

"I'll miss you too," Aleia said as she caressed his chin thoughtfully and placed a loving kiss on his forehead. "But it is only temporary. We will be together again."

"We will?" Elysian looked pathetically hopeful.

"If you wish it so," Aleia promised. "And if you are willing to do what is needed."

"What is needed?" he asked.

"The same thing that is required of the fallen," Aleia said. "You must repent and be born again."

He grimaced at her message, but allowed her to hug him once more. I was just confused by it.

Raiya stepped up to Aleia. "I'll miss you." She reached out and hugged her. "I can't thank you enough for coming to help."

"It was fun," Aleia said. "And I'm glad I could help."

Alora stepped forward. "Starry Knight," she said. "We have unfinished business, you and I. Now is not the time to settle it, but it must be settled."

I frowned at Alora's words, but when Raiya only nodded, I accepted that it would have to wait; we had a dragon to stop.

"Aleia," I said. "We need to get down to the city fast. Can we go through the Rabbit Hole again?"

"You may," Aleia said. She turned to Raiya. "When you are there, you can find the memory that you seek. Wingdinger will know what to do."

"Thank you," Raiya said, grasping her hand once more.

"Go," Aleia said. "St. Brendan is waiting for you."

St. Brendan picked us up silently, and it weighed on me heavily as we passed over the destruction scattered around Time's castle.

THE STARLIGHT CHRONICLES

"I think everything will be alright," I said, trying to cheer him up and helping him back into being his usual self.

"Aye," he said listlessly. "They say on Earth that 'time heals all wounds,' but it's not true."

"I agree."

"Lady Time will need some time to heal," St. Brendan quipped. "But alas, the sadness will go on."

"Not forever," I said quickly.

"No, not forever," he agreed. "I've seen millions upon millions of places; I've seen Stars and the Reborn, and others. Time has an end, and Eternity is all the more breathtaking. Once they are together and Time is recreated, I can only imagine what it will be like."

"No need to wonder until then, right?" I joked.

"Hardly, lad." He didn't seem to catch my kidding. "It's all the more important to keep imagining. Our possibilities are nothing compared to the realities of truth fully revealed."

He turned to me. "It's grateful I am, that you were able to help Lady Time," he said. "She is a most beloved Star and servant of my master."

"No problem," I said. "I only wish I could have saved her before Orpheus attacked, so Aleia didn't have to stay behind."

"Aleia and Alora have always been close. It is no surprise to me that she would stay. It was a choice for her, too."

THE STARLIGHT CHRONICLES

I only nodded.

"We're coming up on her star as well," St. Brendan said. "I've a feeling there's no need to get you to surf over there this time."

"I'm going to stay with my team," I said. "But if circumstances were different, I would take you up on that."

He smiled, his blue eyes gleaming with mischievous fun. "We'll save it for next time's adventure." He nodded toward Raiya, who was leaning on the mast. "We'll bring your lady along too, just to see if she's still got her skills about her."

"Absolutely." I grinned.

The landing on Aleia's star was completely different from landing at Alora's, and I was grateful for this. It was literally just like Martha had said: *There's no need to make your life more difficult.*

I held Raiya's hand as we waved our good-byes to St. Brendan and watched the *Meallán* slip into the torrent waves of space. I was so glad to see her again, to be with her again—even if the situation we were facing was growing more grim by the moment.

She seemed to realize it, too, from the expression on her face.

"Are you okay?" I asked her.

"I don't know," she admitted.

"What's wrong?" Concern etched its way into my words. I knew she couldn't be happy with the situation; we were both

THE STARLIGHT CHRONICLES

tired, and we knew our job still demanded more from us yet. "Was it Alora? What did Alora mean, telling you that you still had unfinished business?"

She shook her head. "That's nothing big. It's not *that* I'm upset about," she said.

"What are you upset about then?"

"I have a feeling," she said, "a feeling in my heart that has been growing for some time now."

"Tell me." I was starting to get nervous.

"I'm sorry I didn't tell you about Grandpa before."

I almost laughed. "That's nothing. He was always irritating. It's not a surprise that he's irritating on two or more levels in addition to the one I already I knew of."

"That's not it." Raiya hesitated. "I've been wondering if he was corrupted by Draco."

"What? When?" I asked. "How long?"

"I don't know," she admitted. "But he knew about us," she said with a blush, "and he's always around Rachel's. He would know about Logan and the observatory, and he would know about Mikey's infatuation with Starry Knight. He could have sent him that night."

"Mikey said that Grandpa Odd had visited him in the hospital, too," I said. "Along with Patricia Rookwood."

"Yes. Aleia said I could check the memory. I wanted to see if he was the one who told Mikey. I thought that might prove he was at least working against us."

I tugged her along behind me as I turned toward the river. "Come on then," I said. "If that's true, then we'll have to hurry and get back. When Draco gets his full power back, we'll have a harder time saving your grandpa from him."

"Thank you." She gripped my hand back in hers. "I was worried you wouldn't want to help him. I know you don't like him much."

"That's true; he is a terrible pain to deal with," I replied, "but I know what he means to you. And despite his goofy teasing, he doesn't deserve to have his soul swallowed up by some dragon bent on unleashing hell on the world."

Elysian was waiting for us by the Rabbit Hole. "Come on," he said, clearly agitated. "There isn't time for you to be making out."

"We weren't making out," I bit back.

"We've got to check a memory," Raiya told Elysian. "Give me a moment."

"Hurry up," he grumbled.

"If you want to help," Raiya said, "go and keep Folly and Foolishness busy. They like to talk too much. It's distracting."

He only grunted in reply, before folding his arms across his chest indignantly.

"Do you want me to take care of them?" I asked Raiya. "I can do that."

"I'll need your help," she reminded me. "I've never caught a memory before."

"Oh. Come on, I'll show you. It's easy." I grinned at the momentary pleasure. It was a soft moment after hours of difficulty.

Together, we picked up one of the crystal clusters which flowed freely from the river's heart.

It was, just as Aleia's orb had been, small and smooth. Holding it together in our joined hands, I looked at her. "Ready?" I asked.

Raiya nodded. "Ready."

I pushed my power into the memory; alongside me, I felt Raiya's power surge. It was a sweet and tender moment when we worked together as one, side-by-side and soul-by-soul. I could almost hear the sound of her music move inside of me, the melody that had first called to me.

I smiled as the memory awakened and pulled us inside, allowing us to slide into the moment it was created.

I wasn't surprised to see that we were inside of Rachel's Café. I saw Mikey come into the café.

He'd just returned from seeing his dad.

"I can't believe he didn't say anything," Mikey hissed to himself.

Okay, so he didn't actually talk with him.

That narrows it down to who sent him to see us at the observatory, I thought.

He moved through the café, his gaze looking across the room. I realized he was probably looking for me, and when he didn't see me, he grumbled some more and headed for the bar.

"Mikey, my lad," Grandpa Odd said as Mikey sat down. "Why are you here?"

Beside me, I felt Raiya's body tense up. Did she suspect Draco was actually using her husk of a grandpa for soul fodder? Evil or not, I would've used someone more powerful or young or at least domesticated.

"Just … just looking for my friend," he said. "Have you seen him?"

"Who is it you seek?"

"Uh, my friend, Hamilton Dinger," he said. "You know, the one that comes in here all the time to parade himself around like a star?"

I frowned and decided I would remember to correct his thinking on the matter later.

"Ah, I see your loyalty knows no bounds," Grandpa Odd said approvingly. "Just as Arthur trusted Lancelot."

"Ugh, sure," Mikey asid.

Does he seriously not know about King Arthur? I shook my head.

THE STARLIGHT CHRONICLES

"He went to the observatory," Grandpa Odd said. "Apparently, there's someone there waiting for him."

How did he know that?

I heard Raiya's response inside of my head. *He knew I would go to check in on Logan and the meteorite from time to time after Logan was attacked. He was the one who told me to watch it, in case it attracted other demons. But then, I don't know if he knew exactly when I would go.*

I watched as Grandpa Odd took a drink of his coffee. "Maybe you should go catch up to him. He didn't leave that long ago."

"Alright, thanks." Mikey turned and walked dejectedly out of the room.

Raiya relaxed. "It was just an honest mistake," she said. "That's—"

"Hold on a sec, lad." Grandpa Odd came over and handed him a coffee cup. When Mikey took it, Grandpa Odd grabbed his wrist.

A shockwave of angry surprise washed over both of us as we saw a red glow leak from his hand to Mikey. Mikey's eyes glazed over, and I could almost see his mind grow blank.

No, not blank. His mind was being altered and protected.

The flood of power into the memory stopped, and Raiya and I found ourselves standing in the River of Life once more.

THE STARLIGHT CHRONICLES

Before I could stop her, Raiya slumped onto her knees, letting her tunic flutter along with the river's ripples. "So, he has been attacked by Draco."

"We'll free him," I said, pulling her up and hugging her close. I was sure of it as I said it. "He doesn't know that we know yet. We can get to him before Alora resumes time. We can beat him before he gets a hold of his dragon powers."

Raiya straightened. "You must promise me," she said, "that we will. We don't know how long Grandpa has been captive. Draco could know *anything* about us."

"Anything?" I was skeptical.

"Grandpa knew about me, about you, about Elysian and Aleia, and—"

"And Mary," I added.

"Who's Mary?" Raiya asked, and then she nodded. "Never mind, I remember. Yes, Mary too. Grandpa would know if it was me or not. But my point remains. He easily has the upper hand, and if he gets the rest of his power, we're at a severe disadvantage."

"Are you done yet?" Elysian asked. "I've managed to shut up these talkative rocks for the time being."

"You'll have to tell me the secret to that," I called back, "considering they'd caused me a lot of trouble last time I saw them."

THE STARLIGHT CHRONICLES

Elysian blew a ring of smoke toward me. "Even stones will melt under fire," he told me, and I almost gulped. He sounded as though he was seething, and impatiently so.

Elysian had always egged me toward battle, but he always seemed content to combat me with conversation as we headed toward the physical battle. He never threatened me physically, so this was the first time I really realized just how scary he could be.

I was beginning to realize just how badly things could go wrong when people made bad decisions.

"Let's go," Raiya said as she glanced up at me.

I nodded and shifted, still keeping my arm around her shoulder as we walked toward the Rabbit Hole.

"Finally!" Elysian cried, before he jumped into the swirling wormhole. He disappeared less than a split second later.

"It's quiet now that he's gone," I said as I looked around for one long, quick moment. I didn't know how long it would be before I saw it again, and I wanted to remember it. Aleia's star was no less majestic than Alora's, but while Alora had all the crystalline beauty of the night sky, Aleia's star had a vibrancy that made every shade and color seem more bright and more full of life.

"You know," I said, "the 'Rabbit Hole' is kind of a weird name for this place."

My comment managed to elicit a small smile from Raiya. "It's from *Alice in Wonderland*," she explained.

THE STARLIGHT CHRONICLES

"You sure seem to know a lot of people who like books," I said. "I must be the exception to that rule."

"*I* like books," Raiya told me. "Aleia named the portal to Earth the 'Rabbit Hole' for me."

"That was a crazy book," I said, recalling how I "read" it in junior high. "I'm not sure why you liked it."

"Life can be crazy," Raiya said, "just as it can be painful and beautiful and frightening. But you can still see truth behind it all, a star constant against the night sky, while all the universe swirls around it."

I eyed her quizzically. "And you read that book before you fell?"

Raiya laughed. "You're a fallen Star living on Earth, too. Don't you wonder about the others? Don't you think we've met other humans, too, before we fell?"

No.

I knew there were other Stars on Earth. I just didn't think about it that much. So far, none of them had really bothered me. Or tried to reach out and help us.

That alone gave me grounds for refusing to care about them, I decided.

I tightened my grip on her, before I drew her against me.

Tenderly, lovingly, and achingly slowly, I kissed her. The moment was quicker than most, but the sentiment was as fiery and soothing as it had always been.

When I leaned back and saw her eyes glaze over in quiet passion, I grinned. "There's only one fallen Star I'm worried about right now," I told her. "But we have other things to worry about. Let's go home."

"I am home now," Raiya said. She glanced around, and I could see her looking over the realm around us. I wanted to comfort her, to assure her that she would be back one day, that we both would be, but before I could, her eyes met mine again and she whispered, "You are my home."

Her voice was solemn and steady against the whirl of worlds around us, marking a moment in time when time had stopped, where we could be bound forever inside of its current.

I wasn't strong enough to say anything back. I felt my heart reach out in response before my arms reached out for her.

Before she could stop me, I picked her up—no easy feat, considering the extra awkwardness of her wings and armor. But regardless of the obstacles, I cradled her against me as I jumped into Memory's whirlpool, feeling nothing but the rush of emotion as we swirled down toward Earth.

THE STARLIGHT CHRONICLES

Battle for Power

It seemed to take less time for me to blink than it did to get back to Earth. Weariness of the world sank into me as I felt myself land on the earth; it was almost like trying to squeeze into a pair of clothes that no longer fit.

I blinked again and saw it was still raining, even though time had stopped, and the rain was paused in its falling. I was on back, my wings sheltering me from the cold, wet ground, while Raiya was beside me, watching over me, the same as before. "Where are we?" I asked, my voice sounding like a scream against the relative silence.

Elysian's face appeared over my face at once, his staunch glare aimed at me. "We're at the marina again," he said. "Just the same as before, when St. Brendan picked us up before."

"Wow, you need to calm down," I said.

"I've been waiting for over ten minutes! You just got here a minute ago."

"Space-time travel is trickier to deal with than you think," I said. "You're bigger than me, and, I assume, able to deal with more of the pressure, since you're a dragon and not a human."

When he only snorted smoke in my direction, I knew I'd scored a point. "Ha!"

"Come on, Humdinger," Raiya said. "There's no point in teasing Elysian. Especially since you're still not as adept at handling your power as I am at mine."

I caught sight of her smirk and felt a rush of pleasure. She was back. We were back.

Elysian must've caught it too, because he turned to her. "We left your grandfather at Rachel's," he said, and that's where we should start—"

Pain lanced through my wrist as my mark burned.

"Ouch! Ugh, that hurts," I nearly shouted, grabbing my wrist in pain.

"Oh, great," Elysian muttered. "Asteropy's come out to play."

"I'll bet anything that she's doing this intentionally." I gritted my teeth against the grinding pain.

"She would," Raiya said, taking my wrist and sending some of her healing comfort up my arm. (It didn't work that well, but it was nice of her to think of me, so I didn't say anything.) "She's technically under Draco's command now, too, remember? Orpheus is gone, but the chain of command still matters."

"We'd better split up," I said. "Elysian, head out to find Asteropy. It's probably better if you're not involved in fighting Draco at first anyway."

"What's that supposed to mean?" Elysian huffed.

"You're emotionally compromised," I said. "It's as simple as that."

"That's nothing!" Elysian countered. His tail pointed over to Raiya. "Remember all the times that you were too

THE STARLIGHT CHRONICLES

overcome by your own emotional problems to work with her? You were way worse than I am," he insisted.

"Well, it's not like we're going to let him run free," I said. "Raiya and I will go and seal him away. And then we'll finish off Asteropy, and then everything will be over."

"That's true," Raiya said, her voice full of quiet awe. "Once Draco and Asteropy are sealed, we'll be finished with our mission. We would just have to return them to Alora."

"We'll worry about that when it's over," Elysian declared. "Let's move out."

"I don't know if I've ever seen him this determined," I said, watching him stomp away, prepping for takeoff.

"He's worried about Draco," Raiya reminded me. "We should follow his lead on this. After all, Draco *is* his brother. Out of all of us, he's the one who would know best what we are up against."

"I suppose you're right—" I broke off in sudden realization.

Brother …

I nearly fell over. "I forgot about Adam."

"What about Adam?" Raiya asked.

Before I could tell her that I left Adam in the care of Mary and her possessed grandfather, a sonic boom sounded throughout the night.

The world under our feet groaned, calling out for peace and crying out for rest as Time's power resumed once more.

"Whoa," I yelled, trying and failing to keep my balance; momentarily, I saw that Raiya had jumped up, using her wings to hover above the ground. Admiration and envy simultaneously hit me. *That* was a smart move.

She met my gaze as I dusted my knees off. "That was harder than the last one," I muttered angrily.

"That's because of that," Raiya said, pointing toward the city skyline.

I felt my heart sink as I looked up. A smoky trail of a fireball, freshly sprouted from the sky, poured out from the heart of the night and settled into the city.

"Another meteorite," I noted. "Great. Draco's skin is here, I guess."

Elysian reared. "We need to make sure Draco doesn't get his skin," he said. "If he does, he'll be impossible to beat."

"We'll have to deal with Asteropy later," I said. "I'm going to go and get Adam. Elysian, you go and stop Draco's skin from finding him. Raiya and I will go and get Adam and her grandpa."

Elysian snorted a stream of fire as he flew off, while I spread my wings, their flames roaring with a deadly fire as I took flight. Raiya appeared beside me less than a second later, her bow pulled out and ready to go. She followed me close, allowing me to take the lead; it was a nice feeling, but it meant the world to me that she was there right behind me.

245

THE STARLIGHT CHRONICLES

We arrived at Rachel's within moments. As we landed, I could hear sirens going off, the echoes of trial and trouble resounding through the streets.

People, now in motion, were stunned to see Starry Knight and me as we burst through the door of Rachel's Café.

"Wingdinger."

I nearly fell over in relief when I saw Mary, sitting quietly at the bar. "Mary," I said. Ignoring the strange glances from the other people, I headed over toward her.

When I was close enough, I lowered my voice so only she could hear. "Where's my brother?" I asked.

"He's upstairs in Raiya's room," she told me. "He was tired, so I put him down to bed a while ago."

Relief washed over me. "Thank goodness," I muttered.

Mary glanced over my shoulder and looked at Raiya. A kind smile came over her face. "I'll go and wake him up for you. Be right back."

Raiya came up beside me as Mary headed up the stairs. "So that's Mary?"

"Yeah. She's going to get Adam for us."

"Did she say where Grandpa is?"

"No—"

As if on a cue, a small explosion rocked through the second floor of the building. Raiya and I were flung to the

THE STARLIGHT CHRONICLES

floor as others were shaken. Above me, wood splintered, glass shattered, and over the cries of the concerned guests in the café, I could hear two distinct voices screaming coming from outside.

Adam! Mary!

I rapped my head against the barstool above as I tried to stand up. "Ow!"

"Come on," Raiya said as she grabbed me, hauling me up and hurrying out the now-cracked café entrance.

Pushing past my momentary pain, I hurried after her.

We did not need to hurry. When we came outside, I saw that Adam and Mary lying on the ground in the middle of the street.

"Adam," I called, hurrying over. I picked him up. "Are you alright?" I asked.

He was conscious and alert, even if he seemed scared. I forgot I was still my superhero self, but after a moment of careful studying, he glanced up at me. "Hammy," he murmured, before sticking his head into the heart of my chest.

Raiya came up behind me. "Let me see him," she said, her hands already glowing with her power.

"I've got him," I told her. "Go ahead and take care of him while I hold him."

She gave me a proud smile, and I was confused at it. But as her power sank into Adam's skin, I figured she was just happy that I was more appreciative of my brother. And she most likely had the right of it, too, as much as it chagrined me to admit it. Since learning of her connection to him, and how I owed her my brother's life as well as my own, I *did* feel more like I was truly a part of his life.

"Is Mary okay?" I asked.

Raiya turned around, no doubt, when I heard her gasp. "Grandpa!"

I turned to see Grandpa Odd was also lying down on the street, not too far away from Mary and Adam. His frail form shook, and his hand pressed against his heart as he breathed in short breaths.

"Grandpa!" Raiya called out to him again, rushing over to his side. She knelt down next to him. "Let me help!"

Raiya tenderly took hold of her grandfather's wrist as he continued to wriggle around. For a moment, I softened, and I thought about how good of a doctor she would make if we were ever going to get out of our superhero gig.

"Mary," I said, turning my attention to her while I still held onto Adam. "What happened?"

Mary's eyes opened at her name. "He nearly killed us," she said with a gasp as she shot up into a sitting position.

"Who?"

"Him!" She pointed toward Grandpa Odd. "I thought everything was okay, I didn't realize … "

As Mary rambled on, clearly upset, I turned to see Raiya still at work. I was about to ask Mary what she meant when I saw it. As she called up her power again, I saw an aura of darkness leak out from Grandpa Odd.

"Raiya," I called. "Watch out! It's—"

The aura lashed out, unleashed from Grandpa Odd's body. His eyes burned from their kindly, twinkle-filled eyes to the sharp red I'd seen before, in Mikey's memory.

Raiya weathered the blow as his power rushed at her. I pulled Mary and Adam to the side, providing cover for them.

As the surge decreased, I turned to Mary. "Can you take Adam for me?"

She nodded, her eyes full of surprise and wariness. I didn't wait for her to tell me to be careful. I dumped Adam into her arms, and headed off to help Raiya.

"Grandpa!" she cried.

I came up beside her. "Subdue him," I said. "Get him tied down, something. See if your arrows can hold him. Then I can take care of his heart."

Raiya nodded, but I could tell she was shaking.

This is not going to be easy.

Draco's eyes gleamed. "Lady Astraiya," he rumbled. "We officially meet at last."

It was odd—no pun intended—to watch as Grandpa Odd's body contorted to fit the fullness of Draco's personality. He moved stiffly, his legs and arms rigid with a possessed quality; a black cloak—one I recognized from seeing it in the shadows before—suddenly appeared and surrounded his body.

Raiya's tension melted as she pulled out her bow. I bet anything that it was helpful to see Draco, rather than the face of her grandfather, staring back at her.

"Get out of my grandfather," she ordered. "He's of no use to you. Let him go, or we'll make you!"

Draco laughed, cruelly and crudely. "I'd love to see you attempt it," he said. But as he marched toward us, he stumbled.

"I need … more power," he muttered, frustrated.

Raiya ran up beside him, her bowstring taut. "Hold still," she commanded, before releasing her arrow.

It missed his body, but it bound him to the ground by his robe. I felt the familiar hum of its staying power as I reached for Draco.

"Good job," I told Raiya. "Use a few more while I see if I can break him free."

"Alright," she said. "But be careful. He's clever."

"You know I'm right here, right?" Draco muttered. There was a charismatic grin on his face. "Oh, Wingdinger, the mighty, please, do your best to save this wretched old man from his folly."

I frowned at him, and (for once) refrained from snapping
back at him.

I grabbed his arm, pushed his cloak back, and then used my
power to transport the two of us into the world of his heart.

It came as a shock to me that he had a heart at all, to be
honest. When I felt the rush of my power leading me through
to the other side of himself, I was nothing less than surprised.

I think I was even more than surprised.

Especially when I only came up on Draco, standing in the
middle of vast, empty land. There were little stars all around,
or at least that's what I thought they were at first. When I
looked closer at one, it was more of a memory bubble, like
the one Aleia had running through the River of Life.

Draco said nothing to me while I observed, gently poking
some of the bubbles, making sure they wouldn't explode or
something like that.

After being reasonably satisfied they weren't booby traps, I
turned to face him, meeting him eye for eye. "Where is he?" I
asked.

"Where is who?" Draco asked. He was still cloaked, but I
was close enough to see his skin had scaled over, while his
eyes remained large, narrowed, and red with malice.

251

"Where is Grandpa Odd?" I asked. "I've come to set him free."

"If only you could," Draco lamented, scorn dripping through every syllable. "He doesn't exist."

"What did you do to him?" Knowing how upset Raiya would be, I felt my power simmer inside me.

He laughed again. "He never existed."

"Of course he did, you liar!"

Draco began circling me, something that I hated, but I let him do in order to keep him close to me. I knew he was crafty, and I would need to strike quickly.

Recalling Elektra's intent, I also knew I had to defend myself at a second's notice.

"Do you know how interminably long life is when you're an immortal?" he asked. "Waiting, and waiting, and waiting. It gets old."

I was still confused. Which, in all fairness, was to be expected. I was inside of Grandpa Odd's heart, a man who seemed to know more about everything I would consider largely outdated and obscure. Nothing was supposed to make *much* sense in here.

But the idea that Grandpa Odd was an illusion, a role in a play with no other actors and the world as its audience ... well, that just seemed too out there.

"You talk about good things," I said. "You recite poetry and philosophy and theology and—"

252

Draco laughed again. "It's wonderfully amusing, how many people will be swayed by the words of those who disdain the very meaning of them."

"What about Raiya?" I asked, desperate for any sign that this was some kind of demonic hoax. "You took care of her after her parents died."

"Yes." A hungry look came into his eyes. "Lady Justice finally fell, and I went to her and made sure she was under my care."

"Why?" I was genuinely baffled. "Why train her to do what she is supposed to do, when she's supposed to bring about your downfall?"

"The Prince," he murmured. "The Prince's words are never wrong. But this time, I have the advantage. His world has repeatedly rejected him, and I have found a way into the very heart of the one who is supposed to bring me to meet my end. I fully intend on surviving the encounter."

"You think Raiya's just going to fall over?" I asked. "You're the one who taught her to stand."

"And you're the one who was stupid enough to save her," Draco grumbled. "She would have consigned herself to a spot next to Alküzor if you hadn't stepped in and saved her and the Sinisters."

"So you think," I said, putting it all together, "that because I'm here, you'll succeed in beating Raiya?"

"Precisely." He grinned. "Do you have any idea how easy she is to manipulate?"

THE STARLIGHT CHRONICLES

"You're the one who told her to go and drink from Aleia's star," I said. Anger flared inside of me.

"Of course." He cupped his hands together and his voice went high as he mocked Raiya. "'Oh, Grandpa, I do love him, but I want to do the right thing!'"

"Shup up!" I warned him.

"Please, don't get overly excited." He gazed down his nose at me, smugly. "After all, are you really going to be the one who kills her beloved grandfather?"

I faltered.

"I am the one, remember, who came and got her when she was the only one to survive that car accident in Norway—"

"The one who probably arranged it, too," I muttered.

"The one who told her stories of heroes and adventure and true love—"

"So you could undermine it in real life!"

"The one she would come crying to after school, when the other kids would make her angry or sad, triggering her growing powers when she was young or testing her discipline when she was older—"

"Stop it!" I said again, too unwilling to recall my share of that.

"The one who made arrangements for her to give blood at the hospital and held her as the needle pressed into her arm for the first time—"

THE STARLIGHT CHRONICLES

"You did that?!"

"For power, naturally," he said, interrupting his list of rights to Raiya's trust for the first time.

All of the pieces suddenly fell together in a strange way. Grandpa Odd—Draco—had been using Raiya and the hospital as a way to gain her blood.

He had been living on the earth as a human for thousands of years. He never died.

He was looking for Justice. He knew she was a Star. He likely found several ways to get a hold of a lot of money. He wanted to monitor the universe for signs of her coming. He was a crazy old man who had waited for millennia to gain what he wanted.

Suddenly, it made sense. In the weirdest, most diabolical way. "You're Ogden Skarmastad, aren't you?"

Draco laughed again, this time with pleasure in his eyes. "Figured it out, did you? Pity you won't be able to prove it."

Prove it? I still had trouble believing it. Dr. Skarmastad had come to Apollo City years ago and set up his astronomy hub. He claimed to be looking for the secrets of the universe. He was rumored to be this passionate, mad, brilliant man.

"I'll tell Raiya what you told me." I gripped the hilt of my sword. "I'll tell her that you were using her. There's got to be a paper trail to prove that I'm right."

"Changeling dragons are hardly registered citizens," he reminded me. "I'll admit, it's getting harder to fake an identity in America, but there are still plenty of ways around it."

"Raiya will still trust me," I insisted. "She loves me."

"She also loves me, her poor, old, sweet Grandpa Odd." The scaly face darkened. "What makes you think love and trust are the same things? Aren't you the one who teased her, argued with her, called her names, trashed her in front of your friends?"

I frowned.

"Aren't you the one who 'took a vacation' from using your supernatural powers to help her, leaving her weakened in battle?"

That was my breaking point; I had to defend myself. "Hey, she wanted me to quit!"

"Aren't you the one who has consistently been her greatest weakness?"

"Only because she's afraid of losing me," I insisted.

"Aren't you the one who is lacking in discipline, with temper tantrums and arguments and fights? The one who rejected her despite always promising to love her—

"Enough!" I thundered, drawing out my sword. I leapt and swung at him, determined to show him I was not who he said I was. At least, not all the time.

He easily dodged me, ducking and laughing as though it were some kind of game.

THE STARLIGHT CHRONICLES

"Augh!" I yelled as I swung down the deathblow.

Instantly, his face transformed, and his eyes were suddenly the ones I recognized; it was Grandpa Odd.

"Are you going to kill me then?" he asked, his voice soft and weary.

My eyes went wide and wary, but I shook my head. I moved slightly to the left, cutting into his shoulder before I stopped completely.

I breathed deeply, in and out, huffing.

And then I watched as his face transformed back, and Draco grabbed hold of my sword. "See?" he said. "You can't even hurt me. There's no reason to think my granddaughter will be able to defeat me, even if you do tell her about my real identity."

"You'll pay for this," I said.

"Not as much as you will." He sneered at me, tossing my sword to the side. "I'd hate to see us on such poor terms, young Hamilton."

"It never bothered you before," I said, before it registered.

Hamilton? Why is he calling me by my ...

That's when it hit me—just how dangerous he was. Draco could not only hurt me and Raiya, but he could expose us. He could go after our families and friends.

He already damaged my favorite coffee shop, didn't he? And that doubled as Raiya's home.

THE STARLIGHT CHRONICLES

"You're a monster," I hissed. Resolve hardened inside of me again. *We have to stop him. No matter what!*

"Then you should know," he said, "just how imperative it is you destroy me."

"I'll agree with you there."

"You can do it right in here," he said, "if you're okay with throwing your relationship with Raiya away."

"I already told you, I can explain things to her," I reminded him, drawing my sword back again. "She would trust me."

"But for how long?" he asked. "How long until she suspects you just wanted to finish your duty up, so you took the easy way out, sacrificing her grandfather along the way?"

That nagging voice at the back of my head, disguising itself as reason, said he was likely right. I should include her in the decision.

The other part of my brain—the part I liked better—said that Raiya had made her own plans on her own before, and I was perfectly justified in following her precedent.

While the silent debate was going on inside my mind, I saw him suddenly speed toward me, his hand transformed into a dragon's claw, with the sharp edges of his nails full of darkness and power.

Still undecided, I raised my sword to defend myself. *Please, please. I need help.*

He rushed at me, and I felt nothing as he passed through me.

THE STARLIGHT CHRONICLES

"Huh?" I blinked few times, only to see my body disappearing. I was going out of Draco's heart. I was returning to reality again.

I heard myself groan as I found myself slammed back into my physical body.

The real world was much brighter, even though it was close to evening, and its beauty, hidden away or discarded from the heart of the dragon before me, flooded through me upon my return.

"Are you alright?" Raiya's voice was muffled a bit as I looked up at her.

On the ground, Grandpa Odd/Draco was still captured, held in place by four of her arrows.

"I'm fine," I tried to say, but I think my mouth didn't quite get the message. I heard my words running together a bit, so it sounded more like a restless warthog than a response.

I snapped back to myself as Grandpa Odd moaned, sounding so sad and alone and fearful, I wanted to chuck the sword away and wrap my hands around his bare throat myself.

"What happened?" Raiya asked, before I gave into my temptations.

I didn't want to tell her. I *knew* I had to tell her. But I didn't want to think about telling her. So I just told her.

"He lied," I whispered. I cleared my throat. "He lied to you."

"Lied to me?" Raiya frowned. "Lied to me about what?"

"Everything." Then I shook my head. "No, not everything. Just most of it."

"Most of what?"

I stood up and straightened. "He's not your real grandfather," I said. "He's always been Draco."

Disbelief came swiftly to her face. "No, that's not right," Raiya said, shaking her head. "He's an ambassador from the Celestial Kingdom—"

"Probably just like Elysian, then," I said, nodding toward the inner city. "A forced exile."

"But—"

"He told me. He bragged about it. He told me that you wouldn't believe me."

She faltered. "This isn't about you and—"

"I *saw* his heart. There's no Grandpa Odd in there!" I said. "There's just a sick and twisted fallen dragon, trying to sink his claws into your heart so you can't destroy him, like you're supposed to!"

Raiya's face went ash white at my words, and I instantly regretted my tone.

Grandpa Odd—Draco—wheezed down on the ground below. "Raiya?"

"What is it?" she asked.

"Will you help me?"

"How can I?" she asked, ignoring the hateful glare I was giving her.

"You must kill me," he said, and I nearly fell over in angry shock.

"What?" Raiya glanced back at me. Just as I had been while inside his heart, he was tearing into her two.

"You must kill me. It's the only way."

Raiya hesitated. "Are you sure?" She pulled out her bow, an arrow of light conjuring up in her other hand.

"Yes," he said. "Yes, you must kill me."

"Raiya—" I stepped forward, but she shook her head at me, and I said nothing.

She took careful aim, but as she drew back the drawstring, I could see the tears up in her eyes. "I ... I don't know ... "

She doesn't know if she can do this.

What was his game in all this? I wondered. Why make Raiya do this? If she did kill him, he would be finished. Was it to prove something to me? Was it a distraction?

THE STARLIGHT CHRONICLES

Maybe it was to prove something to himself. Or to her.

Before Raiya could do anything, a tear dropped onto her cheek, and she shuddered.

At the slightest movement of her hesitation, Grandpa Odd's face disappeared, and I would argue the rest of him did, too, as he broke through her arrows and her power.

Raiya fell backwards, while I jumped to the side.

Draco rose to his feet, easily brushing the scattered bits of her broken arrows away into the wind. "It seems all my teaching was for naught," he said.

"Grandpa?" Raiya's voice was weak.

He laughed as he launched out an attack; his fist caught her right in the torso as he sped past her. Draco's eyes gleamed red again as he looked over us.

I turned back to see he was watching Adam, as he squirmed in Mary's arms. I knew immediately we were in trouble—all of us.

"Mary!" I screamed. "Run!"

Mary sprinted off down the street instantly, and I felt a second of relief.

A second of relief before moments of pain, as Draco's power slashed through me. I responded by lashing out at him, gathering my energy into my fists and launching out a stream of attacks against him.

THE STARLIGHT CHRONICLES

Raiya seemed slow to react, as though his blow to her had not only knocked the wind out of her, but knocked the sense out of her, too.

"Come on," I called to her. "We need to stop him."

She nodded, and I felt worse for pushing her; I was supposed to be the one protecting her, after all.

Behind me, I heard Adam scream.

"Adam!" I called back as Draco was making his approach.

Before I could say anything else, Draco managed to grab Adam out of Mary's hands and shove her to the ground.

He picked Adam up and squashed him against the wall of a nearby building. "I've been waiting to get my hands on you," I heard him say. "As a child with the power of Star blood in his veins, you can give me the energy I have longed for."

His dragon claws reappeared, and he pulled back, no doubt ready to slash the heart and soul out of my brother.

"No!" Raiya's arrows sped alongside me as we both attacked.

But it wasn't enough. We were too slow and too far away to do anything but scream.

A moment later, I heard Adam start to cry. I almost didn't look up, and sometimes I still wish I hadn't.

Mary had managed to step between Adam and Draco; she absorbed his blow, his claw disappearing into her body.

"Mary," I gasped. My steps, faltered by the thought of Adam in pain, spurred on forward.

Adam dropped out of Draco's claws and ran toward me. Raiya's arrows landed all around Draco, but he was unable to move as Mary held onto him.

I caught Adam as he passed by and quickly tucked him up on my back where I could count on some extra protection from my wings.

While he settled in, my eyes met Mary's imitation violet eyes.

I watched as there were no tears, only tenderness. The violet faded to brown, and the golden color of her hair darkened, and I was allowed to glance at her face—her true face—for the first, and last, time.

"Time to go home," she whispered. I was too far away for her voice to carry over, but I had a feeling she was speaking right into my being, the way a mother's love called to the heart.

And then, she was spirited away.

As the last of her light dissolved, Draco turned and headed away down the block.

THE STARLIGHT CHRONICLES

☼<u>20</u>☼

Battle for Justice

Adam curled his arms around my neck before I remembered to move.

I'd never seen any of our side die fighting. It was beyond horrifying.

Raiya came up to me. "She's been called back home," she said.

"What does that mean?" I snapped. "Aren't those just nice words for death? For murder?"

"To a human," she said with a sigh. "Mary was a Reborn."

I shook my head, trying to rid myself of all the emotional turmoil that had just thrown itself at me. It didn't work. "What do we do now?" I asked.

"We need to go after Draco," she said quietly.

"Are you going to be able to fight at all?" I asked. "You didn't seem like yourself just now."

"I … I'm sorry for that," Raiya said. Her tone hardened. "If Grandpa is really gone, for sure—"

"He told me!" I shouted. "He told me."

"Exactly," she said. "He doesn't have to tell you the truth."

"But that's exactly what he would have wanted you to think," I argued back. "He told me the truth, to prove to me that you wouldn't believe me."

"Then wouldn't it make more sense for him to lie to you, so you would be wrong, and then undermine my trust in you even further?"

"It wouldn't matter," I said, "if you already didn't trust me."

She sighed. "I'm getting confused by this conversation's turn."

"Me, too," I admitted. "Look, he said he was Ogden Skarmastad, and he admitted to lying to you about the River of Life!"

She stilled as I rambled on.

"The Skarmastad Foundation is the one who's been making Mikey's medicine and they're the ones who hired SWORD— what? What is it?"

Her hands came up to hide her face, while distress, anger, and bitterness overflowed from her.

"I didn't want to believe it," she said. "But I have no choice now."

"What are you talking about?" I asked.

"Remember that day before Thanksgiving break we went to go see Mikey in the hospital?" Raiya asked. "That day I left you to go check on something?"

"Yeah," I said slowly. "What about it?"

"I stole Mikey's records," she admitted. "I wanted to see what they were doing. I know that my blood has been used in some different treatments before, so I wanted to see if they could give him something—"

A new level of awareness hit me. "Mark knows, doesn't he?" I asked. "My dad knows who you are."

"Yes," Raiya admitted. When she saw my anger, she doubled down on her arguments. "Of course he knows! He wouldn't have let me give Adam a blood transfusion otherwise."

This is just a terrible day for finding out terrible things, I silently decided. "So he knows who I am?" I asked.

"I don't know," she said. "But he knows enough about me to know you're in danger if you hang around me."

"After saving my brother"—I jerked my thumb at the four-year-old on my back—"you're hardly dangerous." I shook my head. "You know what? We need to catch up to Draco. Tell me about the connection between Grandpa Odd and the Skarmastad Foundation on the way."

We took off, flying throughout the city, checking through the different streets.

"When I saw Mikey was getting the medicine containing Star blood, authorized by the Skarmastad Foundation, I knew something was wrong," Raiya said, calling out to me from across our windy flight paths. "I know Grandpa had the connection to the founder. I just never imagined he *was* the founder."

A memory stirred inside of me. "Rachel told me once that he was related to the founder."

"Grandpa was the one who told me of its importance, originally. When I was younger, and I started coming to the hospital for treatment, I didn't know what was happening. I knew about my powers, so I didn't understand why I needed treatment. Grandpa said the founder had started up the foundation just for people like me—people with broken hearts and special powers. It makes a sadistic sort of sense, if what you said about him is true."

"I wasn't lying."

"I know. Just as you weren't lying about the bloodwater." Her eyes teared up for a moment as she turned away from me and faced the wind. "I had my suspicions then, but even now that I know the truth, it's hard to believe."

Another concern came to mind. "You know the meteorite's been stolen, right?" I asked.

"I remember you mentioned it before," she said.

"Yeah. I talked to Logan about it."

"Did you find out who took it?"

"No, no one knows," I said. "But the police and the mayor were all looking for it. Logan was a bit concerned he would get blamed. Now I have to wonder if Grandpa Odd took it."

"We'll have to find out," Raiya agreed.

Pain began to pinch into my wrist again.

"I don't know where Grandpa Odd—er, Draco—went," I said, "but I can tell Asteropy is nearby."

THE STARLIGHT CHRONICLES

"We should take care of her," Raiya agreed, "but I'm not sure if we should stop looking for Grandpa—"

"*Draco* is not a lovable, kooky grandfather at all, Raiya," I said, "but a sinister, crazy, power-hungry, revenge-driven devil dragon. I know you would like to think otherwise, but he tried to kill me, he tried to kill Adam, and he wants you to die before you end up killing him."

"I know, but—"

"I'm sorry. I really am. I hate being mean to you, but I'm just trying to protect you."

"Angel," Adam spoke up from behind me.

"Yes," I said. "What would Adam and I do without you?"

Raiya looked stunned as she stared back at the two of us. "I—"

Elysian's roar broke through her train of thought. I glanced over and stopped, mid-air, to watch as Elysian wrestled with Draco's white, flotsam-like skin. "It looks like Elysian's well-matched," I said.

"We should go and help," Raiya remarked. "If we can't find Draco, we can at least seal away his dragon skin."

"Can't be much worse than sealing a Sinister away," I figured.

"We'll likely have to weaken it first," Raiya said.

"Hopefully Elysian's taken care of some of that for us."

THE STARLIGHT CHRONICLES

"True."

We headed down to the area where Elysian was fighting Draco's dragon skin. The ghostly figure of Draco's skin was disturbing.

"Hammy." Adam's voice called me back to where we were. *I need to find a safe place for him.*

Raiya seemed to sense my dilemma. "We're close to the place where Rosemont used to be," she said. "I don't think it's really safe for him around here. Maybe you should take him home."

I didn't want to tell her that I didn't want to leave her, while Draco was running around and still capable of fooling people into believing he was part human, instead of all scum.

"I'm going to go and help," Raiya said, pulling out her bow once more. "Draco's skin won't be able to fluster me," she added, probably clearly reading my expression.

"Okay. I'll come and join you as soon as I take care of Adam."

"See you soon then," she said, waving as she took off.

I waved back and allowed myself a moment to just watch Raiya as she headed into the fight. She was certainly strong, and I had to admire her for that.

Plus she looked really good when she fought.

I turned and immediately regretted my inattention to details.

"Well, it's nice to see you again, Wingdinger," Asteropy said, her voice silky with anticipation as she stared down at me. She frowned at Adam, no doubt recalling her failure to steal his Soulfire last time.

"What are you doing here, Asteropy?" I asked.

"Why else would I be here?" she crooned, gesturing toward Elysian and Raiya fighting off Draco's skin. "I'm here to enjoy the show, of course. Although, now that you're here, I'll have to see about getting in on some of the action."

"You can count on it." I pulled out my sword, desperately hoping I would be able to keep Adam on my back while I fought her.

It didn't take long for her to figure out my weakness. I had to fly carefully; eventually, I saw a park bench and headed toward it in a random pattern as I continued to attack Asteropy and defend myself.

She can't touch Adam, thanks to Raiya, so he should be safe from her.

I waited until I scored a hit against Asteropy, managing to strike her leg with my energy. Then, while she cursed and screamed, I shuffled Adam down to the ground. "Stay here," I said, ordering him as nicely, but still authoritatively, as possible.

"Okay, Hammy," he replied, and for some reason my heart just melted.

All my brotherly instincts must've decided to come in this week, I thought, amused as much as bewildered by it.

THE STARLIGHT CHRONICLES

But I knew that wasn't true. I'd been growing closer to Adam for months now, ever since I first tried to manipulate Gwen into watching him during one of my football games.

As I soared up to meet Asteropy in battle, I knew I had to do what I could to protect him.

"Watch out!"

Raiya's voice called out, and I nearly flinched, until I realized it was Elysian she was talking about. Draco's skin had managed to tangle him up, slapping him down to the muddy ground.

Asteropy took the opportunity to strike me.

I felt lightning soar through my blood and my nerves, and a surreal feeling took hold of me, as I was able to channel the pain and power and direct it back to her.

Asteropy, shocked at my redirection, plunged for cover.

Elysian roared, painfully, and I headed over to help. Just then, Draco's skin turned toward me.

It snarled at me, as I came closer, my sword out in front of me. I held firm as it flew toward me, and I raced toward it …

Only to have it fly over me.

"Huh?" I looked back and saw that it was headed for Asteropy. It picked her up and nudged her onto its back. She lapped it up like cream, of course.

"Well, it looks like you haven't managed to defeat either of us," she said. "And now, together, we will be invincible!"

She gripped onto the horns of the head, rearing up in a celebration of power.

What she didn't count on, I think, was that Draco had plans of his own.

Asteropy reared up on Draco's back, but he bucked at the next moment. Surprised, she fell forward—right into his awaiting jaws.

"No!" Asteropy screamed as the dragon skin consumed her, adding another color to the rainbow in its eyes.

Asteropy was captured, and it was very anticlimactic. Her scream eventually died away with the rest of her being.

When silence more or less returned, Raiya and I exchanged glances, and even as far away from each other as we were for the moment, I could tell she was just as confused as I was.

Elysian seemed to have more of an idea of what was going on.

"Draco," he sneered, a scowl twisted onto his angry dragon face.

"Miss me, brother dear?" Draco's voice boomed out from behind him.

As soon as we heard his voice, we were ready Raiya loaded up another arrow, and my sword was immediately out. On some level, I was relieved to see him, even though I knew this was the absolutely last chance we had to stop him from getting his skin back.

Elysian, still tangled up on the ground, hurried to rearrange himself into a more battle-prepared position. "Let's see," he cried back, and sent a shower of celestial fire racing toward Draco's humanlike form.

Draco dodged it, making it look easy, even though I knew it wasn't.

"Keep going, Ely," I called. "Let him have it!" I pulled out my sword and dropped into a fighting stance as we met. Draco slid away from me, my sword hitting nothing but air as he twisted and twirled away from its double-edged blade.

"Coward!" I said.

"Better a coward than a fool," he retorted. He gathered a ball of energy between his hands. "What about you, *Wingdinger?* Are you a coward or a fool?"

He took aim, and I dug my feet into the ground, ready for anything.

A second later, one of Starry Knight's arrows pierced through Draco's energy, shattering it and splintering it into Draco's body. He cried out and flames erupted from his cloak, spilling smoke all about him.

He cried out as Raiya came and landed beside me. "He's not a coward or a fool," she said. "He's a good friend and ally."

"And a lucky man," I told her with a smirk. "Thanks."

She nodded and we turned our attention back to the smokescreen before us.

Only to see Draco had gone.

"Where is he?" I wondered aloud.

I heard Adam scream behind me. "Adam!" I yelled and hurried away, instantly running to the defense of my brother.

I turned to see that Adam had been approached by Draco's skin, but much like Asteropy, it was unable to touch him without getting burned or scorched.

Elysian, thankfully, managed to tackle it a moment later. The phantasm-like body shifted away, moving slowly, almost like it had taken the blow personally.

Adam's safe. Thank goodness.

And then I heard it.

Raiya gasped.

I didn't have to look to know what had happened. I didn't have to turn to feel the sharp nails clawing at her heart.

I didn't have to see her expression to know she was helpless. I didn't have to watch as her Soulfire blazed with spirit as Draco pulled it free.

All I knew was that there was nothing else in the world that mattered more than saving her.

"Raiya," I muttered, and then I hurried toward her, faster than I thought possible. As the blood splattered out from beneath her armor, I managed to catch her. With the force of my arrival, I was able to knock her Soulfire out of Draco's hands and simultaneously send him flying.

THE STARLIGHT CHRONICLES

"Take care of her, boss," Elysian called. "I'll take care of him, and his stupid dragon skin!" Elysian stepped up; from the look in his eye, he was as determined to destroy Draco as I was to save Raiya.

As he charged Draco, following up on my attack, I hurried to get Raiya back to her usual self.

Her eyes had glazed over, and I panicked enough at the sight. *She looks dead*, I thought, half-wondering if this was how I looked when Elektra had almost managed to pull out my Soulfire. If so, I could understand, all of a sudden, why Raiya had been absolutely so afraid at the sight of me.

"Come on," I muttered, using my power to pull her Soulfire to me.

I'd always wondered what my Soulfire looked like, and I'd gotten a chance, a couple of times, to find out; it wasn't fun, but it satisfied my curiosity. (And thankfully, I never had to do that again.)

Looking at Raiya's Soulfire was enchanting. Mine had been a blood-colored flame, surrounded by fire and light. Hers was not really the opposite, but more of a complement to mine; her Soulfire shined a slivery color, with a blue flame at its core, while shimmers of light, like moonbeams, gave off a pearl-like glow, more subtle than blatant.

How did she manage to bring me back before? I'd never thought to ask. Mostly because it had been an extremely awkward situation, and that meant if I was going to ask, the question was going to sound awkward too. And it wasn't like that was part of the Awkward Game!

THE STARLIGHT CHRONICLES

"Okay," I muttered to myself. "Stop going crazy."

I placed my hand over her heart, recalling how she'd done that to me. I could feel her heart beneath her armor, beating wildly.

Using my other hand, I took hold of her wrist. I couldn't hold onto her power very well, at least with my hands. So maybe my power would work?

It did.

Squeezing my eyes shut, I pushed through, moving past myself and heading further on into her heart and her world.

As I opened my eyes again, I saw that Raiya's heart turned out to be a lot like I expected, even as it was something I could never expect.

The realm of her heart was full of fluff and color and painted edges of what I'd assumed, once upon a time, to be a fantasy world. Juxtaposed beside it were stark, angry lines of reality, where scenes of memories alternated into focus.

I saw her Soulfire floating above me, and all around me. I sighed in relief, even though I knew it was supposed to permeate this hidden world.

"Come back to me," I said, remembering how she called me back into myself through her pleas.

More of her soul seemed to settle in beside me. I was relieved. *It's working!*

THE STARLIGHT CHRONICLES

I grew nervous as I heard echoes of her weeping, felt the silence of her functional distress, and saw the pain manifested inside her heart.

Raiya, along with others, told me before that when things don't work the way they were supposed to, bad decisions were made, and bad things could happen.

I could literally see it. Her soul was shattered. Her heart was broken, her emotions scattered, and her will seemed confused—like she should know what do to do, but it was hard to do it, when it shouldn't have been hard to do it at all.

"Her soul is broken."

"Adonaias." My eyes went wide, and I felt the call to retreat to my own self at Adonaias' words. "Can't you help her?"

"She has been broken for me."

Before I could ask him to clarify, Elysian slammed into the cement, not even a hundred yards away from us.

"You always were so desperate to try to keep up with me," Draco called, taunting Elysian.

Elysian whipped his tail across Draco's path, hitting him strong across his side. "No, you were just desperate to get away from me."

"You'd hate it too, if your brother was foolishly falling at the Prince's feet. You worshiped him, and it was disgusting!"

Tension crept through me as Draco and Elysian continued fighting; I wondered how much longer I would be able to keep Raiya safe while they fought.

THE STARLIGHT CHRONICLES

Glancing behind me, I saw Adam sitting on the ground next to a tall building. He was out of trouble—for the moment.

Raiya let out a small sigh. Whirling around, I saw her Soulfire settle into her body again, and I saw her breathe. Raiya's eyes blinked along with mine, and we were both back in the real world.

I'm going to have to come up with a better name than "real world" for that, I thought.

"Raiya?" I asked. "Are you alright?"

She placed her hand over her heart, her fingers brushing up against mine. "I will be," she said, her voice weary. "Thank you."

"No problem," I said. Behind us, I could hear Elysian and Draco still fighting.

"Do you want me to reach up and grab you and kiss you, like you did to me that one time?"

I laughed, more out of relief than humor. "Yes," I admitted, "but I'm not sure you should move in this kind of—"

Raiya interrupted me as she kissed me. Not passionately or desperately, as I'd done to her before, but softly and sweetly. It was more than a meeting of our lips; it was a tender caress of the soul.

"Well, I guess you're able to get back to work if you're well enough to do that," I said.

Raiya sat up and sucked in her breath. "I'm still bleeding," she said, more to herself than to me.

"Why?" I asked. "Can't you heal yourself?"

"This is a broken heart of a different kind," she said. "It might need some time to heal."

Another barrage of shouts behind us made me worried again. "We don't have time," I told her. While she tried to get her bearings in order, I picked her up and carried her over near Adam.

I glanced over at my shoulder, watching nervously as Draco's skin and Draco began to move closer together.

Elysian let out another cry behind us, pulling himself up from the ground. I felt the heat of his fiery flames, as they erupted toward Draco's phantom skin.

☼<u>21</u>☼
Battle for Love

"You're pathetic," Draco cried as he fended off the stream of celestial fire from Elysian's attack.

"I'm not the one who's been parading around as a human for the last several generations," Elysian shot back.

"I can't expect you to understand," Draco replied. "It takes nothing of our energy, does it, brother dear, to transform into a reptilian creature, no matter the size. But transforming into a human takes unbelievable power. Do you have any idea of how many human souls I've had to drain to maintain my cover?"

"Is that why you've stayed hidden for so long? To chase after human souls?"

"Demon blood is a rarity in this world," Draco admitted. "And I needed to coordinate my attack, so I could have the best chances of survival when Justice finally came."

He gestured toward the floaty-phantom of his skin, which hovered on the other side of our established battlefield in front of the old Rosemont school ruins. "I'll feel much more powerful once I get the other half of myself, thanks to the sacrifices of the Sinisters and Orpheus."

Raiya pushed at me. "Go, help Elysian!" she ordered.

I paused. "I don't want to leave you and Adam defenseless," I said.

"We're not," Raiya promised. "I can't move that well, but I can still shoot." She pulled her bow out, and even though I could see the cringing pain in her expression, I knew she was right.

"Adam," I said, turning to face my brother. "Stay here, and listen to Starry Knight."

"Angel," he said, sitting down next to Raiya. His trusting brown eyes were full of resolve, as if he'd actually listened to me.

I left them, leapt into the air, and took off. While Draco had his focus on Elysian, I decided to go for his other half.

"Time to get under your skin, Draco," I said, amused by the word play. (Maybe there was a chance I would get that perfect 800 on my English SAT after all.)

The ghostlike dragon seemed miffed at my appearance. All in all, I decided the feeling was mutual.

My sword made contact and scratched against the hardened, scaly surface. I was a bit surprised at the resistance I faced. I had been expecting the skin to just fall apart at my blade; it seemed like a ghost, maybe, but it had more of a shield than I expected.

I looped around in the sky, deciding it was best to keep up the attacks. I managed to steal a quick look at Elysian and Draco, and saw they were locked in a similar battle.

As I watched, I saw a bright arrow launch out from where Raiya was situated. I was amazed to see the arrow hit its mark perfectly, burning into his chest.

THE STARLIGHT CHRONICLES

He hollered in pain, and I took the chance to throw all of my power behind my sword.

"Starry Knight!" I called.

Even from where I was, I could see her turn. Her attention never faltered, as she knew what I was calling for.

Another arrow launched, this time at the heart of the dragon skin. I held my breath as it flew past me—once it did, I launched myself forward, aiming for the underbelly of the dragon before me.

The arrow struck the dragon, weakening the power of its scaly protection.

I plunged my sword into it, grimacing as I had to convince myself this was some larger-than-life video game to get through it all. When I removed my sword from the giant beast a moment later, I saw the blood scorch the blade with a pattern of scales mirroring the ones I just cut.

Please, no dreams about this!

But it was almost over, right?

"No!" Draco's cry of denial was scraggly, scratchy.

I turned to face him. It was his turn, I thought. It was his turn to be sealed away.

Elysian reared, his smug expression clear over the clouds of smoke and dirt. "It's over, Draco."

Draco scowled, and for the briefest second, victory seemed not only likely, but close.

THE STARLIGHT CHRONICLES

I could see Raiya and me together, with no interdimensional war to worry over; we were happy and free, as we graduated high school and headed off to college—as we grew up and older, our love growing and remaining along with us throughout all of this life.

And then Draco's power slammed into the ground in front of Elysian, sending dark lightning and debris into his eyes.

The dragon skin beside me glowed, and the line down his belly lit up with light as it healed itself.

Momentarily blinded, I found myself falling to the ground as it shook. When my vision cleared, I saw Draco as he reached out and allowed his skin to consume him.

A sonic ripple splashed through the city the moment when their powers combined. The ghostly dragon skin with the rainbow eyes, seemingly flimsy and opaque, burned into a black dragon.

As I watched, black wings, long and sharp, sprouted out of his back, and his tail lengthened, including a pinnacle of sharp horns at its end. His claws extended, shredding up the nearby sideways and grassy areas.

Draco roared, and I could see the heat waves pouring out of his mouth, as his final transformation was complete.

His eyes devoured the rainbow, draining it of its power and leaving it a gateway to an abyss of emptiness. And then, he opened them to face Raiya and Adam.

"No," I said, grabbing my sword and heading over as fast as my feet could carry me. I stopped as his tail came swatting at me.

"Not so fast," he growled, his voice deeper and more menacing.

He turned back to Raiya, now inches from her face.

I was terrified for her, but she looked as calm and cool as ever.

One day I am really going to have to tell her how irritating that is.

"I've waited centuries to prove I could kill you," Draco told her, making my blood boil more than it had when Orpheus had admitted his love for her.

"If that is the truth, why wait so long?" Raiya asked softly.

I held my breath. *What was she doing? Was she trying to push him into attacking her?*

I wasn't sure if we were going to survive.

But then I saw it.

Despite the dragon's face, I saw Grandpa Odd's expression as it popped up for a half of a second. I gasped.

His head turned, and I ducked as he attacked me even more venomously than before.

I saw it and I knew he knew that I saw it, because he attacked me again, trying to swat me away with his tail again. He missed me, but sent me back far enough he was able to

THE STARLIGHT CHRONICLES

focus on Raiya again. As he looked at her, there was no doubt in my mind as to what was going on in Draco's mind.

He loved her. He loved Raiya. Not as a bride, but as his baby granddaughter. He couldn't help it. And he hated her for it, and he hated himself for it.

"I have my own mission here," he insisted bluntly. "Alküzor is waiting for me."

Before he could stop her, Raiya reached out, holding her hand up to his nostrils. She lightly laid her hand down on his nose, and he baulked.

He inhaled deeply, and then choked; I frowned and tried to move forward again. *What was he doing?* I wondered.

Before I could approach them, Draco took off, sending a shiver down the surrounding streets. Rather than staying to fight, he fled, laughing all the way, until he disappeared down into the shadows of the darkened horizon.

Elysian came up beside me. "I can follow him," he offered.

"Go ahead," I said. "But he's too dangerous."

Elysian sniggered, catching my attention. "What?" he asked. "He's not as dangerous as I feared. He's not yet back to his full power. Probably because we did manage to catch almost all of the Sinisters. The collected Soulfire was nearly depleted when that thing swallowed up Asteropy."

"Can he fix that?" I asked. "It's not like a curse or something, like Alora and Aleia placed on the Sinisters?"

"Unfortunately," Elysian said, "he'll be able to get more power. But we have a little time." He nodded toward Raiya, watching her as she stared after Draco's form, her eyes glazed over. "Which you might need in order to take care of her, by the looks of it."

"I'll take care of her," I said and hurried forward. I arrived by Raiya's side just as she stumbled and fell, leaving too much of her blood stained on the sidewalk.

"Raiya!" I called, gathering her close.

"Bring Adam to me," she said, her words slightly slurred.

"I'm taking you to the hospital," I said.

As if he knew she'd wanted to see him, Adam came up behind us. Raiya sat up and took my brother in her arms.

"Angel," he said, curling his arms around her neck.

She snuggled Adam in her arms and started shaking. "You were very brave," she told him. "Just as before." And then I could feel the tremor inside of her as she pushed out a small amount of her power. "That will make that boo-boo feel better," she said, and then she collapsed again.

"Raiya," I called again, cupping her cheek as I checked her pulse. "Raiya, stay with us."

"I'm here," she replied.

"I'm taking you to the hospital. Can you transform into your regular self?"

She mumbled something under her breath, and I repeated the question.

Only then did she press the Emblem of the Prince, the mark on her wrist, and transformed back into the regular girl I knew from class and coffee runs. If I wasn't so scared to see her frailty, I might've stopped to recall she wasn't the only one who should transform out of superhero mode.

I don't even remember the trip to the hospital.

What I do remember is bursting through the door to my dad's office, still in my Wingdinger form, as Adam rode on Elysian's back at my side, only to see Mark in mid-conversation with a group of interns.

The look of shock on his face was telling, as was the quick assessment as he looked down at the girl in my arms.

"You have to help," I said to Mark.

The interns started whispering, and it was enough to knock Mark's focus off my interruption.

"Ladies and gentlemen," he said. "I would respectfully ask you to take over my floor. It seems we have a special emergency."

The interns looked at us as they filed out, some of them trying to nonchalantly take pictures with their cell phones.

"Remember HIPPA!" I shouted as they left.

Mark smiled. "I was just about to remind them of that," he said. "Thank you."

He gestured toward the door. "Come," he said. "Let's get her set up in a private room."

"Daddy!" Adam cried happily.

"Hi, Adam," he said, lifting Adam off Elysian's back. "Have you and your brother been having a good time together today?"

I stumbled. "You know it's me?" I asked.

Mark sighed. "Of course I know it's you, Hamilton. Do you really think I don't know my own son when I see him?"

I gaped at him as he headed down the hall, calling out to nurses, asking for supplies, and checking on other patients.

Or, for all I really did know, signaling to get the police on the line. Belatedly, I did recall that Mayor Mills, before he went mental, had issued a warrant for my arrest. Not that the assistant mayor was likely upholding it.

We entered a room and Mark closed the door.

"Lay her down on the bed," he said, pulling down some chords and hookups and other medical objects I didn't know about or recognize. "Tell me what happened."

I gulped, trying to swallow my nerves. "She, uh, got cut."

"By what?" Mark glanced over at Elysian. "A dragon?"

"Sort of."

THE STARLIGHT CHRONICLES

Mark sighed. "If you were practicing," he said to Elysian, "you might want to keep in mind that even Stars aren't able to defend themselves entirely from a dragon's power."

"You know about that, too?!" I asked.

"Of course." Mark grabbed a pack of gauze. "Here, press this into her wound right here," he said.

"How do you know about the fallen Stars?" I asked. "How do you know I was one?"

"Dante Salyards and I were best friends in high school," he said, his expression grim and hard, nothing like the father I knew. "And there aren't always a lot of leading cardiologists that can be counted on in a crutch. And that's all I'm going to say in the matter."

"Do you know about Starry Knight, too?" I asked.

"Yes," he admitted. "But I've known about her for much longer than you."

"Did you find out when Cheryl told you I was dating her?"

"I don't want to talk about it, Ham," he said, suddenly harsh. "You're not an adult yet, as much as you might like to think so. There are some things that you keep quiet about, no matter how much you might want to tell someone, and there are good reasons to do just that. Reasons you don't need to know about, nor should you want to."

There was an ominous tone to that entire speech. I decided Dante was going to be answering some of my questions, the next time I saw him.

THE STARLIGHT CHRONICLES

"Does Dante know about me and Raiya?" I asked.

"No," Mark said, before he added, "and that's why we're not going to talk about it *anymore*, okay?"

"Okay."

He exhaled. "We're going to need a good story for this, that reminds me."

"Story?"

"I'll work on it," Mark said. "You just worry about that bandage for now."

"Right."

"When you're finished here," he said, "you're going to do exactly as I tell you, and then, tomorrow, you're going to go to school and act like this never happened. Do you understand me?"

"What are—"

"I said, *do you understand me*, Hamilton?"

I rolled my eyes. "Yes."

"Good."

"Can you save her?" I asked.

"She'll need a few days of rest," Mark said, "but she should be able to pull through. She lost quite a bit of blood, by the looks of it."

"Draco attacked her, trying to steal her soul."

THE STARLIGHT CHRONICLES

"Draco?" Mark frowned, turning to Elysian. "Not this one?"

"Hardly," Elysian snorted.

"I didn't realize there were more dragons down here," Mark said. "That's disconcerting."

"More business for you, I imagine," Elysian replied.

"I'd actually prefer to have less business," Mark assured him as he took the bandage from under my fingers and began to rub solution into Raiya's wounds.

"You and me both," I said, stepping back to make room for him as he worked.

For the first time in a long time, that I could remember, anyway, I actually wished my dad would say something to me. I wanted him to tell me more about how he knew about the fallen Stars and the dragons and SWORD. Especially SWORD.

And the Skarmastad Foundation, too, I recalled. I wondered if Mark was in on the medicine that Mikey was taking. Was it possible he was an active member? Or was he just a cog in their machine, pushing meds as part of some world take-over ploy?

What was the connection between SWORD and the Skarmastad Foundation, anyway? If you were going to control the world, what was the point in hiring the people who wanted to control all the power in the world?

THE STARLIGHT CHRONICLES

Clearly, this was a matter of deep intellect. And more government paper-trailing.

I nearly groaned at the thought, but Mark stopped me before I could manage.

"Okay," he said. "She's all ready to go."

"She's not awake," I said.

"She needs rest, Hamilton." He frowned at me. "I'm going to keep her here for three days."

"No meds," I said.

"You're not her next of kin," Mark said. "I'll need you to go and inform her grandfather—"

"Can't." I shook my head. "He's … he's not available."

"Oh, well then her aunt will do. Or her cousin." He glanced at her chart. "It would be good of you to inform them. Though it looks like I won't need a signature from any of them."

"What do you mean?" I asked.

Mark looked at me quizzically. "Don't you know when her birthday is?" he asked. "I mean, you've been sneaking around with her for a few months now, haven't you?"

"We're dating," I snapped. "And we work together, obviously, on supernatural concerns for the city. What does it matter?"

THE STARLIGHT CHRONICLES

"Her birthday is tomorrow," he said. He pulled out one of her forms. "See? January 23ʳᵈ. She's technically an adult, as of tomorrow."

"Oh."

I stared at the numbers, and I swear, it was almost like I couldn't read them. And then I laughed. "No wonder she didn't tell me," I said. "She and Gwen have the same birthday."

Mark gave me a strange look. I couldn't blame him. It'd been a long day. And it had been an even longer day for me than for Mark. After all, I'd been swept away by time stops, attacked by Orpheus, and off on a dragon hunt all in one waking period.

Weariness finally hit me.

"You're tired," Mark said.

"I know," I replied. "Can I stay with her?"

"Absolutely not." He folded his arms. "You're going to go and tell her family after you leave here. And before you leave here, you're going to tie me and Adam up with these extra bandages."

"Huh?" I wasn't sure I'd heard him right.

"You'll see." Mark moved over to the corner of the room, pulling Adam along with him. "Just listen carefully, and do everything *exactly* how I tell you."

☼<u>22</u>☼

Together

Turns out, Mark needed me to make it look like I was kidnapping Adam and holding him hostage in order to get him to give me medicine. Raiya played a minor, unnamed role as a patient, someone I used to lure the famous, loveable, gifted Dr. Dinger into my awaiting trap, no doubt.

Or at least, that's what Mark told the police and the reporters who came to investigate the events at the hospital after I tied him up and then left with Elysian.

While I wasn't happy about the news coverage, I did sort of understand it. Mark was friends with Dante, which made him a contract—reluctant or not, I didn't know—of SWORD. And if Dante didn't know about me, Mark was on my side, trying to keep him from finding out.

So I was going to have some pretty bad press in the meantime.

That was the bad news. The good news was that I could go and visit her after school the next day.

The more bad news was that I actually had to go to school.

And sit there, once more, with my back to Raiya's empty chair in Mrs. Smithe's class, wondering if she would ever come back, and desperately missing her while Martha prattled on about … okay, about some important stuff, but not recent important stuff.

295

The more, more bad news was that, due to the building damage, and a loss in the family, Rachel's was closed to the public for a few weeks.

The more stupid news was that my friends—naïve, ignorant, and simple as they were—contributed the coffee shop's closing to my bad mood. I snapped at them a few times, as if to prove them wrong, only ending up proving them right. Mostly. They were still wrong.

"Hamilton," Mrs. Smithe called from the front of the room. "Are you coming?"

"Huh?" My head snapped up with a start. "What?"

"Class is over. Come on up here."

Anger, frustration, and bitterness washed over me. I wasn't sure why, exactly. I mean, Draco was free, Raiya was in the hospital, none of this would've happened if Adonaias had just stepped in …

There. That was it—the real reason I was angry.

"What's wrong?" Mrs. Smithe asked.

There. That was it—my breaking point.

"What do you mean, 'What's wrong?'" I spit back. "Don't you mean 'What's right?' Turns out, nothing is."

"I see," she said, non-committedly.

"Doesn't it bother you?" I asked. "Doesn't it bother you that everything *doesn't* really happen for a reason? Doesn't it bother you that good people suffer? That people who are trying so hard to fight for the good in this world are overrun by all the bad?"

I turned away. "What kind of leader would allow his people to suffer? Especially when he has the power to take it away?"

Martha remained silent for a long moment as I fought against the angry tears in my eyes.

Raiya worked so hard for the Prince! All she wanted was to go and see him and live with him again in the Celestial Kingdom. And I knew he had the power to make her life better. But no, she had a grandfather figure who turned out to be a vindictive monster raising her, learning all her weaknesses, and stacking the odds in his favor for when he finally decided to strike.

"Well," Mrs. Smithe finally said. "I don't know what you're talking about specifically, but let me tell you a little story, Hamilton."

"What?" I snapped. "I don't have time for stories. I'm too busy trying to live my own life." Which was getting more and more out of hand, I thought.

"Just put your lips in park and listen." She straightened her glasses. "My husband and son were not killed by a car accident, though that is the story on record."

That managed to capture my attention. "Huh?"

"They were murdered," she continued, "by members of my former company."

"That's terrible."

"They've done worse," she assured me.

"That's … that's terrible," I repeated, unable to say much else.

"Yes, it is," she said. "Listen. There are times when we don't know the reasons or the answers to questions, if there are even such things in this life. All we have to do is choose what do with the time and skills we have."

She patted my arm. "Save your anger for those who truly deserve it—your *true* enemies. Save your anger to fight another day."

I nodded, slowly, thinking of Draco. First and foremost, he was the one who tricked Raiya and hurt her the most. I had to worry about him before anyone else, especially compared to my heartless, braindead friends. "That makes sense."

Elysian said we had time, didn't we? Not much, maybe, but enough to formulate a new plan. One in which Draco would pay dearly.

"That's a good idea," I said slowly. Then I looked up at her. "Why did the company you worked for kill your family?"

"They needed my cooperation," Mrs. Smithe said.

"I see."

She scooted her chair closer to the desk, inching closer to me. "Do you know why I'm telling you this?" she asked.

"No. Not really. Sort of. But not really."

THE STARLIGHT CHRONICLES

"Because they will likely do it to you," Mrs. Smithe told me. "Especially since they'll likely need your cooperation, too."

"My … cooperation?" A tingling feeling tugged at me.

"Yes." Mrs. Smithe gazed at me intently over the thick, black frame of her glasses. "SWORD is notorious for finding convincing ways to make people work with them."

For the first time in my life, ever, I couldn't wait to go to the hospital.

After Martha's admission, I needed Raiya more than ever. I needed to talk to her, to discuss everything, to sort everything out. We had a lot of trouble up against us, and it was starting to feel dire.

This time, I made sure Mark wasn't around when I walked in as quietly as possible.

While it was second nature to me not to try to stand out at a hospital, I was more than a little displaced by the feeling of trying to be invisible. While it suited Wingdinger more than Hamilton Dinger, invisibility was never something I was good at on a public front.

I reached Raiya's room and knocked quietly, more to check to see if there was a nurse stuck in there than to see if Raiya was awake. Although I did want her to be awake. I wanted to see her.

299

I should have been used to disappointment by then.

For a good hour after I stepped inside to see her, Raiya continued to sleep, while I continued to watch the steady rise and fall of her chest as she breathed in and out in a rhythmic pattern.

She's added such music to my life since she came, I thought half-jokingly. And for all she made my life better, hers seemed to just drag.

It doesn't take you long to get bored, especially if you're smart.

I thought about how I'd seen her heart, the realm of art and music and messiness. It was a world so different from mine, but still one that called to me.

Thinking it over, I decided it wouldn't be a bad idea. I could try to see her realm of the heart and see if I could help mend the division in her heart, soul, and mind, to see if it could help her with her body.

I placed my hand over her heart again, surprised by the slight warmth. She wasn't wearing her armor this time, just one of the silly sleeping gowns that hospitals provided. Clear of armor, her body seemed a lot more fragile. I took her wrist in my other hand, same as before.

Pushing my power forward, I reached into her heart.

Instantly, I regretted it.

This time, there was no solid place, but worlds overlapping with different ideas and memories.

THE STARLIGHT CHRONICLES

Some of the memories caught my attention.

I saw a car accident through her eyes, as the Norwegian night sky crashed into the murky waters of a disguised lake, hidden from the moonlight.

I squinted and paused; as horrifying as it was, I couldn't look away.

But that wasn't all that was surprising. When the car hit the water, and the water rushed inside, a bright light sparked against the cold and the dark.

It was Adonaias.

I watched as he reached out and grabbed a hold of her.

"I am waiting for you," he said, the same as when he told her that before, in Lake Erie, when Maia had attacked her and I'd gone after her.

My mouth dropped open as I watched him pick Raiya up out of the waters, his hand pulling her toward the edge of the water.

"What was that?" I blurted out.

Before I could get an answer, another memory was called forth.

There was Grandpa Odd, unchanged from how I knew him. I watched as he picked a small, seven-year-old Raiya up, hugging her and taking her home, and promising to take care of her.

THE STARLIGHT CHRONICLES

I watched for a longer time as Grandpa Odd told her the truth of Adonaias, the Prince of Stars, and oversaw her training. He strengthened her dedication, fed her desperation, and encouraged her daydreams.

This is too much, I thought. *I need to get out of here.*

But then, I saw me.

I saw me at the play, with Mikey and Poncey and Gwen and Tim Ryder. I saw the backdrop where Raiya had painted the background.

I saw myself walking on it, tripping over it, and falling on it.

I flinched. *Was I really that clumsy?*

Confusion came when Raiya saw me close up; a moment later, I felt the strange sensation of remembering me, and remembering her longing for me …

And then, as I opened my eyes to the real world again, I saw her eyes, dewy and damp with tears; and then she was crying, and afraid, and vulnerable, holding onto me with all her strength.

"I'm sorry! It's okay," I told her. "Everything will be alright." *I hope.*

Why did she have such a hard life, anyway?

"Her soul is broken," I said, muttering to myself as she buried her face in my chest. Adonaias had spoken to me before, saying that her soul had been broken. "Why make her go through even more pain? Or is it just unavoidable, since we all seem to be broken?"

I sighed. I remembered the comfort and power I felt when Adonaias had come to see me before. I knew he was powerful. I knew he was kind, or he had been kind to me. I knew he was merciful. I mean, I was the Star of Mercy, right? If I knew anything, it was that he should know what that was, at least.

I knew that Raiya certainly loved him; I mean, really, she was just about dying to see him.

"Why?" I asked, still talking to myself more than anyone else. "Why do this? Why let these things happen?"

I wasn't expecting an answer. I'd grown used to the idea that there were just no answers for some things that happened in life. Reason fell short, love wasn't enough, and reality could be brutal.

So I was not expecting an answer. But I got one. Or part of one.

"Because once something has been broken, it becomes more precious than before."

How was that possible?

I guess I could see it in my own life, somewhat. My relationship with Raiya, for one. Mikey's trust, for another. Even on some level, the plans I'd had for my life.

If it was one thing I knew from all of that, people would pursue precious things.

Speaking of precious things …

THE STARLIGHT CHRONICLES

Raiya's arms tightened around me as she finally opened her eyes again and quieted down. A deep sigh escaped from her. "Hamilton."

"What? No 'Humdinger?'" I teased.

"Not today, I guess." Her eyes glowed in the soft lighting. "You seem preoccupied. What are you thinking about?"

Somehow, "Your existential fate" didn't seem like an answer that she would want to hear. I laughed and shook my head, trying to distract her.

"Just thinking about the SATs. They're coming up soon, and school's just been slow lately. Would you want to study with me?" I asked. "I'm going to actually try to study, even though I know it's not usually my style. I don't want to be the person who gets a 798 on the English section because I was busy worrying about slaying a dragon."

Raiya lost her smile. "People forget that in real life, the dragons win more often than we would like."

"Come on, it's the SATs," I said. "It's standard, and you're in some of my classes. I'm sure you'll get a score that's at least above average."

"I don't think I'm going to take it," she finally replied.

"Why not?" I asked. "Are you afraid I'll get a better score than you?"

"No." She shifted uncomfortably in her bed. "I've decided to drop out of school."

"Is this because of your attendance?" I asked.

"No." She shook her head. "I have enough credits through Rosemont and Apollo Central that I can enroll in a GED class."

"Why?"

"It'll be easier to fight Draco if I'm not at school, for one," Raiya said. "You really should be able to see the advantage in that."

"I'll agree less school is generally a good thing. But then I wouldn't get to see you."

"It's a sacrifice we'll have to make," Raiya muttered apologetically.

There was something too strange and too familiar about the way she said that. "This isn't because you're thinking you'll have to die again, is it?"

Raiya flustered, and I knew it. *I knew it!*

Anger boiled up, fast and hard and relentless. "You're going to sacrifice yourself again."

"Look, I know you don't want to hear it, Hamilton—"

"Oh, no you don't," I said. "You promised me. Your word will bind you, remember? You promised me that you would live for me."

I could see her regret and frustration clearly, even without being able to read her emotions directly on her face.

"Grandpa knew me very, very well," she said carefully. "He knows my weaknesses, he knows my family, he knows about

305

you, and Elysian too. How can I not think he'll manage to beat us? And how can I not know that death will come to me before I allow it to hurt you?"

I took her hand. "We can still defeat him. Elysian says it will be some time before he's up to full power. Besides, Justice is going to be the end of him," I told her. "Prophecy is on your side."

"But I don't want to kill him," she admitted. "That's why he didn't kill me when he had the chance. He wouldn't have been able to just kill me. He knew my power better than most, and he raised me and taught me and pushed me toward you, all so he could make me stumble and destroy myself."

"But you didn't," I told her. "You didn't drink the water from the River of Life."

"You saved me."

"See? That's more irony for him then," I said. "He thinks that he'll win because you and I have found each other again. But he's wrong."

It was more than instinctual for me to reach over and kiss her again. The spicy sweetness of her wrapped itself around me, and I knew, as she did, that we had settled into each other.

I liked how she'd said it before: She was home when she was with me. I could easily say the same.

"I'm still worried," Raiya said.

THE STARLIGHT CHRONICLES

"Me too," I said. "But we can't look back. We just can't. We have to keep going on."

She barely nodded, but she agreed with me in the end. "Yes," she said. "You're right."

I thought about trying to make her feel better. What can you offer someone when you're staring down an impossible task and fearful that the end of the world might come before you complete it?

The surge of protectiveness from behind my heart fluttered, and I knew what I could do.

I pressed into the mark on my wrist, gently, only wanting a momentary transformation.

"What are you doing?" Raiya asked.

"You'll see," I said. As my wings began to form out of my back, I reached behind and pulled a feather free.

And tried not to scream. I managed to conceal the sudden spike of pain, I think, but I still needed a moment to make sure my voice would work properly.

"Are you okay?" Raiya asked.

"I'm more than okay," I said, the pain already lessening as I held out the feather. It was long and red, the flames burning quietly. "Here."

When she just looked at me, I finally reached out and tucked it into her hair, just as she'd worn it as Starry Knight when I first saw her. "This feather is for you," I said.

THE STARLIGHT CHRONICLES

"You know this isn't a real feather, right?" she asked. "It's a part of your soul."

"Well, that might explain why it hurt so much to tear it off myself." When she tried to argue again, I shook my head.

I wasn't ready to ask her to marry me. I was young and we were up against the world. I didn't want her to feel more pressure. I also didn't have a job or a high school diploma or a reliable income. Those things would wait, and I would wait along with them.

"Keep it. I want you to have it," I told her.

Despite what doubt or fear she might have felt, I was rewarded a moment later. She latched onto me, her emotions dancing all around in joy, love, and hope.

I held her for a long time after that.

Moments later, Raiya pulled back from our shared warmth, gently running her fingers down the feather in her hair. "I know I'd be keeping you from studying for the SATs," she said, as she fiddled with her sheet, "but let's go over the information we do have so far. It might help us make our next set of plans."

I grinned, sliding down and sitting next to her in the small hospital bed. "I'm an expert in avoiding my study time for the SATs," I told her. "There's no point in changing that now."

We would face this battle together. Whatever the future held, we would find a way to make it into forever.

C. S. Johnson is the award-winning, genre-hopping
author of several novels, including sci-fi and fantasy
adventures such as *The Starlight Chronicles* series, the *Once Upon
a Princess* saga, and the *Divine Space Pirates* trilogy. With a gift
for sarcasm and an apologetic heart, she currently lives in
Atlanta with her family.

THE STARLIGHT CHRONICLES

THE STARLIGHT CHRONICLES

Dear Reader,

I always like to close out my books with a little note to you, to let you see past the curtain of my words and glimpse into the heart of my world. I've struggled with this book's note, probably as much as I've struggled with the book itself, no doubt largely because of its theme, and also because of the application.

I'm sitting here writing this on the eve of a special anniversary. As of this moment, my husband and I have been together for nine years, dating for two and then married for seven. (I refer to this day as "Yay Day.") And while it is a very special occasion, not too many people know the deeper implications it has for me.

This is the same date, three years prior to meeting my husband, that I was dumped by my last ex-boyfriend. He broke my heart some, but my pride more. "Yay Day" was formerly "Yuck Day." That was the day I swore I would never get married, that I would cling only to God and his mission for my life.

That's a tricky thing, telling God what your life is going to be like. I couldn't see past my pain and my pride. But he did. And he not only gave me someone to love, and someone who would love me, but he redeemed "Yuck Day." "Yuck Day" was reborn as "Yay Day."

What does this have to do with this book? I think most of it has to do with this book because there is something absolutely beautiful about innocence.

311

In the believer's journey, trials come up that give us (and our heroes) a chance to see the real vs. the disingenuous, both inside and in the world around us, and the difference between innocent faith vs. virtuous faith.

It's a consistent theme in literature, that the loss of childhood innocence teaches us that life is not all rosy and pleasant, and we must find a way to survive in such a world. (Hint: It's not easy!)

Disappointment and confusion come, and still we must cling to what we know to be true. Our commitment cannot be shaken. The good news is we have a solid place to anchor ourselves in times of storms, we are broken creatures, living in a broken world. Yet we are still pursued by God, and because we have been broken, restoration becomes a more precious prize—to both sides.

With *Continuing*, as with *Calling*, commitment plays a central role. If commitment is a response to acceptance, continuing is the response from the pushback from commitment. This stage is often an underscore, a contra-alto harmony, for the remainder of the believer's life. In my own life, I've likened this idea to marriage. In the best of times, you fall in love, vow to love and honor each other all of the days of your lives, and then, in the worst of times, you get to argue over dinner and gripe over money.

Continuing on from an innocent faith to a virtuous one is essential for the fulfillment of love, both in Christ and in life. I also see this as part of hope and faith. It was instinctual for me to long for a better life as a child; it is deeply intentional now that I am an adult. It was nothing to cling to God as a child, when trust somehow came easier; it is everything to me as an adult. It was easy for me to have faith as a child; it is both easier and harder now that I am adult.

Thank you once more for joining me in Hamilton's journey. We hope you will continue onward with us as we enter into Book 6!

Until We Meet Again,

C. S. Johnson

THE STARLIGHT CHRONICLES

AUTHOR'S ACKNOWLEDGEMENTS

EDITOR

Jennifer C. Sell

Jennifer Clark Sell is a professional book editor and
proofreader. She works from her home in Southern
California. With her years of professional and personal
experience, she offers several quality packages for authors.
Find her at
https://www.facebook.com/JenniferSellEditingService.

Photo Credit: Savannah Sell

AUTHOR'S ACKNOWLEDGEMENTS

COVER ILLUSTRATOR

Amalia Chitulescu

Amalia Iuliana Chitulescu is a digital artist from Campina, Romania. Raised in a small town, this self-taught artist has a technique which is delineated by the contrast between obscurity and enlightenment, using dark elements in a dreamy world. Her areas of expertise include the use of theatrical concepts to create a macabre and surrealistic world that still maintains a highly recognizable attachment to reality. Bridging a diaphanous environment with light elements, an eerie view, she creates a dream world of dark beauty, done with a blend of photography and digital painting. Find her at https://www.facebook.com/Amalia.Chitulescu.Digital.Art

Photo Credit: Amalia Chitulescu

Chapter 1 *from*

OUTPOURING

BOOK SIX of *THE STARLIGHT CHRONICLES*

C. S. Johnson

☼ <u>1</u> ☼

Warmth and Wakefulness

It was not the usual matter of desperation that fueled me forward, as I ran in the rain, heading toward my favorite coffee shop.

Don't get me wrong; despite the early, early morning hours, I fully expected to be greeted with a steaming, warm cup of coffee, one that was perfect for warding off the chill in the air. I knew I was going to need it to get through the day, and it was likely I was going to need the second or third cup I would leave with, too. But in recent months, coffee had become the secondary reason that I loved to stop in and sit for a while at Rachel's Café. (It was not a love easily dethroned, either.)

Coffee had been my true love, until I'd found my *true* true love.

I glanced up to see the soft light coming from the room on the second floor. *She's awake.*

I pushed open the back door to the small café and headed up the stairs, silently as possible, and then all of a sudden there I was, standing in the doorway to her room. The echo of the rain was slightly louder, as the newly renovated wall in her room still needed some work, and the soft glow of her desk lamp was on, casting a small shadow of relief against the thunderstorm outside.

"Raiya."

319

She was sitting on her bed, her eyes glowing with wakefulness as she remained curled up in the warmth of her covers.

"What are you doing here, Hamilton?" she asked, her voice bracing against the subtlety of the night. There was no accusation in her tone, just surprise.

"I wanted to check in on you," I admitted, suddenly feeling dumb.

"At five-thirty in the morning?" Raiya asked. "I know I told you I've been having trouble sleeping, but it's—"

"Sorry." I scratched my head, suddenly very aware of how wet and cold I was. "I had a dream about you. I wanted to make sure you were okay."

"So you ran all the way here?" Raiya's lips curled into thoughtful smile. "You didn't want to call me?"

I considered arguing with her, which I would have delighted in, but thought the better of it. She was more beloved to me than arguing, too. "No."

"No?"

"I wanted to see you."

She pushed back her covers, allowing me a good grin at her fluffy-pants pajamas, and came over to me. "I'm glad you're here," she admitted, "and I would hug you, but you're all wet. Come on. I'll get you a towel and a cup of coffee."

"I feel like a king already," I said, although I probably looked more the part of the pauper. Even moments later, as

THE STARLIGHT CHRONICLES

my hands wrapped themselves tightly around my mug and a towel was draped over my shoulders, I felt more of the part of the humble and helpless, while I'd meant to be the hero.

"How's that?" she asked. "I can't imagine you're warmed up yet, but hopefully it'll help."

"You're the only *Raiya sunshine* I need," I assured her.

As she rolled her eyes and walked past me with a handful of creamers, I tugged on her shirt, pulling her in close. "Thank you," I said, as I finally got to kiss her again.

Raiya chuckled as she drew back. "It's my pleasure."

"No, *you're* my pleasure," I replied, staring at her long enough to make her blush.

She redirected me immediately; for all the brashness and boldness she had to stand up to me and my opinions, I knew and appreciated that Raiya had a modest side.

"Tell me about the dream you had. It must've been pretty bad if you're coming here this late," she prompted as she moved to the other side of the counter. I knew she was making some tea. She loved her espresso as much as I did, but she was more of a tea drinker in the mornings, and I loved her for it. "Or should I say this early, since Rachel won't be here for another two hours?"

"Letty won't wake up, will she?" I asked, suddenly dreading the thought of Rachel's old-lady mother coming cranking down the stairs as we spent our time together.

THE STARLIGHT CHRONICLES

"Not likely," Raiya said, effectively putting my shallow fears to rest. "I've been taking the morning shifts here at the café since I dropped out of school. Aunt Letty doesn't usually wake up till noon anymore. Unless, of course, she hears me when I wake up in the middle of the night. But the rain should provide some cover tonight."

"I can't tell you how lucky you are, getting to drop out," I said. "Even if AP Gov is not the same without you to argue with."

"I imagine it's much more peaceful," she said neutrally.

"Peace might seem like an attractive offer," I said, "but I'll take arguing with you over semantics and historicity and context any day of the week."

"How is Mrs. Smithe?" Raiya asked. "Has she said anything else to you about SWORD lately?"

"Not since January," I said. "Almost two months later, and nothing in all that time."

"She's not the only one who's gone quiet," Raiya said as she sat down across from me. Her eyes fell to the seat that her grandfather, the esoteric and elusive Grandpa Odd, would sit in, and my reasons for scurrying over to see her immediately jumped to the forefront of my mind.

I reached out for her hand. "Everything will be alright," I said.

She squeezed my hand in return. "I'm not sure *you* know that," she replied easily enough, then she took a sip from her own mug.

THE STARLIGHT CHRONICLES

Raiya had a point, as she usually did, and it was a big one. If I truly believed things would be okay, why did I come running to see her before daybreak?

I shoved that thought aside. I loved her. I wanted to be with her. I knew we faced a considerable challenge, so there was nothing inherently wrong with running through the rain and the dark of the night to see her.

"I'll admit, I'd feel better if we knew where Draco was hiding," I said bitterly. "I guess it didn't matter if he had his dragon skin or not. He's still terrible to try to locate."

"Agreed."

"He hasn't been here, has he?" I asked.

"No," Raiya said, shaking her head. I watched, transfixed, as some of her gingerbread hair broke free from the loosened bun at the back of her head. "Rachel and Aunt Letty were surprised to hear he went missing after the last attack near Rosemont. They haven't made much of a thorough investigation, but that's more because of the 'police' jurisdiction than anything else."

I snorted. "SWORD's going to have to think of a better cover soon."

"They've gotten away with sillier explanations," Raiya pointed out. "They've done more clean-up around the city, as far as damage goes. That's probably the reason that the assistant mayor's willing to let it slide for now."

I shrugged. "Assistant Mayor Dunbrooke doesn't seem as interested in the supernatural stuff as Stefano did."

"That's probably because he hasn't been taken over by a Sinister or a demon monster," Raiya replied.

"So far as we know." I frowned, thinking of the small, wiry man who seemed more machine than man, especially when it came to running what he referred to as "his domain." Which included the city, which included me, for the three or four days a week I would go into work.

I didn't mind that much. At least he was smart enough to leave me alone.

"True." Raiya smiled. "You have me there."

"Did I tell you that he's ordered the judiciary council to give Cheryl a deadline to produce the city superheroes?" I asked. "She has ten days to find them or the case is getting dismissed. Dunbrooke says it's costing the city time, money, and manpower."

"I'll bet your mom didn't like that."

"No," I said. "She didn't, putting it mildly. Blowing up ballistically when she got the report is more accurate."

Raiya laughed. "I would've loved to see her face. It's not often that the famous Cheryl Thomas-Dinger, the Queen of Apollo City Courtrooms, doesn't get her way."

"I'll try to get a picture of it when her time's up and she's left without us to fight in court."

"I'm assuming that your dad hasn't told her the truth about us?"

THE STARLIGHT CHRONICLES

Thinking of my dad made me flinch. I shook my head. "No. He wouldn't. He knows how to keep secrets. And he's mandated to do so, with healthcare laws as they are. Or so he says. I can see him working around them if he wanted. Or," I added, "if Cheryl wanted."

When Raiya's grandfather revealed himself to be not only Elysian's rebellious brother Draco, but also the mysterious Ogden Skarmastad, the founder of Apollo City, he gave us quite a surprise. An unwelcome one, at that. But finding out my father had known about SWORD and my secret superhero identity smashed through me. Since then, it was as if a chasm of secrets had suddenly pushed itself between us, damaging the ideas we had about each other irrevocably.

Mark usually came home late, left for work early—which really wasn't out of the norm—and our interaction was limited to the raw food dinners my mother's latest chef, a sushi master named Ayako, was making for us. We didn't talk much.

Raiya nodded. "I guess if he didn't tell her about me, he wasn't going to tell her about you. He loves you very much."

"Psh." I finished my coffee. "Coffee and intellectual levels, that's really all we have in common. And even with that, I'm pretty sure I'm smarter, and he likes his coffee darker."

"You really think you're smarter than your father?" Raiya arched her brow at me.

"I'm not the one who's best friends with a SWORD operative," I reminded her.

THE STARLIGHT CHRONICLES

"Good point. You're making a lot of good points, despite being up this early," she observed.

"I know you're trying to get me off the original argument because you can't win," I told her, "but I'll humor you because I love you."

"I know you're just charming me because you're afraid I will come up with something better," Raiya responded. "But I'll humor you, because I love you, too."

I grinned. "Intellectual banter is so much fun with you."

"It always was for me," Raiya said. "Although I do miss you getting ticked off with me for winning before you knew who I was. That was pretty amusing."

"Ha, ha." I laughed drily. "If it makes you feel better, I'll start getting more angry when you attempt to win. But anyway, there are good reasons I'm awake and I'm here."

"Yes, you should tell me those." Raiya sipped her tea thoughtfully. "You mentioned the dream. Is there something else? Is Elysian bothering you?"

"I wish," I admitted. "He's been pretty alert and disciplined since Draco's reappearance. He probably sleeps less than you do."

"A considerable feat," Raiya said with a laugh. "Although I probably sleep more than you realize. I take naps after Letty relieves me, before you're out of school and swim practice."

"Thankfully the season's over now." I shook my head. "No new records this year, but still a lot of wins."

"Maybe you'll break some records next year," Raiya said.

"Will we be done with this mission by then?" I asked. *That would be super. Absolutely perfect, actually. The sooner this is over, the happier I will be.*

She shrugged. "I don't know. But there's no harm in hoping."

"I'm just hoping that I'll stop having these premonitions in the middle of the night." I sighed. "As much as I love you, and I love seeing you, Mark's already not exactly happy with me, and Cheryl's passive-aggressive enough to make me worried. I don't want to be punished for feeling like I need to come to your rescue."

"Couldn't have been that bad, even if you did run all the way here, and in the rain, no less."

"It was bad enough." I tapped my empty cup on the counter. "In my dream, I just saw you looking sad, like you were upset, so I wanted to come and rescue you."

Raiya pursed her lips. "I know that when I was in the hospital and attacked, you were scared," she said carefully, "but there's no reason to believe I was in immediate danger."

"Attacked" was the neat way to summarize getting her heart smashed and her soul ripped out of her body just weeks ago. I clenched my fingers together, trying not to shout at her for her flippancy.

I calmed down enough before replying with, "I know."

I know, but I couldn't help it. Maybe I wanted to come more for me than you.

"Are you sure you weren't the one who wanted me to comfort you?"

Hearing my own thoughts echoed back to me just made me more frustrated. "No," I insisted.

Raiya was smarter than that. "I know you better than you realize, you know." She laughed. "I still remember that whole issue last year with your birthday cake."

"I can't believe I apologized to you for that. I take it back."

She smirked. "It's too late, I already took it."

I stuck my tongue out at her, before sinking into silence.

"I know it doesn't help you any with Mikey still in the hospital," she added after a while.

I still said nothing. Mikey had been my best friend, like my brother at one point. Now, he might as well be permanently planted in the hospital bed where we could occasionally go to visit. As swim season dwindled down, I had a harder time not telling him he was going to pay for just lying around all day and night. At least the poor quality hospital food was keeping him from getting fat.

His mind and heart had seemed to heal more. He was, apparently, doing better with the tutor Central had sent over, and he seemed more like his old self when we went to see him.

Sometimes.

Then Mikey would remember he was supposed to hate me and I'd been the one who'd caused the demise of his true love, or whatever he wanted to call her, who just happened to be my ex-girlfriend.

I didn't think it was my direct fault that Gwen got her Soulfire stolen by Asteropy, the last of the Seven Deadly Sinisters. If I had to make a case for it in court, I could probably make it convincing. When I argued the case in my head, it went back and forth enough between the "innocent" and the "guilty" verdict that I was uncomfortable.

The best thing I could do, as far I as could figure—and Raiya agreed with me on it—was work to free Gwen's Soulfire from Asteropy.

Who just happened to be eaten up by Draco's dragon skin last time I saw her. It was probably going to take some time to destroy him, and *that* was of no comfort to Mikey, especially since he'd witnessed her pain.

I still had trouble seeing his PTSD diagnosis, but I did know that part of the reason for it was true, and the other reason was for his protection.

His estranged father, Dante, my less-than-agreeable and less-than-amicable, most-of-the-time contact from SWORD, was keeping him there. And I could appreciate it, because he was keeping him from my mother interrogating him about the identities of Wingdinger and Starry Knight—me and Raiya, respectably.

"Maybe he'll get out once the timeline on the case is over," I said. "Stefano said before only Cheryl could get to him now.

Maybe once she's out of the way, the statute of limitations will be over and Dante will allow Mark to give him a clear discharge."

"Maybe." It was Raiya's turn to shrug. She glanced outside the windows, where the rain was picking up, pitter-pattering down as it washed the world clean.

She picked up my empty cup and poured me a new one. "Let's not worry about it now."

"What?" Incredulously, I looked at her as if she'd gone crazy. "How can we *not* worry about this?"

"Talk to me about other things," she said. "Tell me stories of all the other girls at school terrifying you, thinking that you're not secretly in love with your coffee barista. Tell me about the swim team drama this semester."

When my mouth just dropped open, appalled at her appeal to the meaningless, she smiled. "I can tell you about some of the daytime soaps that Aunt Letty leaves on upstairs, if you can't think of something more interesting."

"Don't we have to worry about this?"

"We've worried about it for a long time," she said. "I need a break. Just a small one." She came around and sat down next to me.

Tentatively, I nodded. "Okay. I can think of more interesting things than Letty's soap operas. If you're sure you want to."

THE STARLIGHT CHRONICLES

"I do," she said. "We'll go crazy trying to figure out everything right now. Let's just be normal for a bit."

"I can't argue with that," I said, and then I obliged her with stories of Poncey's latest pranks, the swim team's gluten-free swim-ghetti disaster, and Via's constant attempts to push her new boyfriend in my face, despite my eternal apathy.

I watched in wonder as she made faces and comments and more coffee.

It was a good two hours I got to spend with her, on a cold, rainy, late March morning, with nothing else to look forward to except coming back to her at the end of the day. As Rachel came in, and customers soon after her, I wondered if I would have a "normal" life like that, where I wouldn't have to say good-bye to the "normal" parts and slink back to into the dread that accentuated my day.

Thank you for reading! Please leave a review for this book
and check for other books and updates!

THE STARLIGHT CHRONICLES